PAX AFRICANA

DAVID JENKINS

VAULT

A Vault Paperback

ISBN 978-0-9926436-2-1

Typeset in Garamond

Published by Vault
36 B Mornington Terrace
London NW1 7RS

Also by David Jenkins:

Pax Britannica

The Story so Far

An extraordinary anomaly has come to light on an archaeological dig near Hadrian's Wall. Sterland Morris, a British Museum curator, has uncovered a modern military crest among the genuine Roman artefacts.

A week later, an army helicopter ditches in the Solway Firth. Eleven crew escape in two life rafts, one of which contains the senior officer, Birch, his female co-pilot, Sands, and four soldiers. Once ashore, this group is attacked in the dark by unknown assailants, resulting in the death of one private and two attackers. Next morning the fog lifts to reveal Hadrian's Wall, confirming Sands' assertion that they've travelled back in time, and that they've been attacked by Romans.

Meanwhile, back in London, Morris phones the local coroner, Jamieson, to reveal that he is Sands' uncle. There is no sign of the crashed helicopter and thus begins a fruitless and frustrated struggle by the two men to uncover the mystery of the crash.

Back at Hadrian's Wall, a power struggle culminates with Sands, as the only Latin speaker, seizing command of the platoon. The story culminates in a frantic and bloody night-time mission to free the sole surviving soldier in Roman captivity. Scores are settled, revenge exacted and mayhem visited on the fort. The platoon members flee to freedom across the Solway Firth, where they are granted the prospect of kinship by the local tribe. Trapped and overwhelmed by what lies ahead, Sands feels the need to escape the control of others. Unknown to her, Morris and Jamieson are also in hot pursuit, keen to re-establish influence over her fate and ensure that past and present continue to be inextricably linked.

For more information about David Jenkins
please visit his website at www.paxbritannica.co.uk

PAX AFRICANA

ONE

"Tea, Dr. Morris? Ars aboot a make a brew when thew knocked."

"Not for me, Jed, I'd like to get started right away."

"Nae problem."

"And thanks for the tip-off."

"Aye, it was reet lucky thew was in Burgh by Sands the day," Jed calls from the kitchen.

Sterland Morris is standing in the hallway of a scruffy farmhouse. He kicks the mud off his shoes while thumbing through a pile of Jed's unopened letters. A grandfather clock strikes seven.

"And you're certain you haven't told anyone about this?" Morris shouts. "You haven't mentioned it to anyone else since you spoke to me?"

"Nae fear, Dr Morris. I reet ken when to keep my gob shut. Nae news of your niece or the missin' helicopter, then?"

"No, Jed, they're scaling back the search, I think."

Morris pokes his head into an adjoining sitting room and surveys the scene. "The whole thing's been a damned fiasco from day one."

"Aye, how can all this be happenin' in 2013? It's no' exactly the bloody dark ages. It's a bloody disgrace, is whar it is, I'm tellin' thew."

Morris steps back into the hallway, his skin tingling with anticipation. He's just spotted the object that's been the motivation for his sudden visit.

"Jed, d'you mind if I have a closer look at what you've found?"

Jed's head appears around the kitchen door. "Aye, sorry Dr Morris. Go ahead, help thaself, that's whar you're here for. It's on yon table in the front room."

Morris pounces, his heart racing as he approaches the table. He's working hard to contain his excitement.

"How many more d'you think there might be?"

"Hard to say, there's a pile in yon field out there, a good few mebby. I found 'em when I was diggin' a new drain. It's geet waterlogged ground, right clarty, but I didn't want to risk pulling 'em all oot, you ken? I nivver, ivver sin owt like it in my life. I thowt they was wood shavings to begin wi'."

Jed has begun to move back to join Morris, stirring his tea as he enters through the sitting room door.

"You did the right thing, Jed. The wet conditions underground will have helped preserve them, especially if this one's any indicator."

Jed watches in fascination as Morris puts on a pair of spotless gloves and begins to scrutinise the object on the table in front of him.

"Look, it's discolouring already due to oxygenation and it's only been out the ground for, what, ten hours?"

"Aye, less mebby. Whar do thew reckon it is, then?"

"I can tell you exactly what it is. It's a Roman tablet, probably their equivalent of a postcard or airmail letter."

The two men lean in closer as Morris prises the object open with immense care.

"If you look carefully you should detect some lettering?"

"Oh, aye."

Morris pauses to place a magnifying monocle in his right eye. "And it's clearly written in ink. And, if previous finds are anything to go by, it's most likely to be in a Latin script known as old Roman cursive."

"Do thew ken whar it says?"

"No, without infrared photography it's going to be impossible to decipher it in its present condition. I'd hazard a guess that it's most likely a military report or a letter."

"Do thew ken whar it's made oot of?"

"Almost certainly local wood: alder, birch, ash, lime. There're hundreds of examples similar to this in the British Museum, all unearthed in Cumbria and Northumberland."

Jed moves a lamp closer to the table. Morris angles the tablet to one side, allowing the light to fall more clearly on the edge of the object

"Can you see how the wood has been scored down the middle to enable the tablet to be folded in half once it has been written? Look, the writing is clearly visible. And it should be legible when properly treated. That's a formidable hand at work there, compact and confident. But most importantly, the tablet's in an extraordinarily fine state of preservation."

Jed rubs the grey stubble on his face. "Whar's in it for us, d'you reckon? Is it worth owt?"

"Not to you, Jed. But it's worth an incalculable amount to a historian like me."

"How-ee, Dr Morris, are you skittin us? I may just be a thick farmer to the likes of thew, but I've been around long enough to ken it must be worth a bob or two to the museum."

Morris fixes the other man with a determined gaze.

"I'm not in the habit of having people on, Jed. And I don't believe in beating around the bush. I can assure you that you'll not make a penny out of these tablets, not unless you do exactly as I tell you."

"How's that, then?"

"It's simple really, even for someone who pretends to be a thick farmer."

Morris puts the object down and turns to face Jed eyeball to eyeball. Neither man blinks as Morris continues.

"You're a plain speaking man, so I'm going to spell it out for you in words of one syllable. You will do just as I say and not tell a soul of this find. Then, you're going to hand over all the tablets, at least what's left of them, to me personally, and forget you've ever laid eyes on them. This is to be our secret and it is never to be shared with anyone - friends, family or anyone connected with the British Museum in particular. Have you got all that?"

"Have I got all that? Aye, I can tell thew whar else I've got - a reet nasty feeling, reet here in the pit of me guts. I can tell thew is up to something downright dodgy. Whar's tha game? I was doing thew a favour inviting you out here like this wi' all this subterfuge. I could have gone straight to the British Museum like before when I found the Roman hoard out back."

"And where did that get you? You landed up to your neck with a problem that's likely to prevent you getting a single penny for your troubles."

"Whar the bleedin' hell's that got to do wi' thew? That other treasure was found on my land. I found it meself, didn't I? That money should be mine."

"Should be, I'll grant you. But will it be yours? It's highly unlikely as things stand. You know that a coroner's court will have to declare that find to be treasure trove for you to collect your entitlement to its value. And you've got no chance of getting the money unless I can convince the coroner that in the opinion of the British Museum it is yours by rights."

"Whar's stopping you doing that then?"

"That Roman military badge you found."

"Aye, whar aboot it? It was found in the pot wi' the coins and all the other stuff."

"Are you sure about that, Jed?"

"Course I'm reet bloody sure."

"Because that badge is going to stop you getting your hands on what is rightfully your reward."

"You fuckin' whar, laddo? That badge was found wi' the rest of the hoard. I must have told thew that a dozen times."

"And so you have. But it would be perfectly understandable if you'd become confused about the exact events of that day - all that gold coinage glistening in the cold light of day. It would be enough to knock anyone sideways. I know I'd find it impossible to remember the exact events of that day, and the order in which they occurred. D'you see what I'm getting at?"

"You want us to say the badge was found separate to the hoard, is that aboot the size of it?"

"Look, the coroner can't declare the find to be treasure trove unless we can convince him that the badge didn't form part of the Roman hoard you found. The badge is modern, which means whoever placed it with the hoard may still be alive and, therefore, entitled to the spoils. Do you understand what I'm saying?"

"Aye, of course I do. But I'm tellin' thew, I did find yon badge wi' the hoard."

"Is it not possible you may have accidentally added it to the top of the hoard once you had found it? The amphora had been broken by the plough and some objects were strewn around. You kept digging out the amphora, correct?"

"Aye."

"And is it not possible that the badge could have been dug up alongside the amphora? And is it not also possible that you could have assumed, understandably, that it belonged with the contents of the hoard and placed it back there unwittingly?"

"Aye, now that I think of it, it was hoyin it doown and there was kack everywhere. I didnae ken whut I was djarn."

"Excellent, it's as I thought. Both the amphora containing the hoard and the badge were dug up at the same time by the plough and were buried near to each but in separate locations. Due to the appalling weather and your confusion on the day the objects subsequently became mistakenly placed together and were incorrectly assumed to have been buried together as part of the same hoard."

"Aye, that sounds ahreet."

"Good, now we're getting somewhere."

"Whar aboot yon coroner then?"

"You leave the coroner to me. Jamieson's a decent sort. The last thing he wants is a complicated treasure trove case on his hands. It's in everyone's interests to get this sorted out cleanly, believe me. You'll get your money, the British Museum will get their Roman hoard and Jamieson will get home nice an early from his coroner's court."

"And whar aboot you, Dr Morris? Wharra thew get oot of it?"

"A few harmless wood shavings, Jed."

"Is that all you're after, like?"

"That, and a guarantee of your complete and utter silence. Have we got a deal?

"Have we got a deal? Aye, ye crafty old sod, we got a deal."

TWO

Location: Barsalloch Point
Coordinates: 54°43'60" N and 4°34'0" W

Time and Date: 21.30, 21st June, 258 C.E.

It was a calm evening. The sun was beginning to set on the longest day of the year. Six men and a lone female, seated on a semicircle of boulders, were gazing out to sea across a sandy beach. It felt as if the forlorn cry from a circling seagull was the only sound that existed.

"When's the baby due, George?" the woman enquired of the young man sitting opposite her.

"Dinnae ken for sure, Kal."

The youth squirmed in his seat. His limbs danced in nervous disorder, as if impelled by some inchoate external energy. His slender arms had acquired a patina of chaotic, rite-of passage tattoos, bearing eloquent testimony to his troubled encounter with adolescence.

"Aye, the womenfolk say the next day or two, most likely."

"No way you're coming with us. You're staying for the birth."

"Fuck it, Kal, give the lad a bloody break," interjected the hulking man sitting on her right. "His missus'll be alright – these native women are all built like Shetland ponies. One squeeze of those haunches and the kid will pop out like a bar of soap. No offence, George."

Kal Sands shook her head and sucked on her teeth. "You've not lost your way with words, Stog."

"Come on, get fucking real, Kal," Stogdon retorted. "You tripping, or what? You forgotten that this is the third century? George ain't fannying about with no bloody paternity leave. We need all the power we can get on that boat tomorrow."

"Relax, Stog, you can manage fine without him," replied Sands. "I cleared it with Talorc earlier. He'll take George's place, and he'll provide a helmsman too. I know you're wound up about the Mull of Galloway tidal system. Everybody is, but we've just got to deal with it."

An athletically-built black man stood up to throw some wood on the fire. "She's right, man, these are the best weather conditions we're going to get. You guys'll be fine." He opened his arms, as if to embrace the elements. "Look at how proper calm the sea is. Come on, Stog."

"Fuck that, Ojo, you twat. It's gonna be a piece of piss for you. You're gonna be, like, proper safe and sound in that little sailboat of yours, cosying up to your two officer buddies."

"Actually, there's been a change of plan," said Sands. "Ojo, you're going to have to shift over to the other boat to give them an extra oarsman. There'll be six of you, more than enough to get you out of trouble if you get caught in a foul tide with the wind turning against you. Once you start racing with the tidal stream you could easily be making ten knots."

"Come on, Kal, that ain't playin' fair, man. You know I can't even swim," protested Ojokwu.

"I wouldn't waste time worrying about swimming, Ojo. Capsize that boat, and you'll be riding a non-stop tidal express to oblivion. Trust me, whether or not you can swim isn't going to be an issue."

A single loud laugh rang out. "Feeling better now, Ojo?" Stogdon taunted. "You'll be taking over George's paddle while he gets used to wiping his sprog's arse. Happy days!"

George McKay attempted to intervene. "I dinnae mind coming along wi' youse, Stog. I'm prepared tae come if you really want."

Rattigan, the oldest man in the group, had heard enough. He needed to assert himself. He rubbed his balding scalp in irritation. "Nah, fuck that, my son, you're staying right here. Don't pay no attention to old Stog, he's a fucking troglodyte. Stog the trog. He's just bitter and twisted 'cause he ain't found a good woman like you 'ave."

"Sergeant Rattigan's right, Stog," Sands said, "give it a rest."

Stogdon held up his hands in mock supplication. "Okay, chill, man. I'm getting' the picture, pure and clear. My lips are sealed from now on. Don't pay no attention to me, Georgie boy, I'm just a proper little wind-up merchant." He turned to the man sitting opposite him for confirmation. "Ain't that right, Birchy?"

Birch shot him a dead look. "It's Captain Birch to you, Stogdon. Much as I yearn for greater intimacy, why don't we combat the temptation and just stick to proper names?"

"Oh, I get ya, once an officer, always an officer - that's how it is, right? Still can't bring yerself to mingle with the troops, eh, Birchy? That's just plain rude, man. I wonder what dear old Mumsy would've said about that?"

Stogdon stood up, put a hand on his hip and affected a woman's voice. "Do buck oneself up Birch, darling. You know it's important to be nice to the scumbags under one's command. Old *Pater* would have a hernia and a half if he could see you now."

"Shut it, Stog," interrupted Rattigan, "and *that* is an order."

"Alright, Sarge, just messing with him. I won't speak to no one else, never again, not unless they speak to me first."

"Well that *will* be a bloody first," said Corporal Crawley. He was the last member to join the discussion. He wore a troubled expression. "Any danger of us cracking on with things? What's the plan, Birch?"

Birch leapt up. "I'm grateful to you, Crawley – a sane voice in a sea of inanity," he replied, glancing in Stogdon's direction. "According to Talorc the round-trip should take us about a week. It's a maiden voyage so we shouldn't push it too hard."

"Push it too hard?" Crawley responded. "That sodding thing's hand-hewn from a fifty foot tree trunk. What's the worst that can happen? It ain't gonna sink, surely to God?"

"I was referring to the crew, not the vessel," Birch replied.

He was starting to clear a space on the sand in front of him. "Most of you are complete novices. Sands and I are the only ones who've had any experience of sailing at sea."

"Yeah, true that, but you'll be cruising along in a proper cushy sailing boat. You won't have no paddling to do."

Birch shrugged his shoulders. "Fair enough, but what's the alternative? Once you've dropped the boat off, there's no way of returning without us. Not unless you fancy yomping back for five days."

Sands opted for a different tack. "Once that boat's handed over to the king, we've discharged our obligations to Talorc."

"Now you are making sense," nodded Crawley. "He's the only reason we're still alive. We all owe Talorc, big time."

Rattigan sprang to life. "He's worth ten of any of us at any price. That boat is compensation for all the grief we've caused him. Cheap at half the cost."

"True that," added Stogdon.

"When do we set off?" Crawley asked.

Birch picked up a stick and started drawing a map in the sand. "Talorc says we should leave tomorrow at first light," he began. The others watched in fascination as he outlined the route on the sand. "The fine weather and prevailing winds will help us across Luce Bay. It's about a twenty-five mile paddle but the sea should be calm and the winds light. We aim to shelter overnight in a small bay just north of the Mull of Galloway. The next day is going to be the big one, but fingers crossed we'll be able to round the Mull in one piece."

Birch paused, aware of his audience's growing apprehension. His tone softened as he continued. "Talorc is an experienced seaman and he knows what he's doing. He's going to take you in as close to the cliffs as he can. Once you clear the boiling waters of the tidal race, you're home free, you're riding a runaway train north for as long as you can keep going. If everything goes according to plan you'll arrive in Rerigonium no later than lunchtime on the third day."

Birch finished his presentation by impaling his stick on the spot that marked their final destination. He rubbed the sand from his palms with a self-satisfied flourish.

"And what about you guys, while we're slogging our guts out on board that half-arsed tree trunk?" asked Crawley.

"We should be there shortly before you," Birch replied as he resumed his seat. "We hope that Kal and Talorc will be granted an audience with the King more or less as soon as we arrive, maybe the next day. He is expecting us, though. It seems our reputation has gone before us," he emphasised, directing a glance at Sands.

"So let's assume the King ain't unhappy with the gift of his new boat," asked Crawley. "What then?"

"Straightforward. We all return in the sailing craft. About a hundred and twenty miles sailing into a gentle south-westerly breeze should take us three days or so, depending on how shipshape she turns out to be."

"Shipshape?" queried Ojokwu, his face disfigured with anxiety. "Nine months we spent working on that sodding boat. She should be bloody well shipshape. What's to say the bastard thing won't sink while the eight of us are crossing an open sea."

"Look, let's be frank, I'm no boat designer," replied Birch. "I know that and you know that, but I reckon that little vessel is the most advanced craft ever to have sailed these waters. Look at all the firsts: first to have a proper keel, first to have a triangular sail, first to use clinker built construction methods. It's hundreds of years ahead of its time."

Ojokwu stared at him. "Yeah, very impressive, Birch, but will it float?"

Birch shot him an outraged look.

"Float, you cheeky bastard? Of course it will bloody float. But we'll have to bail water like buggery to stop it sinking."

The group emitted a spontaneous laugh at Birch's brutal assessment. His mixture of blind optimism and exasperation struck a chord in all of them. Months of back-breaking, tedious toil, much of it spent using unfamiliar iron-age tools, had tested their mettle and tried their patience, but it had also bonded them together in a shared, worthy endeavour that all were proud of. Those two boats, utterly different though they were, held a special symbolism for their builders: one vessel was a massive hand-hewn, hand-powered canoe, built to Talorc's exact specifications, the other an anachronistic, experimental sailing ship, entirely born of their own creativity and ingenuity. The former represented a link to the past, and the latter a bridge to the future.

"What are we going to do with her once we get back?" asked Crawley.

"It depends," replied Sands. "You guys still planning to try your luck south of Hadrian's Wall?"

"There's easy pickings, Kal, you know that," replied Rattigan. "It's like the wild west down there. The local Brits need someone to maintain a bit of order. They're our people, remember?"

"And who do you think you are - the Old Bill? Do us a favour, Rattigan. You're talking about crossing back into the Roman Empire."

"Tell me something I don't know. What's your point, Kal?"

"My point is that we're *all* bloody Romans now. Don't you get it?"

Rattigan's face started to flush. "Tell the poor sods who're treated like second-class citizens in their own bloody country."

"They won't thank you if you start killing Romans in their back yard."

Rattigan looked to his comrades for support. "They're a bloody downtrodden mob, a rabble, they need someone to come in and straighten things out a bit."

"And you think you're the boys to do it?"

"Why not, why shouldn't it be us? We're entitled. After all, you gotta start somewhere - you know what I mean?"

"Yeah, I get the idea," she nodded. "I've overheard what you guys have been saying. But what you're considering is way beyond the pale; it's not a million miles from organised crime. Is that the best you can do, Rattigan?"

"Organised resistance, more like."

Sands shook her head. "I'm not naïve, I know how this goes, Rattigan – dress it up with fine sentiments if you like." She started to address her remarks to the wider audience. "It starts off with a bit of muscle, keeping some drunken Roman soldiers in line, exacting a little revenge here and there, sorting out a few uncooperative tavern keepers, then it moves on to controlling the gambling, a bit of protection money on the side, and soon you're running the local brothels and things are getting really nasty. I can predict the trajectory a mile off."

"So what the hell else do you suggest we do, eh?" responded Rattigan. "Become exiles from our own bloody country?"

"Sarge, youse have forgotten, Scotland *is* my country," replied George. "You're welcome to England. These are my people round here. There's nae chance I'm leavin' them. I'm stayin' north o' the wall."

"That's fine, George, each to his own, son," replied Rattigan. "You're too decent a young fella for this fucked-up war-zone anyway. Good luck to you if that's what you wanna do. Just don't think the world will simply pass you by, though. You're still gonna have to watch your arse, even in this backwater. Keep those tattoos covered up, for starters. You know what I'm saying? They're a dead give-away. You'll stand out a mile."

Sands had been watching the exchange with a fascinated intensity. "Each to his own, Rattigan? Maybe you're right. If so, who the hell's to say who should do what?" she asked.

"Each to his own," he repeated.

Sands surveyed the group. "Maybe in this upside-down world you're right and I'm wrong? I'm finding it hard to tell any more. Maybe we should all just make our own choices and to hell with the rest. Who's planning to go with Rattigan?"

"Stogdon, Crawley and Ojo," he interjected.

"And Birch, what about you?" she asked.

He looked startled by the question. "I'm going where you're headed, Sands. I've already told you that you're my best chance of getting out of here in one piece."

"And what are youse plannin' to do, Kal?" asked George. "Are you still under pressure to tie the knot wi' Talorc, like?"

Sands shifted in her seat. "He only suggested it because he's trying to protect me. He's simply concerned for my safety."

The men cast knowing glances at each other.

"I'm serious," she insisted.

"If you say so, Kal," smiled Crawley, his mood lightening up for once. "So, does he really think the local king might be gunning for you?"

"Yeah, likely as not," she replied. "Talorc thinks he's being squeezed by the Romans. He says that Selgovae spies are crawling all over the place trying to pin down my whereabouts."

"But why are they looking for you? It don't make no sense."

"We left them two Roman commanders alive, that's why," spat Rattigan. "We should've rubbed those bastards out good and proper when we had the chance."

Sands ignored his remark. She was tired of revisiting the site of old battles. "Since when did any of this make any sense to anyone?" she asked. "There are bigger forces at play here than any of us can control."

"Or understand," sighed Ojokwu.

"So why don't you come with us? Why don't we all stick together?" asked Stogdon.

Sands looked at him in surprise. She examined his rueful expression with care. "You never cease to surprise me, Stog. You getting sentimental in your old age?"

He ruffled his hair in a distracted manner. "We've been through a lot together, man, don't forget that. I may be an arsehole, but I'm an arsehole who sticks by his mates. And that even includes you, Birch, sitting over there with that smug, fucking smirk on your face."

"Cheers, Stogdon - likewise, I'm sure."

"No, I'm serious, Kal," continued Stogdon. "Where's your protection at if you don't stick with us? We'll bare watch your back if you watch ours."

"Sure, Stog, but whatever I decide, it's got to be for a positive reason, not out of fear. I won't be intimidated by what the future holds."

"Ain't that what we all think, Kal?" interjected Crawley. "We ain't hardly sitting waitin' for some geezer's permission to act."

"I know," she conceded, "but aren't you just taking the easy option of conforming to type?"

Crawley looked at her in surprise. "What's that even mean, conforming to type?" he asked. "How the hell else we gonna survive? We ain't no farmers and we ain't no fishermen. We can't even chat the local lingo. We ain't got no options."

"What's wrong with you guys?" Sands demanded. "Think about it, you've more options than you realise. You're bloody men for a start, a brotherhood. You could use your muscle power for honest endeavour. Don't give me that 'ain't got no options' shtick. You can read and write, you can do mental arithmetic, you can measure, you can reason. You could become traders, shopkeepers, scribes, builders, tradesmen, entrepreneurs. You've got everything going for you."

"We're soldiers, Kal. Always have been. Don't try and dress us up as something we ain't."

"But that was back then. Way back when you had no choice. Now you're free of that baggage. You can reinvent yourselves in ways you've never dreamed of. Face facts, twenty-first century capitalism never did you guys any favours. It squeezed the options out of you. It chewed you up and spat you out."

Ojokwu smiled. "Third century Britain ain't exactly no cakewalk neither."

"Nobody's denying that, Ojo, but don't you feel that your destiny lies in your own hands in a way that it didn't before?"

"Destiny – what, are you having a laugh? Destined for what - the slaughterhouse? We're condemned, Kal, that's all I can say."

"I don't disagree with you," she replied. "We're condemned from the moment we're born. But not in the way you mean."

"Oh, here' we bleedin' go," replied Rattigan. "How does that help? Don't you ever give it a rest, Sands?"

"No, Rattigan, if there's one thing you should know about me by now, I won't ever give it a rest."

Rattigan crossed his legs and leaned back in a mocking fashion. "Ok, so in what way was I condemned, was any of us condemned, from the moment we was born, as if I didn't already know? So I've had a tough life – my mum didn't love me, boo-fucking-hoo!"

Sands cast him a pitying glance. "We're condemned to struggle, to suffer and to die."

"Oh, right," he sniffed. "Is that it?"

"No, that was just the good news. The bad news is that first and foremost, from our first breath, we're condemned to be free. That's the most terrifying prospect of all. It's a life sentence and there's no chance of remission."

Rattigan snorted with derision.

"But if there ain't no remission, how do we deal with it?" asked Ojokwu. "You're offering us a quick trip to the abattoir and fuck-all else. We need bare hope, man."

Sands hesitated. She emitted a long sigh. "We deal with it by embracing freedom as a gift, not as a curse."

"Exactly! That's why we gotta get out of here, start bigging ourselves up," replied Rattigan. "We've been hiding behind Talorc's apron strings for way too long."

"That's something we can all agree on," she replied. "The big question is how do we stand on our own two feet? What choices should we make? Will we shape the future or will it shape us? Dialectically speaking, both conditions are possible. I'd argue that nothing is pre-ordained. Everything is up for grabs. We're living proof of that, if ever it was needed."

"What does that even mean, Sands?" laughed Rattigan. "I'm sorry, but you don't half talk some ruddy garbage sometimes. If that's what a college education does for you, then you can bloody well keep it."

"He would appear to have a valid point, Sands," Birch replied with an amused glance. "So exactly where *are* you headed - dialectically speaking, I mean?"

Sands was finding the mockery hard to take. "Alright, enjoy your little joke. The truth is I haven't decided yet. If you other guys don't need the boat, I'll use it to get as far away from here as I can."

"You're welcome to it," replied Crawley. "You ain't going to remain in one piece if you hang round here much longer; the Romans will see to that. Birch, make yourself useful. You can help her sail that thing, right?"

"You've got it arse about tit, Crawley," Birch replied. "When it comes to seamanship, Sands will be helping *me*. We've already got the chain of command sorted. When we're at sea, I'm the skipper, she's the deck hand. The same applies to you lot. Wherever we do decide to go, I'll be in charge."

"You must be partial to mutinies," taunted Stogdon.

"Don't wind him up, Stog."

"One on land, one at sea – it'd make a bare perfect set," Stogdon continued.

"I doubt you'd have the same swagger if you were caught in a force nine gale," Birch replied.

Stogdon projected his lower jaw in a threatening manner. "Just listen to him. Are you frightened to go around the Horn, Mr. Stogdon? Are you a coward, sir? Old Birchy's only gone and bleedin' turned into Captain Bligh."

Birch squirmed.

"Advantage Stogdon," pronounced Crawley.

Birch glared at his adversary. "I doubt those two words have ever been conjoined before," he muttered.

Sands intervened. Like most of the others, she was keen to avoid needless conflict. "Is Carlisle where you're really planning to go?" she prompted Rattigan.

"Yeah, what's its Roman name again?"

"Luguvalium."

"Is it a good choice?"

"Best of a poor bunch, but it's the only town of any size along the wall. You'd be better off heading for York or Chester instead. Have you thought about how you're going to avoid being recognised?"

"It's been a year. Last time they saw us, we was in Roman army uniform. And the only one who's likely to recognize me, that bastard jailer, he's rotting in his grave."

Birch intervened. "If you want, we can try and get you across the Solway Firth and a fair distance along the River Eden. It'll depend on the river conditions, but if we can't make it to Luguvalium, itself, you should be pretty close."

Ojokwu got to his feet. He looked agitated. "You know what, I'm gonna take a hike. All this talk's doing my head in."

The others looked at Ojokwu in surprise. As he started to make his way down to the seashore, Rattigan motioned to Stogdon to follow his comrade.

"What's up, Ojo, you okay, guy?" Stogdon called as he jogged after him.

"No, I ain't okay, Stog. I'm a long way from okay."

"What is it, man? What's going on?" Stogdon was looking at his comrade with concern.

"My head – it's all screwed up. It's something that she said," Ojokwu mumbled, gesturing at Sands.

"Don't let her get to you, man."

"I ain't complainin', Stog. I'm trapped. I wanna be free."

"We are free, man, you know that. What she's sayin' is just bollocks. She's messing with your head, is all."

"No she ain't, it's just like what she was saying. It makes some kind of mad sense to me."

"Can't you see what's goin' on? She's driving a wedge between us. Look at how she talks to us. She proper looks down on us, man, I'm telling you."

"That's plain bullshit, and you know it."

Stogdon bristled. "Come clean, Ojo, where's your shit at, man?" he demanded. "Are you with us or not?"

"No, I ain't Stog, not in the way you mean. I don't belong here, man. I can see it now. I want to get outta here."

"Yeah, but that's what we're all planning to do, man, just as bare soon as we get back. We're going to cause an ass-load of mayhem in Carlisle, man. Just think about it, Ojo, all that Roman pussy, man."

"No, Stog. Not for me, man. No more. That's the old me you're talking about."

"Are you tripping, or what, guy? 'The old you', what the fuck you talkin' about? What else you gonna do?"

"I think I see what I gotta do," Ojokwu replied.

"Listen to me. *What* you gotta do, motherfucker? Tell me."

"I gotta go with her," he said, pointing at Sands.

THREE

In the bowels of the British Museum, underneath the museum's Great Court, lies a spacious auditorium. In common with the UK's few remaining publicly-owned assets, the auditorium's precious acoustics and serried ranks of plush leather seats - and the bloated sense of entitlement that they confer - are subject to private, commercial hire. This is 2034 after all, a full twenty years after the events described in the first chapter, and by the fourth decade of the twenty-first century it has long been assumed that the state should occupy itself, on behalf of the taxpayer, with extracting the fullest-possible value from its national treasures.

In most respects, the museum, particularly in its external aspect, is indistinguishable from the solid, timeless institution that Dr. Sterland Morris had been connected with in previous decades. Morris, in vivid contrast, has aged in the intervening years. Time, acting like acid rain, has ravaged the external surface of his features, while failing to corrode his inner core.

This evening finds him standing in the wings of the auditorium. He keeps glancing out at the packed audience. A noticeable tremor of anticipation, carried aloft on the wings of a flock of audio technicians, hints at the momentous event that is about to unfold.

A countdown begins and the auditorium lights dim. Morris braces himself for the announcement that will kick-start the proceedings. He glances at the young person, his acolyte, who is standing next to him, poised to step out on the stage and looking anxious. He gives his companion's hand an encouraging squeeze. "Ok, Andrea, just stick to what we've agreed and you'll be fine."

"The name's *A*."

"My apologies. I keep forgetting. I must be getting old."

Finally there is complete silence. And then a disembodied voice begins to intone.

"To the specially invited audience assembled here tonight, and to the millions tuning in live around the globe, we're simply thrilled that you've been able to join us for this historic entertainment event. It's been five years coming. During this time it has become the most keenly awaited product in the history of computer gaming. But now, the long wait is almost over. Ladies and gentlemen, welcome to the official worldwide launch of Pax Britannica II. And without further ado, please welcome your host for this evening - *A* Crossan."

A single spotlight illuminates the young person striding towards the podium.

"My apologies for the bombastic introduction, everyone," *A* begins. "If it's all the same to you, I'm going to crank things down a notch or two."

A smattering of laughter echoes around the hall.

"You may have heard that I'm not one to make a habit of apologising. What I'm about to say may come as an eye-opener to some people who've worked alongside me for the last five years, but I want to be clear where I stand. I know that some of you out there watching this broadcast will find the hype surrounding the launch distasteful. A "sell-out" is a term that's been bandied about in some quarters. You may have written off the commercial excesses as pure gimcrackery, and I'll confess to a degree of sympathy for that viewpoint. Those who know me well will also know that if I full-on agreed with you, I'd have no hesitation in admitting it. But you know what, in one important respect, the most important respect, the excess is justified. In one hour's time, we can demand to see a few questions being answered. At exactly 11pm London time, 7pm New York time and 7am Tokyo time, Pax Britannica II will finally come alive and commence 24-hour realtime VR broadcasting to an estimated 60 million mobile devices and computer consoles. And are you seriously telling me you're won't be one of the millions accessing the game through some device over the next three months?"

Shouts of encouragement can be heard around the auditorium.

"Everyone out there is going to have their own story for why they've bought into the adventure. Most of us, I reckon, well, we'll just want to check out what fate has in store for Sands, Birch, Ojokwu and the others. The first game climaxed with them evading the clutches of their Roman pursuers and seeking sanctuary with some resentful Scots tribesmen. Want to know how that's going to pan out? Log in at eleven to find out. On the other hand, some of you will want to have a blast travelling through a virtual landscape that has been designed to encompass the whole of the Western Roman Empire; that means we're talking about the provinces of Britannia and Gaul and Hispania and all the land surrounding the western Mediterranean Sea. Others will want to explore the physical remains of the era, or maybe experience the communications links unifying the Empire. For the real adventurer, the hard-core gamer, we've built the largest, best-equipped sandpit in the virtual playground. You guys are going to have a complete blast. For the scholar, the student of history, we've produced the most accessible and best supplied learning resource centre in the online academic world. And what's in it for the player who just wants to see what all the fuss is about? Maybe you've never really bought into online gaming, in which case it's a near-certainty you're a woman. Or maybe you've got a purposeful life already, with friends you talk to and have meaningful relationships with, in which case it's a near-certainty you're also a woman. Well for all you sisters, daughters and mothers out there, for the 52% of the world's population who insist on doing useful, human-centred things with your time, we have a Pandora's Box of possibilities: you can choose who and where you are going to be, not just for today, but for each consecutive 24 hours, for the next three months. For absolutely everyone, Pax Britannica II promises a mind-expanding experience. Trust me when I say that all you need is an open mind that is flexible, responsive and generous enough to engage with the enormous life-enhancing possibilities on offer."

"So what is it that will be so unique about this game? It's simple – you'll have your own guaranteed, front row seat where you'll be totally immersed in the scene, just inches from the characters, right in the middle of the action. And how can you become part of the adventure, day in, day out, whenever you want for the next twelve weeks? Equally simple: you go online now, pay for a subscription and, using our onscreen camera, upload three full-length photos of yourself, front, side and rear views. Our technical wizards will do the rest. Within thirty minutes you'll be in possession of your own customisable likeness in the form of a 3d avatar, which you can insert into the game at any point of the action, day or night. No matter where the action is there will always be space in the scene for you and at least one other avatar – so you can always time-travel with a friend whenever you feel like company. But remember, while you can see the game characters, they can't see you. And you will be unable to personally interact with them or influence the story as it develops."

"But, I'm telling you, none of these tantalising prospects would exist if it weren't for the work of our amazing crew of researchers, advisers and visionary programmers. When all else is said and done, Pax Britannica II, like its predecessor, is a serious research tool. And this is where I really get excited. Please welcome the inspiration behind the Pax Britannica franchise, and a personal hero of mine, Dr. Sterland Morris."

As *A* completes the introduction, the beaming face of Morris appears on the giant screen behind them. Spontaneous applause breaks out around the hall.

"Welcome, Dr. Morris. I'm thrilled you are able to join us here this evening."

"Thank, you, *A*, I wouldn't miss it for the world."

A glances at the autocue. "I understand there's an important piece of news you'd like to share with us all tonight."

"That's right. I'm delighted to announce that at 11pm tonight we will be able to unveil a ground-breaking collaboration with the British Museum. At the precise moment that the game goes live around the world, we will jointly publish online the first of

12 authentic and beautifully preserved Roman hand-written tablets. These tablets were recently found in a site located close to Hadrian's Wall. They are all written in the same hand and they form a continuous narrative that will be central to determining the course of the action once the game gets under way."

"So what makes you think that the content of the tablets is so relevant to the game?"

"The evidence is circumstantial but still highly compelling. The writer consistently refers to events and characters closely related to the precise era when the game takes place."

"And the location?"

"The location, too."

"And how often, and when, will the tablets be published?"

"We plan to publish a new one every week for the next twelve weeks. The tablets run in a clear chronological order and they will be released for public scrutiny in proper sequence."

"And what role has the British Museum agreed to undertake in presenting these historic artefacts?"

"Every week the British Museum will unveil a new tablet to coincide with its publication in the online game. The tablets will be presented one by one in sequence, until all twelve are available for public view. They will form the central axis of a specially curated exhibition, which will culminate with the presentation of the final tablet and the climax of the game."

"And what will happen to them once the game's completed?"

"Once the exhibition is finished, the Morris Archive has agreed to donate the *Aballava Tablets* to the British Museum."

A wave of approval rolls down from the auditorium.

"Future generations will be able to enjoy and study these magnificent scriptures, which rank as some of the earliest and most revealing hand-written artefacts ever discovered in Britain."

"And do you really think they will help shed further light on the fate of your niece and her fellow soldiers?"

"Ultimately, that will be up to the general public and the academics to decide. Until we are able to uncover their physical remains, the gamers and historians will continue to be the final arbiters of their fate."

Morris' final words are masked by a cascade of sympathetic applause. After a cheery acknowledgement to the audience, his face fades from the big screen on the wall behind A's back.

A waits for the applause to subside, before continuing the presentation to camera.

"Once the programme starts running later on this evening, we expect that the outcomes will add significantly to our social and historical understanding of third century Rome. But, more importantly, this group journey will allow millions of our fellow citizens to draw an international perspective from the errors and failures of our shared past. Not to put too fine a point on it, that means the screw-ups, but also the successes too. For most of us, the past is too often just a mystery. It appears to have slipped out of focus, out the back door; it's a world in which too many people have been erased or filtered. The future, by comparison, is up for grabs. The future belongs to us collectively, but only if we seize the right to shape it."

A's words are met with a short burst of applause and cheering. A sole dissenting voice crackles out from the dark.

"Stop manipulating the past. You're just rewriting history."

The protester is shouted down. The comment is masked by the applause but it is still clearly audible, visible almost - as if calcified and hanging like a stalactite above the heads of the audience. It is stunning in its unexpectedness.

A looks startled, but is used to such interventions. Ambient noise erasure will ensure that the offending comments are edited from live broadcast.

"And as for those alarmists, those who accuse us of wanting to manipulate posterity for our own evil ends, I've got a simple message: it's time to back up and let the rest of humanity start harvesting the fruits of the past. Your myopic understanding of human interaction has been blocking our view of history since time immemorial. It's time to open up new frontiers in interpretive historical research."

A new wave of applause cascades across the room, obscuring a few angry shouts.

"And towards that end, the producers of Pax Britannica II have agreed to make a £60 million endowment to the International Centre for Comparative Historical Research, which is to be based right here in central London. And that's something that everyone who plays Pax Britannica can be really proud of. We're not just about bricks and mortar, though. We also want to support the nation's youth. We've also made available free institutional subscriptions to any UK university department still offering degree-level courses in Classics or History. I'm proud to announce that in the last week every eligible student has received the full 90 day enhanced interactive pass, plus, of course, a free customised VR headset each."

As they speak, a huge screen behind *A* starts projecting details of the hardware and online subscription packages available for purchase.

"Now that's enough from me. We got a short film to show you before the game kicks off, so don't disappear. Be ready to enter the world of Pax Britannica II in exactly forty-five minutes."

A quickly vacates the stage through a side door, pushing through the throng in the foyer. At the far side, Morris can be seen waving.

"Come join us," he bellows. "There's some people here I'd like you to meet."

A's long-time confederate and colleague, Jermaine Oredieu, is smirking with apparent amusement. He is signing an indecipherable gesture over Morris's shoulder. His eyes guide *A*'s gaze towards the backs of two men in their company.

"What's up, Jermaine? Your probation officers tracked you down at last?"

"No, no, *A*, it's you they is proper looking for."

Jermaine smiles at the astonished look on his friend's face as the two men turn.

A is standing transfixed in front of one of the powerfully built strangers. "Bloody hell! Who are you?"

Slowly A holds out both arms and points at the man, as if picking out a suspect at a police identity parade.

"Stogdon! It's bloody Stogdon," A yells.

The four men guffaw with unfeigned delight.

"Not quite," replies Morris, "but not far off". He gestures towards the stranger. "This gentleman is Professor Marcus Stoddart. Marcus, in case you hadn't heard, is Britain's most eminent evolutionary psychologist."

Stoddart shoots Morris a self-indulgent smile. "You're far too generous, as ever, Sterland, but out of respect for your judgement I won't dispute the accuracy of your introduction."

Morris chuckles. "And quite right too, my dear boy, but don't expect your charm and deference to work quite as effectively on young A, here."

"For God's sake, spare us the Oxbridge drivel," A spits.

The two men share an amused glance. "I rest my case," replies Morris with a knowing smile.

"What's going on?" demands A. "What the hell are you two up to? And what are you doing in the game?"

"Over to you, Marcus," replies Morris. "A's all yours."

A's eyes have not left Stoddart's face for an instant. "Have you been involved from the start? And how come I don't know anything about all this?"

"Listen carefully and all will be revealed," Morris replies.

"Yes - to answer your question directly - I have been involved from the start, but only for the first couple of years. Sterland brought me in during the development of the original game to ensure that the perspectives of evolutionary psychology were fully enmeshed into the gameplay and artificial intelligence system."

"And what a job you made of it, Marcus," adds Morris. "There's an enormous amount there that we need to be grateful for."

"But what the hell is Stogdon doing looking like you?" demands A. "And what's with the similarities in your names?"

"That was just a conceit. He had to look like somebody."

"But why?"

"You want to know why he had to look like somebody?"

"I'm asking why he had to be modelled to look like someone in particular, and like you specifically? It doesn't seem like a very objective, scientific approach to take; especially coming from 'Britain's most eminent evolutionary psychologist'."

"Bit rude, *A*," admonishes Morris.

"He's a big boy, Sterland. He can look after himself. If he *has* reached the top of his profession, he won't have got there without dishing out some good kickings along the way. Ain't that the size of it, Stog?"

Jermaine couldn't contain his delight; that *A* just couldn't give a damn, no matter what the person's reputation. "Oh my days, *A*'s gone and thrown down the gauntlet now, Marcus, good and proper. Over to you, boy - you gotta start hitting back, man, or you're a gonner. *A* don't take no prisoners, this one - trust me."

"Look, come on, Andrea, just back off a bit," Stoddart protests. "There's no need to be so adversarial. Stogdon isn't me, as you full well know."

"For a start, the name's *A*. And, secondly, you're not like Stogdon? Are you fucking joking, or what?"

"No I'm not. And more to the point, Stogdon isn't like me. I could just as well argue that you're like Sands."

"Oh, fuck off - gimme a break. Are you serious?"

"And you expect *me* to buy *that*?"

"That's just lazy conjecture."

"What? Same age, similar looks, same politics?"

"Meaningless coincidence, I've just told you. I wasn't even around when her role was conceived. I was only a teenage games' tester back then. Ask Sterland."

"Identical personalities?"

"I wish."

"Oh, come off it, Andrea, face facts. It's almost as if your two characters are converging. Who's influencing who? Is she becoming more like you, or you more like her?"

A's face is beginning to redden. "You've got some fucking nerve. You're just trying to deflect attention from yourself. I'm not the one with a purpose-built avatar who's running around killing people for fun. That's you, in case you'd forgotten. "

"Considerate of you to remind me."

"My pleasure - partial memory recall must be a bastard. How do you cope?"

Morris steps in quickly before things get totally out of hand. "Ok, are you both done?"

"Absolutely," replies Stoddart. "I'm happy to move on."

"One final point," interjects *A*.

"Be my guest."

"You say there's no similarity between the two of you now. Why's that? Did you originally plan to make Stogdon's personality and character more like your own?"

Stoddart hesitates. He glances at Morris. "Maybe partly it was the intention, but let me phrase this carefully. Let's just say we experimented with a few behaviour modification algorithms. They were designed to influence his essential character but they all failed. They all went down the tubes from day one."

"Meaning what?"

"Meaning Stogdon is simply ill-equipped to adapt. He can't deal with the challenging circumstances that he's found himself in; at least, not in the way that Sands or some of the other characters have been able to."

"So you reckon he never stood a chance then?"

"Not based on the evidence I've seen. I mean, come on, do you? The guy is simply de-evolving. It's most disheartening, especially from a personal point of view. Even when he was attacked on the beach on the first night in the fog it was clear he'd been written off."

"How's that?"

"It's obvious. Remember how the book described it?"

"What bit?"

"The exact wording? "Birch marked the soldier down as the worst kind of insensate brute". Those words are burned on my memory: "the worst kind of insensate brute". He's been defined as a stone-age caveman from the outset and it's all been downhill since then. He's simply living down to type."

A examines Stoddart, animosity giving way to curiosity. "You think he's de-evolved?"

"I'd really love to think that on a moral and spiritual level he's redeemable. But I have to keep reminding myself that it's just a game, after all?"

"It's a game," agrees Jermaine. "But I'm telling you man, it's also a real-world social experiment. The psychology of religion and superstition, sexuality and morality – all that stuff, it's all in there, up-front and centre. I guess we've probably got you to thank for that, Marcus. I'm telling you, I wouldn't wash my hands of any of those characters, especially Stogdon."

"What about me then?" asks the fifth member of the group, whose presence so far has gone unnoticed by *A*. "I better introduce myself. I'm Brigadier Julian Ruffin, commonly known as Jules to his friends. But you may recognise me as Julius Rufinus, Commander-in Chief of Aballava."

"Oh, for fuck's sake, not you too," *A* gasps. "What the hell were you playing at, Sterland? Sometimes I feel like giving up, I really do."

.

FOUR

Caeluibianus, Cohort Tribune and Praepositus of the Company, to Julius Rufinus, Tribunus Laticlavius and commander-in-chief, I send my greetings. In the matter of determining the fate of Galla Placidia (undertaken in the utmost secrecy as directed) I have done so in full accordance with your wishes and have set out my findings below, although I would caution, my Lord, that proof of my report is still far from certain. On your instruction I traversed north of the Vallum Aelium and have received word from our spies among the Selgovae that a young female stranger, answering to the description of Galla Placidia, was met with uncommon courtesy by the king of the Novantae in that place formerly known to us as Rerigonium. It is believed that the king offered her his royal protection in exchange for the surrender of a sailing craft and her agreement to warm the royal bed whenever it pleased his majesty. And if such accounts are to be believed, she rejected his proposal out of hand and roundly abused him for his troubles! To pile insult upon injury, it was not the fate of the boat in question that caused the dispute, as my Lord may well have supposed, but, rather, it was the sanctity of the young woman's virtue that proved to be the sticking-point! May Jupiter and all the Gods preserve us! As a consequence of her headstrong behaviour, both she and her followers, although it is not clear how many, have been denied further sanctuary within the borders of the king's lands and also those of his allies. Knowing what we do about the harridan, my Lord, these reports have the ring of authenticity about them. As to her possible whereabouts, I have received conflicting and troubling reports. One account has her returned to Hibernia, the bog-infested land whence she and her followers are thought to have sprung. As long as she remains outside the borders of the empire, that barbarian country is welcome to her. Her infamy appears to have spread wider than my Lord had supposed, which in itself is troubling, but conflicting sightings of her over the last year - east, west, north and south, and all points in between - have been so regular as to cast doubt on their veracity. I have one good piece of news to report. Proceeding northwards along the coast towards the mouth of the Abravannus Fluvius we espied a barbarian escarpment where Galla Placidia is reported to have found protection earlier in the year. I proceeded ashore to check the strength of the defences and there surprised a strapping youth, clearly one of her conspirators, who attempted to flee. And escape he would have, too, if it hadn't been for the urgent intervention of my two faithful hunting dogs who brought him down and injured him most grievously. They would have separated him limb from limb, as would I, but it was necessary to restrain them in order to preserve the Latin markings inscribed on his inner forearm. In doing so I took care to offer up his life to the Gods before skinning his upper corpse. I duly rewarded my beloved hounds with a thigh bone apiece to sate their appetites and hone their jaw muscles. I know that my Lord may consider me a man disposed to every species of depravity, fixed and immutable, a charge that is unjustly levelled against me by my enemies, but surely indulging my dogs thus reveals a kinder side to my character that may merit approval? My Lord will find the skin along with this letter, and I take pleasure in presenting it to you as a measure of my highest esteem and comradeship. But what should one make of the Latin inscription engraved on the rebel's arm, my Lord? The phrase "VENI VIDI VICI" is attributed to Caesar by the esteemed historians Plutarch and Suetonius. I am at a loss to know how an illiterate barbarian would be familiar with the words of two great men of letters, or, indeed, of the noble Julius Caesar, himself. By the Gods, the more I ponder these puzzles the more I remain convinced that my Lord is right in pursuing Galla Placidia and her gang of unholy conspirators. By discreetly dispatching them, we can prevent rumour of their plot spreading abroad and further impugning our reputations. To that end I am this evening embarked for Luguvalium in response to rumours that have lately been brought to my ears. My spies report that a small group of her cohort may already have breached our defences and may be in hiding there. I will investigate these suspicions personally and will await there until my Lord sees fit to issue me with further instructions. I will do what I am ordered and at every command I will be ready.

FIVE

Location: Irish Sea
Coordinates: 53°56'30" N and 3°35'39" W

Time and Date: 15.30, 2nd July, 258 C.E.

It was early July and it was perfect weather for sailing.

A long midsummer's day had delivered a welcome dose of sunshine and a south-westerly breeze just stiff enough to keep the three sailors on their toes. Throughout the afternoon, the light had reflected with coruscating intensity off the surface of the sea. The waves had yielded without complaint to the effortless passage of the boat's hull. Progress had been steady, if unspectacular, but no-one, least of all the two deck-hands, was complaining. Since dropping their three colleagues off at Luguvalium, life had begun to offer an unexpected, almost forgotten prospect. Here, at last, was a chance to experience a flicker of pleasure, in stark contrast to the persistent pain that they'd all become accustomed to. The future could be glimpsed with something approaching optimism, in contrast to a perpetual sense of dread. This was a rare treat, and it was one to be fully savoured by those who were aboard the small sailing craft. And the boat was more crowded than the three sailors could ever envisage. Millions of individual avatars, in disparate ones and twos, were seated alongside them. These stowaways came and went, minute by minute, mile by mile, day and night. They formed as disreputable an assembly of digital hitchhikers, virtual passengers, cybernated freeloaders and automated fellow-travellers as ever came together in joint enterprise.

The previous evening had seen them anchored in a sheltered bay, close to where the town of Whitehaven was to be built a thousand years later. By the third century, however, there was no evidence of human settlement to be seen, save for a small

Roman fort located on high ground about a mile to the north. Individual gamers, should they have chosen to disembark, would have had the right to wander far and wide. They would also have had access to a time travellers' contextual database, *Guide to Provincia Britannia*, referring them to several sites of local and historical interest.

Location: Whitehaven Bay
Co-ordinates: 54°32′56″ N 3°35′02″ W
Information: Travellers to this part of the world are often surprised to learn that military conflict during the American Revolutionary War didn't just occur in the colonies of North America, but also extended to the very shores of mainland Britain. In 1778 John Paul Jones, father of the United States Navy, led an armed attack on Whitehaven and attempted to set fire and sink the 400 strong merchant fleet anchored in the harbour. Whitehaven is also the last resting place of George Washington's grandmother, who lies buried in the grounds of St. Nicholas' Church.
Recommended Shore Excursion: A thirty minute hike will take you to the site of Gabrosentum, a small Roman fort located 1.2 miles to the north (54°57′37 N 3°57′41″ W) and the final link in the Roman Empire's 'Western Sea Defences'.
Cost of Excursion: Free to all subscribers
Risk Rating: Varies from Low (walk to fort) to Moderately Perilous (exploration of fort compound)

The next day, as they continued their sea journey south, the route seldom strayed far from the sight of land and familiar geography. But the well-known landmarks and views proved to be a mixed blessing, often evoking bittersweet and painful memories among those on board. The virgin landscape was peppered with paradoxical reminders of times past and of times yet to come, from the hills of Wordsworth's Lake District to the rugged peaks of the Isle of Man TT races, from the shipyards of Barrow and Birkenhead to the sand dune golf links of Hoylake and Royal Lytham, and from the muddy foreshore of the Blackpool seafront to the raucous birthplace of John, Paul, George and Ringo.

"You still feeling sea-sick, Ojo?" Sands asked, as they leant back against the starboard side.

"No, man, ever since we passed the Isle of Man I've been feeling a lot better. I'm enjoying this now. And I'm starving, too. Any chance of any grub?"

"Yeah, the swell's gone down. And it's not as humid."

"Yeah, this is the life, man, I'm telling you. Let the wind do all the work."

"Ready to go about?" yelled Birch from behind them. "Ok, you two, on the count of three."

"You spoke too soon, Ojo. Here we go. Mind your head."

Birch swung the tiller over to the opposite side. The boat veered to the right. As the wind angle changed direction it forced the triangular sail and the boom to swing over the heads of Sands and Ojokwu. They ducked in unison, pushing the boom over to starboard and shifting their seats to the windward side of the craft.

"Nice bit of tacking. Haul in your sails a bit tighter, Ojo."

As the sail was close hauled, the boat picked up speed. To counteract the tilt of the craft as it ploughed upwind, all three sailors added their ballast to the port side, squatting with care along the edge of the boat.

"How does this thing even sail into the wind? What's stopping it getting pushed backwards?" Ojokwu asked. "This boat's a proper miracle. Ain't there nothing it can't do, Birch?"

"It's quick and manoeuvrable, especially in fair weather. But there's one down side: you stop baling, we're sinking. The resin's not doing its job. The hull's leaking all over the place."

"How come we can sail so fast into the wind?" The spray was now stinging his face. "It feels like we're going faster than when we got the wind behind us."

Birch pointed upwards. "The sail acts like a giant bird's feather stuck up on end. It's collecting the wind and giving us lift just like a wing would."

Ojokwu and Sands stared up at the billowing sail as if to assess the plausibility of the explanation.

Birch was basking in the attention the boat was receiving. "But by itself, the wind would just push the boat in a direction away from where we want to be headed. To counteract that force we have a fin-shaped keel under the water." He stamped his foot on the hull to confirm that the keel lay under the bottom of the boat. "Simply put, the keel exerts a resistance to the water and forces the boat in the direction we want to go. Without it, we'd probably just end up being blown sideways on to the shore. It's basic physics, really."

"That I get, but how do you compute all them things when you're sailing?"

"No idea. I don't really give much of a thought to the science of what's going on. Sailing's instinctive to me. Once you have a feel for the boat, and know a bit about tides and weather, you don't have to think twice about the physics behind what you're doing. Ask any sailor worth his salt, and if they're honest they'll probably admit the same thing."

"And you think them Roman boats can't do what we can?"

Birch shook his head. "No, no way; we can sail this boat much closer to the wind. Square sails on Roman boats are great when you've got the wind behind you and you have no keel. Otherwise, you're screwed."

Sands threw in her tuppence worth. "The Egyptian grain fleets were stuck in port for eight months of the year. In winter they couldn't make it westward across the Mediterranean to Rome. Compared to them, we've got it made."

"Yeah, we've been proper lucky, especially with this sweet weather," Ojokwu beamed.

Birch's demeanour suddenly changed. "I don't think our luck's going to hold much longer," he replied.

"Why, what's up?"

He pointed over his left shoulder. "Have a look at what's coming directly upwind of us."

Ojokwu shielded his eyes against the glare. "Bloody hell, what's that? It's heading straight this way. It's proper shifting."

"I don't like the look of that boat, Birch," shouted Sands.

41

"Me, neither, and I don't fancy the look of the weather it's bringing with it."

Without any warning or logic, as if on the whim of some unnamed author, the wind had got up and the sky had blackened.

"Bloody hell, this doesn't bode well," said Sands. "Where'd the sun go?"

Her hands gripped the edge of the boat like a vice. She was fighting to keep her anxiety at bay. This didn't feel right. She was becoming too scared, too quickly. Events felt like they were tumbling in on her with terrifying momentum. This sudden change of emotional gear felt very alien, and very out of character.

"I don't like this, Birch. I want to get out of here. Something's not right."

Here, suddenly, out on the dark ocean, under a menacing sky, she felt incapacitated, out of time and out of place. What had happened to the happy vibe she was experiencing a few moments earlier? She'd become mere entertainment for the masses once more. She felt trapped, unable to move, as if spread-eagled helplessly at the bottom of some spiral stairwell. She scoured the horizon for a means of escape. Tumultuous cloud formations pressed in on the boat from every side. Raising her eyes upwards, she found herself facing an avalanche comprised of her own worst fears. Countless memories, regrets, thwarted dreams and ambitions cascaded down, bouncing and crashing against each other as they fell. They smashed and fractured around her on the deck where she cowered. Her chronic anxiety was rendering her defenceless against the assault.

Despite everything, a small piece of Sands had succeeded in detaching itself from the trauma she was enduring. An authentic bit of her could still decipher what was happening. What was she experiencing? It was unnatural, surely? Her sense of self was coming apart. But she could still fight. It wasn't too late for her to re-assert control. "Come on, pull yourself together, do something! Come on, where's your voice?"

"It's a pathetic fallacy," she yelled.

"What's that?" replied Birch.

"The weather: it doesn't augur well." She was pointing at the unnatural cloud formations gathering overhead. The strange words broke the chains of anxiety bounding her. Even so, the wind ripping through the sails was muffling her voice. "We're being set up, Birch. Get us out of here."

"Ok, let's not start panicking yet, Sands. Let's tack to port and see if they change course to intercept us. If they do, then we know we're really in trouble."

As they came about the cold sea spray whipped across their faces. They peered to see what impact their manoeuvre was having on the approaching boat. The advancing vessel was starting to alter course. They were being hunted, that much was now certain.

"If we carry on like this they're definitely going to intercept us," Birch confirmed. "We've got to change course and get them chasing us with the wind behind us. Then we may have a chance."

"Who the fuck are them guys?" Ojokwu muttered, his gaze transfixed on the pursuing vessel.

"What the hell difference does it make, Ojo? Your guess is as good as mine. Irish pirates, maybe? Whoever they are, we need to go about and out-run them."

The two deckhands stared, their faces disfigured with alarm.

"Are you ready to change course?" Birch demanded. "We're going to stay on a starboard tack, but with the wind coming right over our stern. Do you understand me?"

They nodded in unison.

"Do it, man, do it," cried Ojokwu.

Birch pulled the tiller towards him and the boat swung around until the wind filled the sails from behind them.

"Right, let's see what they're made of!"

As the boat built up speed, Sands trained her sight on the pursuing vessel. She estimated the distance between them to be about a mile. She yearned to see the gap between the two craft widen, but it was clear that quite the opposite was occurring, and with a rapidity that was shocking to witness.

"Birch, they're gaining on us fast. Can't you do something?"

"They've got oarsmen as well as a sail. There's no way we're going to outrun them. Look, you can see for yourself."

Birch was right. Only half a mile separated the two vessels now. And with every metre that the gap narrowed, the darker the sky grew and the rougher the sea became. And although visibility was becoming poorer, Sands could make out markings on the ship that compounded her anxiety levels. The vessel's prow was desecrated with a pair of staring eyes, a huge, gaping mouth and a fearsome set of teeth, all of which fell in and out of sight, in symmetry with the billowing waves that crashed on and off the ox-hide hull. And a line of decapitated human heads, fringing the currach's hull, swayed in time to the boat's rhythm, bobbing up and down in a perverse *dance macabre*.

"They've got at least eight oarsmen and a bloody great square sail," she yelled. "Listen, you can even hear them gaining on us." The sound of their pursuers, urging each other on in unison, was carried across the waves to their small craft by the following wind. It was an eerie, awe-inspiring sound that bode ill for anyone in direct earshot.

Ojokwu was now holding an oar with which to ward off the enemy. "She's right, Birch. We're dead and hosed if we carry on like this. What we gonna do, man?"

"Put the oar down, Ojo. You won't need it till I tell you."

"I'm not fucking going down empty handed, man, no way! I'm taking someone with me."

"Just keep calm and do what I say. You're slowing us down."

The gap between the two boats was now reduced to a couple of hundred metres. It was possible to identify the individual outlines of the raiders. Shaggy hair and beards were visible above the edge of the hull and faces could be seen grimacing with the physical effort of propelling a craft through the waves at such a velocity. Their endurance and strength seemed superhuman.

"Look, we can still do this," urged Birch. "Their boat's a bloody currach. They'll be no match for us going upwind. We'll let the oarsmen exhaust themselves as they chase us downwind. Once we change course and head back upwind they'll be unable to steer properly or keep pace with us."

"So when do we change course?"

"At the last bloody minute so they can't intercept us, just as they're about to try and board us. They'll stop rowing to get ready to attack and that's when we slalom past them."

"But they'll be on us in minutes."

"That's why we keep it going for as long as we can, so we can tire them out."

"And then what, Birch?" Sands implored. "What do we do then? Your plan's got a bloody great hole in it."

"Have faith Sands. God put us all on earth for a purpose."

The sea spray was streaming down her face and her clothes were soaked through.

"Are you for real, Birch? What the fuck did God put *you* on earth for? It's always been bloody mystery to me."

"My purpose in life is simple," he replied. "It's to protect you."

Sands shook her head in disbelief.

"Surprised? You satisfied now?"

"Jesus, Birch, why do you do this? Why do you only come good in a crisis?"

"Yeah, and then turn into a fucking miserable bastard when things are looking up?" added Ojokwu.

Sands grimaced. She wiped the cold spray from her face. "Just don't fail us, Birch. If we're going down, let's go out in style. I can't stand the thought of God having any say in the matter."

By now the gap separating the two boats had shrunk to the length of a football pitch.

Birch glanced at Ojokwu. "Okay, Ojo, are you ready? When we tack, we'll be open to assault. They'll hurl everything they've got at us - spears, grappling hooks, the works."

"Bleedin' hell, and how is we supposed to defend ourselves?"

"Here, between you, pull out the stern sheets and have them ready to shield the starboard side when we come about."

With a swift kick Birch loosened the stern sheets from their thwart risers. Sands and Ojokwu yanked the U-shaped wooden seats free.

"They've got handles on the underside to help ward off an attack," Birch yelled.

Presented amidships to the enemy, the stern sheets offered the prospect of substantial protection against spears and projectiles hurled deckwards. "This is more like it," Sands mouthed.

"Get ready to bat 'em away, Kal. My forehand, your backhand - we work as a pair, yeah?"

"Bring it on, Ojo."

"Prepare to repel boarders. Go for it, Birch."

"Ok, here we go, let's move!" he yelled from behind them. "Ready to go about?"

He hesitated, waiting till the last possible moment. "Ok, now!"

Birch slammed the tiller over as far as he could, causing the boom and sails to swing over the heads of his ducking deckhands. The boat swivelled through a third of its circumference and lost speed, the sail flapping with indecision. "Close haul the sail, damn it, Ojo," yelled Birch. "Quick man, let's get moving."

The manoeuvre took the pursuers by surprise. They'd almost caught their prey, but the following wind, which had been their biggest ally, was starting to push them off track. A warning shout went up. The oarsmen had put down their paddles in anticipation of launching their attack and were unprepared for the sight of the small boat cutting across their bows and heading past them.

Angry shouts and curses could be heard as the boats passed within ten metres of each other. The helmsman attempted to intercept the small craft, but merely succeeded in unbalancing his crew members as they prepared to launch a broadside attack. Despite the chaos aboard the *currach*, a hail of missiles and chained hooks rained down on Sands and Ojokwu. Some missed their target, but most rattled off the sides of the boat's hull, showering great splinters of wood up into the faces of Sands and Ojokwu. Both were badly lacerated but they clung to their task of protecting the sail from damage.

But far worse was the next barrage. Cattle entrails and human faeces rained down on them from a great slingshot. The psychological shock of the impact outdid any physical damage caused. The stinking compound of waste and body parts clung with cruel insistence to the limbs and faces of the three sailors as they fought off the next wave of missiles. It covered their feet, their hands and their hair. It hung from the sail, a suppurating sore, a dripping stalactite, anointing their heads and shoulders while they fought for their lives.

As they struggled vainly to wipe themselves clean, a spear flew past them with terrifying power and embedded itself in the inner starboard hull, forcing the boat to shudder upon impact. Next, the stern sheets took the full force of a mighty grappling hook thrown with Olympian power by one of the pirates. It smashed against the wood shield, cracking it in half, but failed to rip through the sail, its intended target. The hook fell on to the deck at Ojokwu's feet and then attached itself onto the boat's starboard thwart riser.

A triumphant cheer went up from the attacking vessel. Now the pirates had them where they wanted them. They simply had to reel them in like a harpooned whale. But this was no ordinary whale they'd hooked. This was as agile and as spirited a sea creature as ever contested a tug of war on the end of a fishing line.

"Cut the line, Birch," Sands yelled.

"No, leave it, let's see how they like being towed backwards."

"Cut the line, Birch, please."

"No. Let *them* cut the line. This is where our keel comes into play."

As the line between the two vessels tightened with a jolt, the violent snap pulled the rear of the pirate boat down, sending a huge wave over her stern and knocking the crew off its feet.

"Cut the line," Sands repeated. Her face was lacerated with small cuts. Blood and faeces smeared her forehead.

"We'll swamp them first," yelled Birch. He grabbed the

pirates' spear from where it had embedded in the hull and yanked it from its mooring. "This is where the prey becomes the predator," he shouted, before hurling the spear back towards the other boat.

It took Sands four hacks with the boat's axe to sever the line binding the two vessels. The first blow was delivered as the spear left Birch's hand. The second landed as the spear launched on its parabola. The third blow coincided with the spear breaching the ox-hide covering of the boat. And the fateful final blow was delivered just as a gaping hole tore open along the waterline of the boat's stern. Shouts of alarm rent the air. The currach was inundated and the crew began to bale frantically in an effort to stem the flow.

The severing of the artery between the two vessels added to the mayhem. Both boats lurched forward, displacing crew and contents overboard. Ojokwu was hurled headlong into the sea but succeeded in holding tight to a line thrown to him by Sands.

His terrified face and bulging eyes could be seen breaking the surface as he rode the waves like a Nantucket sleighride.

"Hang on, Ojo, we got you. Just don't let go."

"Pull, Sands, pull. Reel him in," yelled Birch.

"Help me, Birch, I need help," she implored.

"I'll do what I can," he gasped in pain. He was splayed out in the bottom of the boat, a huge splinter of wood protruding from the flesh of his upper left arm.

"Jesus, Birch, hang in there."

"I can still pull with my right. Pass me the rope."

The sails were flapping in alarm and the boat began to veer off course, but together the two pilots managed, inch by inch, to haul their desperate comrade back on board.

"Nice one, Ojo, you fought like a good 'un," yelled Birch, his face distorted with pain.

"I ain't givin' up on no grove, man, I'm tellin' you. You okay, man?"

Birch was staunching the flow of blood with a cloth.

"I'll live. Now let's get this boat ashore. We've got more chance than they have."

The three of them watched as the crew on the *currach* fought to prevent their craft from foundering. The cries of desolation and despair from the other boat began to fade as the distance between the two vessels widened.

"If we can just make it to Deva, we'll be safe for a while. Talorc's cousin will offer us shelter," said Sands.

"Can you navigate us there, Birch?" asked Ojokwu.

"If you can sail, I can navigate. We're in Liverpool Bay now and then it's a straight up the River Dee to Deva. I'm in your hands, guys."

SIX

"His or her personship in yet?"

"The pair of them have been here all night, Dr Morris - they ain't slept a wink."

"No surprise there. Call down for coffee for six, please, there's a good chap. Mr Jamieson is going to be bringing along a couple of visitors shortly, and, once they've arrived, no one's to disturb us for the next hour. Is that clear?"

Sterland Morris sweeps into the conference room. "Oh, to be in England now that April's there!"

"Oh, to be in bed now that you're here!"

"Buck up, young people, fresh coffee's on its way. What news from afar?"

"The good news," asks A, "or the really, really shit news?"

"I'm feeling optimistic. Let's start the day on the front foot."

"Tell him, Jermaine."

"Twenty-nine point four million online accounts activated in the first ten hours: two point six million in the UK, nearly four million in the U.S. and Japan and Korea about to enter post-work primetime. We should be well happy with them figures. They totally line up with the projections."

"How many are 12 hour free-trial activations?"

"About 55%, but, like I said, that's in line with what we was hoping. So far we've got about twelve million paying customers. The next 24 hours is sign-up or sign-out time for the freeloaders."

"It's a decent start, I'll grant you. Now, what about the other news?"

"Let's wait for Robert to arrive. He needs to hear this too."

There's a knock on the door. A trolley is wheeled in.

"Ah, here comes the coffee."

"Six cups, Sterland?" queries A. "What's going on?"

Before Morris could answer, a familiar face appears around the door.

"Robert! We've been expecting you. Do come in."

Robert Jamieson, Morris' long-time accomplice, enters proud and upright, a sprightly figure in his late seventies. He is followed by two younger men. They're the same pair, Marcus Stoddart and Julian Ruffin, whose appearance had caused A such consternation the previous evening.

"Not those two again," A says. "Are you really serious?"

"Look, you can stop this nonsense right now," snaps Morris. "I won't tolerate this kind of self-indulgent rudeness, so you better start showing some bloody courtesy. These are our guests, and as a senior employee of this organisation, you should damn well start treating them as such. Am I making myself clear?"

A sits back in surprise. It'd been a while since Morris had issued such a reprimand. He could be an intimidating character when roused.

"I think we should all take a deep breath and count to ten," intercedes Robert Jamieson. "Let's not get off on the wrong foot. It's the first morning, for Pete's sake."

"Robert's right," adds Jermaine, "calm the fuck down."

Jamieson throws Jermaine an offended look. "That's not what I said."

"Yeah, but it's what you meant. Anyway, we got bigger fish to fry. Look at the complaints flooding in, man."

"Complaints, what complaints?" queries Morris.

"Overnight, Sterland," says Jamieson, pointing at the large monitor on the wall. "The news feeds are full of them. Look," he continues, reading aloud, "*Outcry over Trauma Suffered by Gamers*."

"And look at this one," interjects Jermaine, "*Vulnerable Gamers at Risk in Online Frenzy*."

"Ridiculous," replies Morris, "they're just playing right into our hands. The bigger the furore, the better it is for us. What do you reckon, Marcus?"

"I tend to agree, Sterland. I'd be much more concerned if we still had a national press in this country, but since the last newspaper stopped printing we've got no natural predators out there. And now that the old television networks are defunct we've only really got the online networks to worry about. Most of them are streaming live updates and highlights packages in some form or another, so they're hardly likely to kill the digital goose that's laying the golden subscription eggs."

"My sentiments entirely," says Morris. "We roll with the punches on this one. The scare will blow over once the drama in the game picks up. No one will be talking about this issue in six weeks' time."

"You don't know that for certain," interrupts A. "I think I should get my avatar in the game. Then we can monitor the subjective effects of the gameplay at first hand. Gamers have been reporting that they felt under genuine physical threat during the first encounter on the boat."

Morris shakes his head. "We've rehearsed this argument a thousand times. The answer is still an emphatic "no". We employ highly-qualified staff to test every feature of the gamers' experience; they're doing exactly what you're suggesting you want to do. Don't corrupt your objectivity. If you put your avatar in the game then you'll become contaminated. Once that happens, you'll be of no use to me, nor to anyone else."

Jermaine taps his comrade on the knee. "He has a point, yeah? You got to rise yourself above the hysteria, not succumb to it."

"I get that," replies A, "but just look at Jules and Marcus here - these guys are actual combatants in the game, not just avatars. How does that work? It's contradictory to have them attending committee briefings if you're determined to avoid cross-infection."

Morris shakes his head in exasperation. "Not now, A, I've made my feelings clear on the question of Julian and Marcus."

"Okay, it's your right to make the ultimate decision. But this is a disaster waiting to happen. Why take the risk?"

"Your objection's duly noted. So, if you're quite finished, let's move on. Now, what can we deduce from the events in the game so far? Any thoughts, Robert?"

"We can safely conclude that poor George McKay has met a despicable end."

"Agreed, it was clearly George that Caeluibianus killed so pitilessly in the first tablet."

"And what of the other three - Rattigan, Crawley and Stogdon?" asks Jamieson.

"Marcus, you know your mate Stogdon better than any of us," remarks A. "Any insider trading you wish to divulge?"

"Nope, nothing you can't divine for yourself. Those three other guys are street-smart - they'd never have allowed themselves to be captured like George - but that Caeluibianus, he clearly has their scent in his nostrils, and he doesn't seem like the type to give up the chase easily. He may have reached Luguvalium by now. The next tablet could reveal more."

"Perhaps it will," confirms Morris, "but like the rest of the population, you'll have to wait another week to find out."

"And you're still the only person to have knowledge of the tablets' contents?"

"I am, and I will remain so until each of the twelve tablets has been publicly unveiled."

"So it must therefore follow that none of the tablets' information has been programmed into the game's artificial intelligence system?"

A laughs. "Once again, Marcus, your capacity to divine the bleeding obvious has left me gobsmacked with amazement."

Marcus Stoddart throws her an acid stare. "Let's hope that irony isn't your strongest suit, Andrea, because, if it is, you're playing with a losing hand."

"It's alright, Marcus, ignore her. It's been a long night," intercedes Morris, before turning his gaze on A and addressing his young disciple. "I, for one, will not release privileged information and threaten to contaminate the game. Let me remind you all that that the reason we have these daily briefings is to sort out precisely what we can confirm from what we may simply suspect."

"Can we confirm in which direction they're heading at least?" asks Jamieson. "Are we all agreed their destination is Deva Victrix, modern-day Chester?"

"We might be able to say much more than that," adds Jermaine. "I think that's just, like, their starting point. We need to be looking much wider afield, do you get me?"

"Go on, Jermaine, what are your thoughts? The floor's all yours," says Morris.

"Ojo's driven to survive, man. It's like he's on a mission now. He ain't just along for the ride. Look at how he fought for his life to get back on that boat. "I ain't givin' up on no grove yet, man," he said. He's chatting about olives; they're heading south, somewhere way south, somewhere hot in the summer."

"France, Spain, Italy, I agree - it could be anywhere in southern Europe, then, but where exactly?"

"Somewhere further south, somewhere that's gonna feel like it's calling him home. Somewhere he's heard about, that means something to him."

"He ain't making it all the way to West Africa, Jermaine, I got to break it to you, guy," says A.

"No shit, little Miss Travelcard - what about Morocco, then? You even think about that possibility? You think the tube line don't stretch all the way down there?"

"Morocco, what's with Morocco?"

"Think about it, real hard. Go on - what's with Morocco?"

A look of realisation dawns on A's face. "Volubilis! The two African soldiers in the bathhouse - Volubilis was their home town."

"The whole division was recruited, man for man, in Morocco."

"True enough, but the connection is purely circumstantial, all the same" says Morris. "You'll have to present a more convincing case than that."

"How about DNA evidence?" Jamieson interjects.

"Go on, Robert, what've you got?"

"You know you've always said we Scots are a strange breed?"

"You're doing yourself a disservice. The term 'strange breed' scarcely does you justice."

"Well, it appears that Scotland's national DNA might bear your assessment out."

"You'll be referring to the 'Scotland's DNA' project undertaken by Edinburgh University in 2012?"

Jamieson looks rattled by his colleague's response. "Good Lord, yes. How in heaven's name did you know that that was what I meant?"

"And you'll be referring to the fact that 1% of Scots males are of Berber descent?"

"I was, I mean I am," he stutters in reply. "Good Lord, man, that's just what I was referring to. But you've obviously known about this all the time."

"Not quite, I only heard of the research findings in 2012 when they were first published."

"2012? But that was over twenty years ago, man."

A interrupts. "Hang on a minute, what are you two on about? What do you mean, they're of Berber descent?"

"It means scientists have been able to directly pinpoint the DNA marker of roughly 35,000 present-day Scottish men as belonging to the ancient Berber and Tuareg tribesmen who currently inhabit the fringes of the Moroccan Sahara. These are the same people who were widely scattered across the Roman province of Mauritania Tingitana in the third century, at exactly the period when the Romans were recruiting auxiliaries."

"Well, I'll be buggered. And how do scientists account for all this Berber DNA in Scotland?"

"They can't," replies Morris with a self-satisfied grin, "but with a bit of luck we can afford them an intriguing hypothesis."

Stoddart nods his head. "Very interesting possibilities begin to suggest themselves. Do you really think that our three could make it all the way down to Morocco?"

"Most certainly they could."

"But how far is it exactly?"

"At least three and a half thousand kilometres," Morris replies.

"Jesus Christ, you must be bloody joking," splutters Jermaine. "They could never make it. Not in that floating coffin, there ain't no way they're going to make it."

"I agree," says Morris. "They couldn't make it through the English Channel in that vessel, never mind the Bay of Biscay."

"So what do they do, walk?"

Morris shrugs his shoulders as he considers his response.

"Could do, I guess. Travel by foot is a distinct possibility."

He then leans forward and types into his personal device.

"Have a look at the big wall monitor," he directs, pointing at a large-scale map of Roman Gaul. "You can see that there's a more than half-decent road and transport network down through France and Spain. Plus, they're all extremely fit. If they had access to money they could make life easier for themselves by jumping on a horse-drawn carriage."

"You think that's their best option?"

"No, I don't. Travelling overland poses too many risks. It forces them into contact with too many people. It brings them into potential conflict with too many soldiers. And it leaves too many footprints for assassins to follow."

"Caeluibianus, for instance?"

"Caeluibianus, in particular; but don't discount any others who may feel like trying their luck."

"So we're back to square one and the sea route then?"

"It's safer, quicker, and a lot less arduous. But they're going to need money, a lot of money. It's not a cheap passage."

"Hang on, before we start discussing money, how are they actually going to get to Morocco?" asks *A*.

"That's relatively straightforward. Stanford University mapped the likely routes over twenty years ago. Their Geospatial Network Model of the Roman World could have provided Birch and Sands with all the relevant transport information back in 2012, way before the two of them disappeared into the ether."

"If they'd known about its existence," ponders Jamieson.

"Kal would have known about it," Morris insists. "She's a classicist and historian and it was freely available online to all users back then. Check it out - I've got an original archived version of the site right here." He opens up the interface on the large monitor. "This is just as it would have appeared to Kal at about the time of her disappearance."

Morris leans over his keyboard and starts to type.

"So, if we input an enquiry for the fastest sea route between, say, Deva - or Chester, as we now know it - and Tingi, which was what Romans called Tangiers in Northern Morocco, then we get the following information."

The group watches, mesmerised. A heavy red outline appears, detailing a route across a crude image of Western Europe. Boxes of additional information pop up on screen in an apparently random manner.

"Bloody hell, twenty-three days, is that what it's saying?" asks Jermaine.

"That's the quickest route. Then they're still going to have to make it overland by foot from Tingi to Volubilis, and that's easily a couple of hundred kilometres."

"So, if all goes well, and they manage 30 kilometres a day," postulates *A*, "it's still going to take them an additional week to get there once they've disembarked in Morocco."

"If all goes well."

"So, they've got to undertake a sea route with, what?" *A* queries, before pausing and counting to complete the answer to the question. "Seven different legs over three and a half thousand kilometres."

"Looks like it."

"Beginning with Durnonovaria. Where the hell's that?"

"Dorchester, near Weymouth - English south coast."

"And then Civitas Namnetum?" *A* continues.

"Nantes."

"And then across the Bay of Biscay to Portus Blendium? Where's that?"

"Suances, near Santander."

"Then over to Flavium Brigantium. That could be La Corunna?"

"You mean A Corunna, from where the Spanish Armada set sail? Not a bad guess, but if you're a stickler for accuracy, it's actually Betanzos."

"And then down the coast of Portugal to Olisipo."

"That's present-day Lisbon, Vasco de Gama's home port."

"Thought so, and finally Gades: I'm guessing that's now Cadiz?"

"Correct, A - Cadiz, from where Columbus set sail on two of his voyages of discovery to the Americas."

"Just a casual observation, Sterland, but has anyone ever mentioned that you seem incapable of imparting basic information without turning it into a history lesson?"

"Just a casual observation, A," replies Morris, "but has anyone ever mentioned that you seem incapable of distinguishing between a basic observation and a question?"

"Ah, A, I'm relieved that you've noticed his tendency to elucidate at every turn," responds Jamieson with a smile.

"You're proper rude, Robert," says Jermaine. "No matter what you say, Sterland ain't no old windbag."

"Hang on, that's not what I said. I do wish you'd stop putting words into my mouth, Jermaine."

"If you say so, Robert. I thought you was being well harsh. I was just trying to stick up for the boss."

A and Jermaine exchange an amused glance. "Stop teasing him," A whispers. "He'll expire from exasperation one day."

"The point I was making is that these are all heroic cities with a heroic past," Morris insists.

"You're seriously extolling the heroic?" questions A. "The structure of heroism was dismantled by James Joyce over a century ago."

"Was it now? Nobody told me. And what did Mr Joyce extoll in place of heroism?"

"You mean as the motive force of everything? Individual passion."

"But these three cities, by their very nature, have been defined by the heroic. In their own way they've all stood witness to epoch-defining events."

"Maybe they have, maybe they haven't. I wouldn't know, and I'm not disputing that, but how is anything you've just said of any relevance to the possible fate of Sands and co?"

"It's an interesting question. Or is it an observation?"

"Take your pick."

"Whichever it is, my response would still be the same. It all boils down to one's preferred methodology."

"And how does your 'preferred methodology' bear any relevance to our characters' fate?"

"Unlike my good self, *A*, you still exhibit a frustrating tendency to regard history as if it were a one-point perspective drawing. In your world view, events and individuals inevitably appear foreshortened. They become less significant the further they recede into the background. Ultimately, they're all destined to disappear along a single vanishing point, as if being sucked into a black hole. In this sort of perspective view it becomes increasingly difficult to judge the relative size, significance and scale of individual features; as you have just admirably demonstrated."

"Is it just me, or is that *not* sounding like a compliment?"

"On the other hand, if you will pardon my protracted analogy, *I* prefer to approach history as if it contained the information and qualities of an orthographic drawing."

"Meaning what, exactly?"

"Meaning, that history would be better served if it was considered as a form of parallel projection with a front, side and plan view."

"You mean a technical drawing."

"Indeed. The great advantage of such drawings is that all elements appear full-size, irrespective of their relative position to each other, or to the observer. Every detail is recorded and given equal importance. It allows one to reconstruct a fully-formed scientifically accurate model. From where I'm positioned my preferred historical perspective, with no single vanishing point, is entirely superior to yours. I believe it's necessary to examine the past from multiple perspectives if one wishes to understand the future, but there is nothing to stop the past running concurrently with the future, or the present, for that matter."

"You're beginning to sound more like a structural engineer than a historian."

"One observes the historical landscape from whichever vantage point one happens to be located, but it certainly helps to have access to all the blueprints if one intends to eliminate parallax error."

"That's easy for you to say, perched up on that high horse of yours. But once you've hogged the best view, is there any room for anyone else?"

"Why shouldn't there be? Come and join me whenever you feel like it. It's a magnificent sight from up here, but I have to warn you that accessing the view is a hard won privilege. It accompanies sixty years of scholarship."

Jermaine laughs out loud. "He proper got you there, *A*. Oh yeah, admit it, you got owned."

A grimaces with ill grace. "Go ahead, Sterland, pull rank, that's another privilege you've earned."

Marcus Stoddart licks his right index finger and chalks up a metaphorical point for Morris.

"Now, if you two have settled your differences, I have a question for you," says Brigadier Julian Ruffin.

"Forgive our bad manners, Jules. Ask away," responds Morris with a smug grin.

"Where's the money going to come from to pay for their passage to Morocco?"

"Are you writing all this down, Jules? I really don't want notes going out of this room. I thought I'd made that clear to everyone."

"Yeah, and you do realise, don't you, that it's you, Julius Rufinus, Roman commander-in-chief, that they are running away from?" says Jermaine.

"Oh yes, absolutely, I'm quite clear about that. And I'm planning to do everything in my power to ensure that their journey is as short and as unpleasant as possible. You see, unlike Marcus Stoddart here, I'm not in denial about my role in all of this."

"Now hang on, Julian, don't try and speak for me."

"Well, at least he's being honest, you gotta hand him that," ripostes *A*.

"I'm just doing my duty to my emperor," says Ruffin, in a matter-of-fact manner, as if this was a confirmation of the blindingly obvious. "It's every soldier's first responsibility. Surely you bods in civvy street should have realised that by now?"

"Yes, Jules, we're grateful to you for reminding us," adds Morris. "But no notes from now on, there's a good chap."

A and Jermaine fix each other with a bemused stare.

"Is that it then?" *A* asks. "He's just hand-sewn his colours to the Imperial standard and that's the best response you can come up with – no more notes, there's a good chap?"

"No more notes," confirms Morris.

A emits a guffaw and stuffs a couple of croissants into a coat pocket. "Right, in that case, I'm off to bed then. No point in hanging around here. Give us a shout if anything untoward happens."

SEVEN

Aballava Tablet No. 2, Inventory No 13.21 (Morris Archive)

Caeluibianus, Cohort Tribune and Praepositus of the Company, to Julius Rufinus, Tribunus Laticlavius and commander-in-chief, I send my greetings. In the matter of determining the fate of Galla Placidia (undertaken in the utmost secrecy as directed) I have done so in full accordance with your wishes and have set out my findings below. My Lord, on my own cognisance, and as reported in my last letter to you, I endeavoured to follow our prey's trail to Luguvalium. Upon arrival, and conducted with a discretion that raised no hint of suspicion, I was able to ascertain that our slippery young fish had not only evaded the net laid for her capture, but had also succeeded in depositing her rebellious spawn in the nearby shallows. On further enquiry, my spies later reported seeing three strangers engaged in a murderous, drunken brawl with a group of our auxiliaries from the *Legio Vicesimae Valeria Victrix*. The encounter spelt a messy end for a number of our lads and substantial injury to the good name of the Legion. It seems that *Legio XX* had a wolf by the ears and knew not whether to let it go or hang on for dear life. By the Gods, they paid for their indecision! To pile insult upon injury, the rebels were able to slink from the scene of their crime and have not been apprehended subsequently. Descriptions of the men confirmed that it was indeed they who desecrated our standards at the fort of Aballava on the night of our greatest humiliation. Wild reports circulate that one of the criminals – the most vicious combatant, or so I'm assured – possesses a physique of such prodigious proportions that it would cause Lucius Aurelius Commodus to blush with envy. Estimates of his length vary between six and a half and seven *pedes*. In the name of Jupiter, what wouldn't I sacrifice in order to whet my carnal and gladiatorial appetites on this magnificent specimen of manhood? Trust me when I say, my Lord, that I will take the greatest pleasure in hunting him down and impaling him in your honour. I am presently embarked for Deva Victrix in response to anonymous reports that this is where our foxes may lately have fled. By tracking the cubs I intend to uncover the lair where the vixen lies. I'll surprise the whole gang of conspirators in the very home of the *Legio XX*, where revenge is served at its hottest and sweetest. From the smoke into the flame, how beautiful is that irony? They may yet have cause to regret ignoring the old tenet that a wise man does not piss against the wind. With your permission, I have selected the Berber auxiliary, Bostar, the corporal who first arrested Galla Placidia, to attend to me on my journey. He knows the girl as well as any, possesses a ruthlessly cruel streak that I admire, and can act as my eyes and ears when occasion demands. May I not shrink from my purpose, my Lord. I will do what I am ordered and at every command I will be ready.

EIGHT

Location: Deva Victrix
Coordinates: 53°11'36" N, 2°53'28" E

Time and Date: 21.30, 9th July, 258 C.E.

The sun was preparing to sink below the horizon. Deva Victrix, the home fort of the XX Legion, was enjoying every last second of daylight as it basked in the tumescent embers of the evening's glow. The fortress lay warm and secure in the embrace of the river *Deva Fluvius*, its western and southern ramparts wrapped inside its protective, soothing tributaries.

Seen from the vantage of a hovering kestrel, Deva presented a magnificent site. The fort, the largest in Roman Britain, covered fifty acres, almost ten times the area of its equivalent in Aballava. Over the previous two centuries, its strategic location had suggested that it might rival Londinium as Britannia's provincial capital. By the middle of the third century such a prospect had passed it by, but little had inhibited the town's expansion as a commercial and trading centre. The buildings outside the fort spread across the face of the land like a benign lesion. Docks, slipways and warehouses were arrayed for five hundred meters along the shoreline to the west of the fort and in a series of streets running parallel to it. On the river's southern bend lay a five-arched bridge that led to the fort's south gate through a thriving area of residential dwelling houses. Immediately adjacent to the south-east corner of the fort lay Deva's most spectacular building, a two-tiered amphitheatre capable of accommodating 10,000 spectators, the largest structure of its kind in Roman Britain. From our bird's-eye view it would be clear that the most populous area of the town lay to the east of the fort. Many dozens of houses could be espied, arrayed in serried ranks on a semi-formal grid system. And it was within this packed neighbourhood that Sands, Birch and Ojokwu had been granted sanctuary by a local trader, who also happened to be a Novantae tribesman and a distant cousin of Talorc's.

For the past week the three comrades had kept a low profile, not venturing out on to the street during daylight hours. Sands had decided to confine herself indoors, convinced that she would be recognised the moment she set foot in public. The two men were more sanguine about their chances of passing unnoticed. The previous night, Ojokwu had been cajoled into accompanying Birch, his wound now healing, to a nearby gambling house. He then watched in reluctant admiration as the officer ran rings around his opponents at the gaming tables. This was a new Birch, still arrogant and headstrong, certainly, but now more astute and confident in his ability to manipulate situations to his benefit. The previous nine months, during which Birch's gambling and language skills had been honed under Sands' wary tutelage, had been put to good use. It was apparent to Ojokwu that here, at last, was a man to be reckoned with. Not only was he adept at adjusting to changing circumstances, but he appeared to thrive on the challenge of doing so. Birch was a man who expected the environment to adapt to his needs, to bend to his will, to concede ground on his terms, rather than the other way round.

Tonight promised to be a perfect opportunity for Birch to press home his advantage. He was sitting at a gaming table with six Roman soldiers, a number of whom appeared the worse for drink. As his winnings started to grow, his confidence appeared boundless.

In contrast, Ojokwu looked uneasy and self-conscious. He'd selected a shadowy table on the periphery of the room, from which vantage point he could both observe the action and deflect the attention of curious locals. His sequestration appeared complete.

After an hour his isolation was disturbed by the unwelcome attention of a dark haired young man in a hooded cape. Ojokwu was aware that he was being eyed with interest. The youth sidled over and sat down on the bench next to him. Ojokwu could feel his insolent stare and smell his pungent, unpleasant aroma. The interloper sat so close that he could feel the man's arm and thigh pressing hard against his own. And then the young man spoke.

"Budge up, Ojo, for fuck's sake."

"Kal, what the hell?"

"You didn't recognise me?"

"You kidding me, what you done to yourself?" He pulled her hood to one side.

"Roman gender makeover."

"You what? You look like a boy."

"Uh, yeah... like that's the whole point."

"But what the hell you done to your hair, Kal?"

"Caesar cut - the latest look for adolescent males."

"But you been and dyed it black?"

"Yup."

Ojokwu shot her a grimace of disapproval. "Don't take it wrong, Kal, but this ain't you. I liked your hair the way it was. Now you don't even smell like a girl. You fair stink, man."

"Hey, thanks, Ojo. That'll be the hair dye."

"The hair dye? Oh my days, what the hell kind of muck you been spreading on you, girl?"

"It's a special concoction - courtesy of Talorc's cousin: leeches rotting in red wine for forty days. It works a dream."

He shot her an offended glance "A nightmare, more like. You ain't pulling tonight, trust me. Not smelling like that, you ain't. Now back up a touch, you hear?"

Sands smiled at his open disapproval. "Don't fancy me no more, huh? Admit it, you didn't recognise me, did you, Ojo?"

"No, I gotta give it to you, Kal, you're proper changed, man."

"So now you can think of me as your little brother."

"You tripping or what? I had lotsa thoughts about you since I first met you, Kal, I ain't ashamed to admit it." He bent forward and whispered. "But I got to tell you, none of them has ever been in the utmost bit sisterly, never mind brotherly-inclined. That's way too far a stretch."

Sands' face was reddening. She shot Ojokwu a shy look and nudged him. "Come on, Ojo, please let's not go there again."

Ojokwu bent his head back and emitted a resigned sigh. "That's bare easy for you to say."

"Maybe not as easy as you always make out. I'm not entirely without feelings."

"Brotherly feelings?"

"Come on, Ojo, things aren't as simple as you keep pretending. I have to hold myself in check if I'm going to survive. There's a price on my head, remember?"

"So why would that stop you getting with me?"

Sands shook her head. "I don't believe you. You guys are all the same. So what the hell am I gonna do if I fall pregnant? You ever stop and think about that?"

"That didn't seem to bother you none when you was with Talorc. Did it now?"

"See, this is just what I'm talking about, Ojo. This way of thinking is dangerous. You don't know what Talorc and I got up to. No one does, and it isn't anyone else's business anyway."

"You saying you didn't have no sex with Talorc?"

"That's not what I'm saying. I'm saying it's none of your business whether I had sex with Talorc or not."

"All them guys think you did."

"Do they now? That hardly surprises me. And what about Birch, has he expressed an opinion on the matter?"

"Him, no, he's pure persuaded you're a lesbian."

"Jesus, don't you guys have anything better to talk about?"

"Well you did ask."

"A lesbian?"

"You did ask, Kal."

"You serious?"

"Big time."

"He's gonna love my new look then."

"One way you could prove him wrong."

"Oh, shut up will you."

"Just saying."

"See where this all leads?"

"Uh huh."

"Things just get mixed up and complicated."

"Sure do. You like to keep things straight and simple, right?"

"That's what I've been trying to say."

"Not sure life plays by them rules."

"What rules? We need to set our own rules if we plan on surviving. You know me, I'm not going to give up control to anyone else, particularly you two guys."

Ojokwu gave a resigned smiled. "I get you. But my offer still stands, any which way you feel like taking it up."

"Come on. You're my best buddy, Ojo. But we're not meant for each other like that. You know that as well as me. We need to know we can always rely on each other."

Ojokwu nodded.

"So let's not be going there, yeah? It's just going to screw up our friendship, I know it."

He gave her hand a discreet squeeze. She reciprocated with equal pressure.

"Okay, how's old Birch doing then?" she asked, keen to change the subject. She peered through the smoke. He still appeared to be immersed in gambling. "He's a game lad, I'll give him that."

"You're not wrong there. He's been raking it in so far this evening."

"Who's got last night's winnings? Not him, I hope. We don't want to risk losing everything."

"Got most of it right here, safe and sound."

"How much?"

"A couple of hundred denarii."

"And how much you reckon he's won tonight?"

"Easily that much again."

Sands nodded with approval. "Has he now? Good old Birch. He's a quick learner."

"He's also cool and sober like a judge. But them Roman soldiers is well tanked-up."

"That'll help."

"Oh yeah."

Sands got to her feet. "I'm just gonna have a peek around. I want a closer look at what he's up to. I'll be back soon."

"Don't get too close now, Kal. Don't you be drawing no attention to yourself, you hear?"

"See you in a while," she replied. Then she was gone.

As she departed, the gambling house was beginning to sag under the pressure of the new patrons pouring in through its doors. Many of these customers had come with the intention of gambling a whole week's wages, others were tooled up to drink themselves into a blind oblivion, while the ragged remnants were determined to sponge whatever they could in pursuit of fleeting redemption at the bar or gaming tables. There were, however, a number of exceptions to this general rule. Principal among these were the female serving staff who, in common with their successors down the centuries, appeared efficient, polite and tireless but were hard-pressed and often abused for their efforts by a drunken, unconstrained male clientele.

This raucous environment provided a convenient smokescreen for anyone wishing to deflect the interest of casual observers, and this was a state of affairs that Ojokwu and Sands were not slow to exploit. But in addition to them, there was one other figure whose presence went unremarked: a shadowy, furtive character, attentive and yet anonymous and withdrawn. He stood in rapt attention as the drama unfolded at the gaming tables; and in particular, his attention was locked on the table at which Birch held court with such spectacular success. An observant bystander might have noted the care with which he hid himself in the shadows. A sober onlooker would have remarked on the piercing intensity with which the man followed Birch's moves. But observant bystanders and sober onlookers were few and far between that night. In fact, they were only made noticeable among the throng by the spectacular degree of their absence; to all intents and purposes, the shadowy figure might just as well have been invisible. But this was not a world in which intent or purpose could withstand close scrutiny or the application of cold logic. Contrary to reason and expectation, this was a world in which a single sharp-eyed, clear-headed onlooker *did* exist. And it was not long before her full attention was focused on the mysterious figure who had positioned Birch firmly in his cross-hairs.

Sands pressed herself close to the wall and watched the man out of the corner of her eyes with a mixture of alarm and dread. Despite his efforts to conceal himself, she had no difficulty in recognising him. He was the same Roman corporal, Bostar, who had arrested her on her first trip into Aballava. She pulled her hood lower down over her forehead and shrank bank into the folds of her cloak. Her heart was pounding hard in her chest and she could feel the bile rising in her throat. She glanced in Ojokwu's direction but he was no longer in her line of sight. Had Ojo seen the corporal? Had the corporal seen him? Either way, Birch's cover was blown. He was being stalked. His identity was uncovered and they were at risk of imminent seizure. Sands would have to act quickly.

NINE

Aballava Tablet No. 3, Inventory No 13.22 (Morris Archive)

Caeluibianus, Cohort Tribune and Praepositus of the Company, to Julius Rufinus, Tribunus Laticlavius and commander-in-chief, I send my greetings. In the matter of determining the fate of Galla Placidia (undertaken in the utmost secrecy as directed) I have done so in full accordance with your wishes and have set out my findings below. Since my last report, my Lord, the winds of chance appear to have swung, both literally and figuratively. With the blessings of the Gods they now appear to be blowing resolutely in our favour. We are so close to the fleeing heels of Galla Placidia that I can detect her scent in my nostrils. I can also report with satisfaction, my esteemed Lord, that one of her fellow conspirators now lies dead, killed by my very own hand within the last twelve hours. However, in the belief that a story half-told is a story best left untold, I will proceed with deliberation to lay out every aspect of our recent undertakings in Deva Victrix. As recounted in my previous report, we proceeded thither in the belief that the conspirators would arrive in advance of us; a conjecture that, while well-founded, proved to be both half-true and half-false. Of the three rebels who attacked our auxiliaries in Luguvalium there was no sighting. But of Galla Placidia, herself, and of two others members of her cohort, there was plentiful evidence of fresh markings and a scent so strong that the hunting dogs of Actaeon might have directed our chase. And so, my Lord, with the willing assistance of the gods, and with the lure of silver as an inducement to the local Britons (who appear as pitifully corruptible as their fellow countrymen in Aballava), we were able to ascertain the conspirators' hideout with exemplary speed. With the support of two auxiliaries we interrogated the

71

inhabitant of the property, a sullen fellow who claimed to be an apothecary by inclination and a cattle trader by family obligation. Under scrutiny he identified himself as a member of the Brigantes clan and a distant relation by marriage of the Selgovae rogue, Talorc. It pains me to remind you, my Lord, but this is the same Talorc who escaped captivity in Aballava through the intervention of Galla Placidia. As for the apothecary, I found his surly disposition to be an open affront to the dignity of my Lord's noble office. Tradition dictates that your personal representative should be accorded the same respect, as you would demand, *in absentia*, my Lord. Matters in this regard improved immeasurably once I applied my attention to the man's incisors. An apothecary's dentistry implements are a blood curdling sight, my Lord. They may be insufficient to incite full-scale panic among a phalanx of drunken Germanic barbarians, but in the inexpert hands of a novice such as myself, they have a rare capacity to loosen tongues as well as fangs. Indeed, I was able to extract the truth with as much ease as I did the man's teeth, much to the consternation of Bostar who revealed himself to be surprisingly squeamish for such a seasoned campaigner. However, among the general blood and oaths, two particular pieces of intelligence were prised from the apothecary's lips before he died. Firstly, it transpired that the harridan and her disciples were at that very moment acquiring funds for their continued passage south, a local gambling house being their most likely port of call. The second piece of information was more disturbing, my Lord, and may cause us to pause before determining our future strategy. It came in the form of a defiant curse, delivered with the man's dying breath, in which he predicted that shrines to Galla Placidia will spring up wherever her legend has spread, particularly among the Brigantes and their allies in far-flung territories. Alas, my Lord, bitter experience has attested that the final words of a dying man, no matter how preposterous they sound, are more likely to contain the truth as not. Empty threats are reserved for the living. After all, who would risk jeopardising a final wager on the hazard of a counterfeit coin? I ask that you commend these concerns to Cerialis Equester, centurion in charge of the region at Luguvalium. With your permission, we may yet snuff out the flame or rebellion before it is truly lit. Of the immediate whereabouts of Galla Placidia, however, I have less certain news. Determining that it was best to await the return of the rebels and seize them in their sanctuary, I despatched Bostar to various gaming houses in order to detect the insurgents and confound their purposes. I regret to report that the god's did not smile kindly on his endeavours. He swiftly identified one of the male rebels - Galla Placidia's brother, no less - but chose not to apprehend him.   Instead, he saw fit to call for reinforcements! By the time he'd readied himself to return to the tavern, our prey had fled in alarm and has not been located since. May the gods preserve me from the folly of fools! I am certain, my Lord, that it is but a question of time before we unearth the she-wolf from her lair and have the pleasure of exterminating both her and her progeny for good. I will write as soon as I have more intelligence to impart. May I not shrink from my purpose, my Lord. I will do what I am ordered and at every command I will be ready.

TEN

"So, first things first; our subscribers want to know how you've reacted to this week's reviews."

A shoots a thin smile at the interviewer. "The critics have been saying all sorts of things. Anything in particular you want me to react to?"

"Maybe we could take a typical example? There's one here from yesterday's *Digital Screamer*."

The headline flashes up with gusto on the huge monitor at the back of the studio.

"Not the *Screamer*, again - are you serious? That's the problem with you online broadcasters, always picking over the same landfill, always recycling the same rubbish. I'd have brought an anti-pollution mask if I'd known."

"You did ask me for an example."

"More fool me. Let's have it then."

The interviewer starts to read: *"The old Sands used to stand and deliver. That Sands would have taken Bostar down when she had the chance. She had balls. But last week, when the new Sands had the opportunity to show us what she was really made of, she turned tail and ran during the game's first big set-piece showdown. And it wasn't just our heroine who was left looking emasculated. All round, the whole session was one almighty cop out. Thank God, at least, for Caeluibianus. He's turning out to be as nasty a piece of work as ever graduated from the pantheon of Roman psychopaths."*

"Your response?" the interviewer asks.

"It's a predictable opinion; it's actually quite coherent, as reactionary rants go. It's not one I would agree with, of course, but that's the nature of the beast we've created. Everyone is entitled to their say, no matter how big their megaphone. I do, at least, agree with their opinion of Caeluibianus."

"But what about the central point made in that review? Fans feel let down by Sands' unwillingness to engage the enemy head on."

"Hang on, wait a second. Last week when I was on this show, you criticised the new game for frightening the audience too much. '*Help, they're all getting traumatised*!' You can't have it both ways. Be consistent, at least."

"Who says I can't have it both ways and still be consistent? Isn't it possible that what's really happening here is that you're just getting it consistently wrong? I'd suggest that you've been equally inept in misjudging both situations."

"No, I don't accept the basic premise that we got it wrong in the first place, in either of the situations. We're getting blamed here for failing to satisfy the media's blood-lust. You'd do better cross-examining *Digital Screamer* for their motivations. Who's calling them to book for their open misogyny?"

"It might surprise you that our on-line polling shows that most female gamers agree with you."

"I'm not at all surprised. Of course they do, that's my whole point. Individual gamers identify with the characters. They understand and accept that Sands is most likely feminine, possibly intergender, but not a surrogate man nor a programmed robot. Imagine what it must be like for her, just for a minute. Imagine the fear, the uncertainty and the self-doubt she must experience on an hourly basis. And yet, despite everything, she continues to show remarkable levels of resilience, courage, humanity and leadership. All this, *all this*, without ever having had a single female character she could trust or confide in. Imagine that the next time some sexist troglodyte accuses her of having 'no balls'."

"But you can understand, surely, why some of your twenty-five million subscribers would have felt let down by her? She failed to rise to the dramatic challenge of confronting her old nemesis."

"Some would object, sure they would, but the same people would probably also object to the fact that we now have a transgender Leader of the Opposition in Britain."

"Are you really accusing your own customers of being transphobic as well as sexist?"

"Am I? No, not really. Not all of them. But some of our subscribers certainly are. What I'm saying is that none of us should allow casual bigotry and misogyny to pass unchallenged. And that particularly applies to media commentators like you."

"You think I'm part of the problem?"

"Absolutely you're part of the problem. That's because you're colluding; you're inviting right-wing crit-feeds like *Digital Screamer* to set the agenda for the debate."

"So, in the world according to *A* Crossan, who should be setting the agenda?"

"Sands."

"Sands, you say; mediated through whom - you, perhaps?"

"Let her define herself. She's a free agent. She's not a surrogate man. And she's certainly not a plaything for the masses. Why can't she be allowed to own a non-binary identity? Is that so shocking in this day and age?"

"But there's your problem right there, see? You've set her up as a plaything for the masses. By any standard she's proved herself to be the most bankable performer of the last decade. If you want her to remain commercially successful, you have to conform to the public's lowest expectations. That's what they're paying their subscriptions for, that and your salary."

"Not necessarily. Most gamers don't object to the fact that she's now found herself in a safe place, on a proper, seaworthy boat heading south to a new life."

"A lot do."

"Okay, some may feel a little short-changed, but that's hardly a tragedy, is it? I mean, so what? Some people may have had a night of Roman gambling cut short when Birch scurried out of the tavern in a hurry. Big deal; we'll underwrite any losses that gamers have incurred. We've already undertaken to refund any outstanding wagers and stakes that can't be cashed in or reused."

"But it was a pretty undignified exit. Gamers were rudely interrupted; they were just settling in at ringside for the evening's main event."

"Hey, what can I say; life and death decisions aren't always choreographed aesthetically to echo the toss of a dice at a gambling table. Gamers had better get used to the unpredictability of this form of gameplay. They may find themselves being cast in the role of disposable pawns more often than they'd like."

"Is this your idea of customer care? Is this some kind of joke? Are you suggesting that subscribers should start getting used to this kind of dismissive treatment?"

"It's the sort of fluid gamer experience that our subscribers want. And I can assure you that future encounters are going to feel a whole lot more challenging, and satisfying, as a result."

"Do you think you get treated unfairly by the media?"

A sat back in surprise. "You mean me, personally?"

"Yes, you, personally. You have an abrasive manner that rubs a lot of people up the wrong way. Is that fair comment?"

"I've been known to not be everyone's cup of tea, if that's what you mean. I am aware that there's been a lot of negative comment about me over the years, yes."

"And what do you put that down to?"

"I put it down to the fact that you're correct - I do have an abrasive manner. I try to stand up for what I believe in, and say what is right, but I can see why some people might get hacked off with me."

"Your self-righteousness?"

"If you like."

"And judging by today's performance, it looks like you haven't changed much."

"Great."

"Apart from your name, of course."

"That's right."

"So tell us about that."

"About what?"

"Your new name."

"My new name? I don't see how my name bears any relevance to the subject matter of this interview. That's taking liberties, even by the questionable journalistic standards of this show."

"Why don't we let our five million viewers be the judge of that? So what happened to Andrea?"

"What happened to dear old Andrea? She metamorphosed into someone new. She wasn't happy with the gender she'd been assigned at birth. There's nothing special or magical about it. It happens all the time."

"But why change your name to *A*?"

"*A* is the indefinite article."

"Meaning?"

"It seemed to fit somehow with how I viewed myself. I liked the ambiguity and open-ended implications of being represented as an indefinite article. It also happens to be the first letter of my old name, and the first letter of the alphabet."

"So what gender have you chosen to assign to yourself?"

"Genderqueer or non-binary; I'm happy with either description. It's all about personal authorship."

"See, now this is where your own campaign of self-colonisation, if I can term it such, begins to intersect with one of the central themes of Pax Britannica."

"Oh man, I can totally predict where this line of questioning is headed."

"I'm referring to the lust of the individual - or Sands, more specifically - to carve out their own history and identity. Or, if you'd prefer, her ongoing struggle for personal authorship."

"People always try and draw some kind of parallel between Sands and me."

"Like it or not, but you are the public face of the game."

"That's just PR. Someone's got to do it. It just helps if it's someone who's in the public eye."

"But some people feel your influence runs deeper than that. What about Sands' sudden decision to disguise her gender, to reinvent her identity? Is that just pure coincidence?"

"No, I don't hold with the whole concept of coincidence. Journalists are always trying to find meaning and significance where there is none. Sands is a free agent. She acts in her own best interests, as she sees fit. It's insanely ridiculous to draw any link to my personal life."

"But some gamers are suspicious of your influence. They suspect you'll exercise an undue sway over the flow and outcome of the game."

"Have you ever met Sterland Morris? Can you see him allowing that to happen?"

"Sterland Morris moves in mysterious ways."

"So you have met him then?"

"That's not what I meant."

"Is that you laughing?"

"Stop it."

"So you are human?"

"There is a rumour to that effect…"

"And you have been known to laugh?"

A disembodied voice shouts out, "Not in living memory."

Laughter erupts among the technicians out of shot.

The interviewer smiles to camera. "Ok, I'm going to try to manoeuvre my way back into this interview before I lose all my dignity."

"Go on, then, it takes some guts to out yourself as a human being in front of five million viewers; you deserve another shot at a question."

"You mentioned Sterland Morris just now."

"I did."

"What can you tell me about his role in the discovery of the *Aballava Tablets*? Their provenance is still a mystery."

"You'd really have to ask him. But my understanding is they came to light as part of an archaeological exploration he was undertaking about five years ago."

"In Aballava?"

"In Burgh by Sands, it's modern name, yes. It's my understanding that this is a matter of public record."

"Well, there seems to be a little confusion surrounding the exact circumstances of the find."

"There's a veil of secrecy, perhaps, but no confusion. It's only sensible that the exact location of the site should be withheld in order to deter scavengers and souvenir-hunters."

"And the twelve tablets that are central to the new game's narrative, these constitute the entire collection of writings that were unearthed at the time?"

"Yes, as you know, they formed a collection that was uncovered by a local farmer who was digging a ditch in a field."

"So, there are no tablets missing?"

"I think I just answered that question. They will all be there, on display, in the British Museum, all twelve of them, for anyone who wants to come along to examine them in person."

"The first three are on show there already, right?"

"Yep, the fourth one will be released for display as soon as the contents are revealed in the game next week."

"And you can't give us a sneak preview?"

"Wish I could. I'm just as much in the dark as everyone else."

"No chance of a scoop, then? Not even for your favourite human?"

"No chance; your Pulitzer Prize is just gonna have to wait."

ELEVEN

Location: Londinium
Coordinates: 51°30'27" N and 0°5'16" W

Time and Date: 07.00, 18th July, 258 C.E.

Four men were walking together across a long wooden bridge. Every twenty metres or so, they stopped and surveyed the early morning scene.

The river they were traversing was wide and grey but the reflection of the sun's rays transformed the panorama into one of heroic coruscation. The scintillating sparks and flashes of the light elevated the spirits of all those lucky enough to share the view. And there were a good many other people on the bridge with them that morning. Some were rushing to work across the other side of the river, some were late for meetings, others were delivering goods or were making their way to the early morning market. A sea of heads bobbed up and down as the human waves beat towards the shore. And demanding the right of way - then as now - was the overwhelming commercial traffic, and the foul pollution that it emitted with every turn of the wheel.

The passageway across the bridge was narrow, scarcely wide enough for two oxen-driven carriages to pass without endangering the life of unwary pedestrians. At a span of 300 metres, this structure was more than just a notable engineering achievement. First and foremost, it was the capital's life-giving channel, its pulmonary artery. Through this throbbing conduit, the great metropolis founded on either side of it was able to feed, replenish and defend itself. And, by so doing, to grow, prosper and thrive. This was old London Bridge, as it appeared in the middle of the third century, and the waters it spanned were those of the eternally muddy River Thames.

The four men were now leaning against the bridge's parapet gazing upstream at the southern shore of the river. They were watching a cargo of Kentish ragstone pass under the open drawbridge as it made its way upstream to a jetty on the northern shore. The men appeared to be in a state of reverie as they drank in the full measure of the city with its splendid, uninterrupted views. Occasionally they nudged each other to point out some feature on the landscape, or to comment on the contents of a boat navigating its way to a nearby warehouse.

"Hey Sarge," said Stogdon, "whadda them Romans call the river?"

"Here's what you do, Stog. You try asking Titus Pontius yourself. He ain't gonna bleedin' bite you."

"Sod that - my Latin's shit."

Sergeant Rattigan shot Stogdon a look of disdain. "Are you for real, you trog? It's only cos you won't try to speak the bloody lingo. How you gonna learn otherwise?" He then turned with a smile to the swarthy man who was standing next to him. Rattigan was a good foot taller than the Roman. All they shared in common was male-pattern hair loss. "Tell me, my friend, what name this water is?" he asked in faltering but intelligible Latin.

"Tamesis," Titus Pontius replied with a look of delight. "Tamesis is the name; *Tam* meaning wide and *isis* meaning water - wide water. Do you see, Quinte Rattigani?"

"Indeed, this river I know very well," he replied.

"You've been to Londinium before?"

"Yes, many times before. But it looks very different now."

Crawley had listened to the exchange with care. "If it's so different now, how come you can piece together the riverfront?" he asked in English. "Did you live near here when you was a kid?"

"Yeah, I was dragged up on Golden Lane Estate, back of the Barbican. Know where I mean?"

"Nope, never heard of it. Near here?"

"Yeah, not far, just north-west of where the Roman city walls are now. When I was a nipper my old man used to walk me though the city every day on his way back home from the boozer. He spent thirty years slaving as a porter in the old Billingsgate fish market"

"Billingsgate – now, that's a place I've heard of. Guess it would've been down by the river somewhere." Crawley squinted across the water to the northern shore as if searching for its location.

"It *would've* been, yeah." Rattigan pointed out into the river. "Somewhere just about there, I reckon; round about a quarter of a mile downstream and 100 metres offshore."

"Bleeding hell, that far out? Look how much the riverfront's changed. I was just telling Stog the Thames looks a whole lot wider than I remembered."

"At least twice as wide, I'd say. Look at how much land they later reclaimed on the south shore." With a sweep of his hand, Rattigan described a massive arc. It encompassed a terrain that stretched as far as the naked eye could see, from the foreshores of the London boroughs of Greenwich and Lewisham in the east, to the clay fenlands of Southwark and Lambeth in the west. A mighty swathe of South London's undeveloped real estate lay pristine and naked in front of them. Instead of a densely packed array of skyscrapers, offices, pubs, museums and shops, there sat a bleak archipelago of tidal mudflats, muddy creeks, fenlands, channels and unoccupied low lying islands. A few scattered buildings and military outposts dotted the landscape, but it was impossible to envisage how this scene could ever evolve into the dynamic waterfront of the twenty-first century South Bank.

"It's a fucking wasteland, completely unrecognisable," Crawley conceded with a shake of his head.

"See that small island over there in the middle of the channel?" pointed Stogdon.

"Where?"

"Just out there, low-lying, several hundred metres off-shore."

"Yeah, what about it?"

"I been trying to suss it out. Reckon that's about where Tate Modern art gallery is."

"Fucking hell, you muppet, are you for real? Since when was Stog the trog such a culture vulture?" laughed Rattigan.

"Fuck off. One of my best memories ever, that was - a school trip when we was in Year 8. Me and my mate, Morgo, we got suspended for flinging coffee cups off the fourth floor balcony. We was trying to hit a bunch of Japanese tourists."

"Scene of one of your greatest triumphs then, Stog?" Crawley prompted.

"For real. We had a right laugh; them was bare happy days."

"Any familiar features over there on the north shore?" interjected Crawley.

"Not as many as I expected," Rattigan replied. "What about you guys, you see anything?"

"See that raised ground over there? Is that Tower Hill?" Crawley asked. He was pointing to an elevated bluff a kilometre or so downstream.

All eyes followed his outstretched arm.

"Could well be, Mal. Yeah, that'll be about right. You can see that's where the Roman wall begins that encloses the city. It's a natural defensive position. You can get why William the Conqueror built the Tower of London there eight hundred years from now."

"Eight hundred years? That is such a mind-fucker," said Stogdon. "Where'd Tower Bridge go then?"

"Just east of it, a couple of hundred metres downstream."

"And how far upstream does the wall stretch?" asked Stogdon. He turned to face westward. "It seems to go as far as the river mouth over there."

"That'll be the entrance to the old River Fleet. The wall must end there, just south of where St Paul's would be."

"So the whole Roman city's a lot smaller than I fancied," added Crawley. "We should be able to walk around its perimeter in an hour and a bit. What d'you reckon, guys, fancy giving our new gaff a quick once-over?"

"Sounds good, but it depends on what our friend's got planned for us. How many citizens in Londinium live?" Rattigan asked Titus Pontius.

"The provincial governor undertook a full census recently. Thirty thousand citizens accounted for, including military personnel and civil servants, with a couple of thousand other odds and sods – slaves, itinerants and suchlike." Titus Pontius paused, smiled broadly and stretched out his arms. "But look over there, here comes my dear friend, Ateaqab Aqqabai."

The group turned to greet the new arrival, a dark-skinned older man of Middle Eastern appearance, who was sauntering towards them with a wide smile.

"Greeting, Tite Ponti, may the blessings of Dolichenus be upon you. I've always said that the finest silversmith in Londinium deserves the wholehearted sanction of the Iron God"

The two Roman citizens embraced.

"Greetings, dear generous friend, and may the good graces of Mithras protect you and your family."

The newcomer smiled at the three strangers who accompanied Titus Pontius. "And who are your three mountainous friends here? Introduce us, please."

"Of course, my dear fellow. Please greet my trusted accomplices, Quintus Rattiganus, Marcus Crawlus and Tiberius Stogdanus. And this fine gentleman is Ateaqab Aqqabai of Palmyra, recently retired after twenty-five years' service at the outpost of Arbeia on the Vallum Aelium, and one of my dearest friends."

"Greetings, friend," they responded in unison.

"Palmyra – I swear that's in Syria, Sarge," Stogdon murmured once the group had shaken hands.

"Dead centre, north-east of Damascus. But it looks like Ateaqab's a plain old Londoner now. Just like you and me."

"Bloody Syrians, who'd a thought it?"

Titus Pontius made an educated stab at the meaning of this exchange. "Londinium is a city of immigrants, Roman citizens from all over the Empire," he explained.

"And from beyond the Empire," added Ateaqab Aqqabai.

"And from beyond," concurred Titus Pontius with a laugh.

"And from which fertile soil did you three giants spring?" asked the Palmyran.

Rattigan looked at a loss. "Forgive me, I don't understand," he responded with a tentative smile. "My Latin is very poor."

"Don't worry my friend," Titus Pontius intervened. "It's fair to say that in Londinium a man's past lies buried alongside his morality and conscience. There's no need for anyone to expect otherwise. You need say no more."

Titus Pontius gave Ateaqab Aqqabai a discreet wink and linked arms with him.

"However, being a man of irreproachable rectitude and piety, no such prohibition binds *me* to silence and I have quite a story to tell about these three fine fellows."

"Titus Pontius has always been an incorrigible gossip," emphasised Ateaqab Aqqabai. "He's a happy combination of the silver trade and the quicksilver tongue – the critical ingredients of all successful businessmen. Now, go on with your story, dear friend, for I am all ears."

"Well, remember how I was granted a lease giving me mining and smelting rights to the lead mines around Lutudarum?"

"Indeed I do. It was high time the administration permitted civilians to exploit the province's lead and silver deposits. As a former military man, I can vouch that such a decision was long overdue."

"In which case, you'll recall that my principal interest in the mines lay not in the lead itself, which has its own monetary value, but in the extraction of the precious silver which lies encased within the lead ore."

"Yes, yes, it's fair to say we were fully apprised as to your primary motivation, my dear friend. Your workshops have a widely-renowned appetite for its consumption."

"Here's where he tells him how we saved his bacon," Rattigan muttered to Crawley in English.

"The smarmy little fucker has no idea how lucky he is to still be alive," replied Stogdon

"Shh, let him get on with it."

"So, there I am, transferring my first cargo of silver ingots south by wagon, and I find myself under the so-called protection of a group of Frankish mercenaries, may the god's damn them for all eternity. And we are but an hour's journey from Lutudarum, passing through an area of rock outcrops, when we are set upon by a band of brigands, six in total."

"Make that four," Rattigan whispered.

"And without a thought for the safety of myself or my wagon-master, or the protection of my precious cargo, my military escort slinks off with its beastly tails between its legs."

"A couple of pensioned-off veterans," muttered Rattigan.

"And then, when all appears lost, who should the good Lord Mithras despatch to salvage the situation? Why, it was none other than my guardian saviours here. Within a minute all six brigands lay dead around my wagon. I've never witnessed such carnage on a battlefield, never mind on a lonely British road. I was so indebted by their intervention that I offered to reward them generously if they would immediately escort me safely to Londinium, which they did with great efficiency. From that moment on, no one has dared to so much as cast a glance in my direction."

"Judging by their size, I must say I'm not altogether surprised. They're built like Greek gods," replied Ateaqab Aqqabai.

"I was petrified when they turned their attention to me," Titus Pontius continued with a shudder. "Once they had despatched the last of the attackers to Tartarus, it seemed that I was to be next for the underworld." He emphasised his point by gesturing at Rattigan and pretending to slice his own throat.

"No, my friend, you're a good and noble man," Rattigan countered with a laugh. "It was an honour to be of service."

"He wasn't thinking that ten days ago," Stogdon mouthed to Crawley. His grasp of Latin was clearly more assured than he'd been letting on. "We was about to stick him like a pig."

"Keep it down, Stog," replied Crawley. "That was then, and times change. Now we got us a Roman guv'nor who owes us his life."

Stogdon beamed at the two Romans. "Sweet," he said with a wide smile.

"And now they work for me as my personal bodyguards," Titus Pontius pronounced. He smiled at the trio of British soldiers. "Just look at them. They are magnificent. They'll soon be the talk of Londinium."

"You mean, *you'll* soon be the talk of Londinium, you old goat," corrected Ateaqab Aqqabai.

"And for very good reason. In my line of business, the gods alone cannot be relied upon to bestow protection. Snubbing my nose at that principle very nearly cost me my life."

"You've clearly absorbed the lesson well," replied Ateaqab Aqqabai, gesturing towards the three British soldiers. "Any man can make a mistake, but only an idiot persists in his error."

"The revered Marcus Tullius Cicero never dispensed wiser words. But, to our eternal discredit, how rarely do we adhere to them? Now then, dear friend, let's start making our way to the forum. My cohort here is anxious to see my shop and storeroom. Over the ten days it took us to travel down here by wagon, I fear I talked of little else."

The group continued their passage across the bridge. The two Romans brought up the rear, walking arm in arm, while the Brits, seduced by the sights and sounds of the vibrant riverbank ahead of them, pushed ahead, three-abreast. The trio looked much more relaxed, adopting the swing and swagger of city boys. They felt at home in the noise, muck and drama of the urban chaos unfolding around them.

"Good to be back in The Old Smoke, boys."

"Ain't it, though!"

For nearly half a mile, the northern waterfront crawled with an army of workers. Docks, quays, storehouses and slipways were alive with activity. A wide array of craft, from flat-bottomed barges to Mediterranean-style merchant ships, was being unloaded. Cargoes of ragstone, hewn from local quarries in Kent, sat piled in huge quantities on the quayside; alongside, lay massive marble slabs imported from Anatolia and Greece and other far-flung corners of the Empire. A harvest of imported delicacies - wine in wooden barrels from Gaul, fish sauce and olive oil from Spain, figs and other dried fruits from Palestine, olives from Italy - all would have arrived by boat that morning, before being transferred into the open fronted storehouses lining the quays. This was a bustling, purposeful environment, one that Rattigan, Crawley and Stogdon could relate to, a world were concepts of commerce, international trade, the mercantile economy and organised labour made perfect sense and represented the correct order of things. These were the principal activities and processes that London would later be built on, and yet here they all were in full view, in prototype form, laid out right in front of their eyes in third century Roman Britain.

Once the quintet had passed through the quayside warehouses, they continued along a thoroughfare that ran through the heart of the city and linked the bridge to the forum. As they processed further inland the initial appeal of the urban environment began to wane. The familiar, reassuring smells of the riverfront gave way to a mind-numbing miasma emanating from the open drains and sewers that criss-crossed their path. They held their noses and hurried past the pools of effluence and excreta that clogged the drains. The quality of the buildings on the main street, too, fell well below expectation. A down-beat array of stone built, terracotta-tiled houses and more primitive whitewashed, wattle and daub structures lined the way. The three Brits commented with regret that the grandeur associated with the public buildings of ancient Rome was absent. To their disappointment, Londinium was assuming the mantle of a drab provincial upstart.

On reaching the forum, however, things began to improve.

"This is much more like it," said Rattigan, rubbing his hands together in anticipation. "Let's hit them shops."

"For an old geezer, you don't half talk some sense every now and then. I been waiting all fucking year for an opportunity like this," echoed Stogdon. "Come on, Corporal, time to step out; we need to jack ourselves some half-decent shit."

"We ain't jacking nothing," Crawley snapped back. "It's the straight and narrow from here on in. Remember what we agreed on the way down?"

"Force of habit, man," Stogdon laughed. "I ain't never had no money on me before."

"Stog, you're gonna have to watch yourself - remember what we agreed?"

"For sure, for sure."

Crawley looked unconvinced. "I ain't kidding, Stog."

"Come on, guys" urged Rattigan, "let's the three of us go and have a bit of fun and games. See if Titus Pontius can't rustle us up a half-decent breakfast."

They strode past the forum's outer colonnade and followed the crowds in through the monumental arched gateway that formed the main entrance to the marketplace. As soon as they crossed the threshold they stopped still, awestruck in wonderment at the scale of the spectacle that confronted them. The open marketplace of the forum stretched for over one hundred and twenty metres in each direction and was enclosed on three sides by a colonnaded peristyle containing countless shops, storerooms and offices. The fourth side of the square, opposite the entrance, consisted of a single massive basilica, three stories high and fully one hundred and fifty metres in length. The scale of the structure was extraordinary. It would be another fifteen centuries before its overall length was surpassed, but only slightly, by St Paul's Cathedral.

"That is one big fucking square," Stogdon said, with an admiring nod of his head.

Crawley emitted a long silent whistle under his breath.

"You ain't half got a way with words, Stog," Rattigan concurred. "You may not have been born a poet, my old son, but if you don't die one, it won't have been for want of trying."

"Fuck you. I mean, just look at the fucking size of it," Stogdon repeated.

Crawley and Rattigan both slapped their comrade on the back with glee. "You're right, it's one big bugger of a square. Now, where's the boss? I think he's keen on us all making an entrance together."

And make an entrance they did, two of the Brits marching either side of Titus Pontius and one protecting his rear. As they advanced across the forum, hundreds of curious onlookers turned to admire the procession of the Roman silversmith and his imposing retinue, each member of which stood a good head taller than the average merchant they strode past. Dozens of booths and tables, laid out in rows across the square, were now deserted by shoppers and stall-holders alike. Titus Pontius was clearly a man of some renown and flamboyance, but this was an extravagant display of chutzpah, even by his standards.

"Quinte Rattigani," Titus Pontius declaimed, "let me show you and your boys around my shop and strong room." He was intent on creating an impression as much on the watching crowd as on his three companions. "This is where you will be living for a while. You'll be able to provide protection to the premises while we're hoarding a large supply of silver here. No one will be prepared to take on you three, I fancy." He then turned and whispered to Rattigan. "Once Ateaqab Aqqabai starts gossiping, the whole of Londinium will be fully apprised of your heroic exploits."

When the tour of the premises was complete, Rattigan led his two companions out into the middle of the forum. He was now able to observe his surroundings in detail. From where they were standing, Rattigan could see through the entrance gate and down to the river along the main access road that led back to the bridgehead. He turned though one hundred and eighty degrees and faced north towards the monumental basilica.

"If my calculations are right - and if this was modern London we was in - I reckon we'd be standing about half way up Gracechurch Street now, and the Bank of England would be a couple of hundred metres over there to the north west." Rattigan was pointing in a direction beyond the left hand enclosure of the square. "That means that Leadenhall Market would be over there in the north east corner of the forum, to the right, where the basilica is now." Rattigan then turned to his right and held out both arms in front of him at chest height. "And, if I'm not mistaken, right about here, my lads, right about here, would be a drafty little cut-through called Ship Tavern Passage. Come on, walk with me, use your imagination and I'll show you something right interesting."

Crawley and Stogdon followed Rattigan as he counted out fifteen paces with his eyes closed tight. The sergeant then stopped, stood stock-still and opened his eyes. "Right then, here we are. Right *here* would be where you'd find my old man's favourite boozer. Right on this spot - I swear to you on my mum's life - is where The Swan Tavern stood."

"Leave it out, Sarge. You're having a laugh, right?"

"No, I'm telling you, Mal, I walked this same sodding route every single day after school for five years. I could walk it blindfolded then, and I could, near as dammit, still do the same today."

"Well I'll be buggered," said Crawley, scratching his head and looking around him in bemusement. "The Swan Tavern, eh? You ever go inside?"

"What, inside the pub? No, don't be daft, not as a nipper. My mum used to send me down to tap on the windows. I'd have to drag my Dad back home after an afternoon's boozing with the lads. Otherwise, he'd get no tea. He was a fucking shocker, I'm telling you; nearly drove my mum to an early grave. Mind you, he'd always take me to the Arsenal on a Saturday."

"So, not all bad, then?"

"Nah, I suppose not, the old bastard."

"Working class had it tough back then."

"You're not wrong there. I tell you something - he was a real grafter, was my dad. When I see the shifts he put in, day in, day out, no wonder he turned to the drink. It's blokes like him what made this fucking city what it is. And on the day he retired, you know what he had to look forward to: a shitty little pension, lung cancer and a premature death. Poor bastard snuffed it within six weeks."

"It's how it was in them days, no word of a lie," said Stogdon. "We should raise a glass to the old boy tonight."

"You're not wrong there, Stog; and you know what, yeah, when we get extricated out of this effing Roman nightmare, the three of us, we're gonna come down here to this very spot and we're gonna have a right skinful in The Swan Tavern. And that is one promise we'll bloody well keep. What do you say, lads - you with me?"

"Yeah, why not?" said Crawley. "You have to be positive in this life and look to the future. Ain't that what Kal would say?"

"Yeah, count me in too. But only if the first round's on you, Sarge" replied Stogdon.

"Hey, every round's on me - me and my old man." Rattigan looked upwards with a smile, as if searching for parental endorsement. "It'll be our shout, ain't that right, Pop?"

TWELVE

Caeluibianus, Cohort Tribune and Praepositus of the Company, to Julius Rufinus, Tribunus Laticlavius and commander-in-chief, I send my greetings. In the matter of determining the fate of Galla Placidia (undertaken in the utmost secrecy as directed) I have done so in full accordance with your wishes and have set out my findings below. Since my last report, the broom of ill-fortune has swept away all vestiges of Galla Placidia's whereabouts. Alas, no clue as to her current hiding place exists, nor that of her two accomplices, at least no clue that falls within the capacity of mere mortals to detect. However, the Gods, in their munificence, have permitted a ray of unexpected good fortune to shine down on us, raising the prospect that all hope may not be entirely lost. Following reports of an outbreak of religious disorder among the ranks of our troops stationed in Verulamium, I felt it prudent to investigate any possible link to the rebellious sentiments associated with her cult. On arrival, I discovered that the military insubordination had already been harshly repressed some days earlier, the execution of a centurion, no less, serving as a warning to others who wished to subvert the religious tolerance vouchsafed to all citizens of the Empire and their allies. It transpires that the subject of the dispute was not Galla Placidia, as I had feared, but another fanatical and intolerant sect centred on the personage of a long-dead prophet from Syria Palaestina, called Iesus Christus. The execution was the talk of the camp and the surrounding taverns, as you can well imagine. As good fortune would have it, I fell in with an ex-comrade of ours, a veteran from Arbeia on the Vallum Aelium. You're hardly likely to recall him, my Lord, but he particularly requested that I remember him to you with his warmest compliments and greatest respect. He is a former Syrian archer from the 1st Cohort of Hamian Bowmen, Ateaqab Aqqabi, now living in retirement in Londinium. Fortunately for me, his gluttony for wine was matched by his appetite for gossip, as was attested by his shamefully drunken state and the amount of useful information he imparted with every vessel downed. He's an amiable enough sort, this Palmyran, but indiscreet and bit of a buffoon when the spirit moves him. He revealed an interesting detail about three newly-arrived *colossi* from the north who fitted the description of the three rebels who crossed swords with our lads in Luguvalium. Of Galla Placidia, however, there was no word, nor sighting. He's convinced that these three have travelled alone to Londinium, an assertion that has been confirmed by intelligence from another hitherto reliable source. It is said that laughter is abundant in the mouth of fools, and this Syrian is a living embodiment of the adage if ever proof was needed, but, in cases such as this, the spoken truth is often found to be as scarce a commodity as the former is plentiful. I intend to continue to the capital myself and, if these suspicions are proved to be well-founded, to have the Governor apprehend these three murderers on the spot. In your latest letter you saw fit to admonish me for my previous hot-headedness in dealings related to this case, my Lord. You were entitled to reprimand me for what you termed my 'casual brutality'. Rest assured that I have mended my ways and will be a veritable paragon of circumspection henceforth. I will write as soon as I have more intelligence to impart. May I not shrink from my purpose, my Lord. I will do what I am ordered and at every command I will be ready.

THIRTEEN

Location: Londinium
Coordinates: 51°30'45" N and 0°05'30" W

Time and Date: 21.15, 1st August, 258 C.E.

Londinium at night is no place for unwary pedestrians. The pathways that criss-crossed the old city contain countless unsavoury surprises for those who fail to watch their step. And on this particular evening, Rattigan and Crawley could be seen picking their way past a network of wooden gulleys as they proceeded westward along the main thoroughfare. Every imaginable variety of filth ended up in these open sewers, the suppurating contents of which emptied into a tributary of the nearby Walbrook stream. Flies, insects and vermin thrived uncontrolled in this festering environment. All contributed, in their own distinct ways, to the capital's catastrophically low levels of life expectancy. Disease, ill-health and pollution cast a heavy pall over parts of the city. But these were by no means the only challenges facing third century London. The effects of poor diet and squalid housing, and the regular shortage of fresh, clean water, also conspired to hand down an imminent death sentence upon the poorest sectors of the populace.

Rattigan and Crawley had not been slow to re-evaluate their initial impression of Roman London. Since arriving, they'd inspected every corner of the capital. They'd followed the entire three-kilometre length of the city walls, marvelling at the ingenuity and workmanship involved in their construction. It was clear that an army of skilled masons had been required to hand shape the million or so ragstone blocks needed to face the enormous walls. They'd admired the city's four massive gates, which later generations would go on to rename Newgate, Ludgate, Aldgate and Bishopsgate. These entrances were a vital element in controlling the flow of people and goods into the city and, more importantly, permitting the efficient collection of any associated taxes and duties. They'd also inspected the old rectangular army fort and found that it had long been repurposed as a centre for clerical workers and civil servants and that there was little evidence of its continued use as a military camp. They'd twice been spectators at the gaudily decorated 6,000-capacity amphitheatre. The first occasion was at Titus Pontius' insistence, when they were forced, against their better judgement and personal inclinations, to witness a public execution. The following week they'd returned of their own accord to experience a combination of gladiatorial combat, which they loved, and wild animal fighting, which disgusted them. On a more positive note, they'd been startled to see how much of the walled city's hinterland was thrown over to market gardens, dairy pasture and cultivatable land.

Tonight, however, Rattigan and Crawley were on a different kind of mission as they accompanied their employer, Titus Pontius, on a trip through the old city. The Roman silversmith looked preoccupied as he guided them towards a small dark temple lying in a subterranean gulley alongside the edge of the Walbrook stream.

Eventually, they came to a halt in a dark, quiet spot adjacent to a narrow waterway. Small shrines could be seen popping up along the edge of the stream as it wound its way to the river Thames, which lay several hundred metres to the south.

"Here we are at last, my friends," gasped Titus Pontius. In the dark they stood before the unprepossessing facade of a dimly-lit, low-lying, stone edifice. "This is the Temple of Mithras."

Titus Pontius was in sombre, pensive mood. He looked tense and preoccupied. Rattigan and Crawley were used to seeing his face wreathed in smiles and were unsettled by his lack of bonhomie. He cleared his throat as he readied himself to address them. "Before we enter the *Mithraeum*, I have a couple of things I'd like to say to you this evening. I should remind you that this is a place of worship that demands the highest moral code of all those who enter its portals." He paused and scrutinised both his companions. "Honesty, purity and courage are the qualities that are valued above all others. These virtues are essential in novices who wish to be initiated into the mysteries of the Mithraean cult. You two men seem to be the very embodiment of these splendid attributes; unlike your absent comrade, Tiberius Stogdanus, whose general moralities appear to have sunk well below those expected of a potential inductee. He's as depleted in character as he is gargantuan in size."

"Poor Stog," thought Rattigan, "he never catches a break."

The two British soldiers were focused on the Roman. He held their complete attention.

"What do we do when we go inside?" Rattigan asked.

"You do as I've instructed you, and all will be well. I will explain more when it is required."

"I'm getting a right uncomfortable feeling about this, Sarge, I ain't going to lie," Crawley whispered.

"Me too, Mal, but what choice we got? He's bestowing a great honour on us."

"But I ain't no pagan, I can't be doing with no sacrifices or nothing."

Crawley was rarely rattled. But his quavering voice was betraying his hesitancy.

Rattigan cajoled his comrade. "Me neither, Mal. But, come on, ain't you intrigued, just a bit?"

Crawley motioned his comrade to one side. "Intrigued ain't got nothing to do with it. I was raised in the Catholic faith. It just ain't right to be doing them things."

"Then just consider it a smart business move, like joining a Masonic Lodge or something."

Crawley tried to smile, but didn't look convinced. "In for a penny, in for a pound, I guess. It's a right shame about Stog, though."

"Ain't nothing we can do about that."

"Come now," prompted Titus Pontius. He'd been observing the two men with concern, and tried ushering them towards the door. "Don't be reticent. There is really nothing to fear."

The two soldiers hesitated. They exchanged a final fateful glance and Crawley crossed himself for good measure. They both recognised that once they'd passed over the building's threshold, there'd be no turning back. They then entered together, ducking their heads low in order to follow their Roman sponsor into a windowless, cave-like interior. Their eyes took a second or two to adjust to the relative darkness of the temple. The fumes and smoke of incense caught in their throats. Crawley could feel his heart pounding in his chest. They could hear a loud incantation coming from the rear of the temple, followed by a series of mystifying vocal accompaniments arising from the assembled throng. Slowly the dim light from the oil lamps started to reveal the interior of the *Mithraeum*.

Titus Pontius ushered them into the crowded right hand aisle, which was raised and afforded a partial view of the proceedings. Rattigan and Crawley absorbed the theatricality of the scene in stupefied silence. Their attention was focused on the temple's interior, which was of modest dimensions, perhaps eight metres wide by twenty metres in length, but appeared strangely familiar in its architectural forms. The low, two-storied building had a central nave with two aisles. Along the nave, two rows of seven columns supported a pitched roof with wooden crossbeams. At the far end of the temple, a priest-like figure was standing in front of a raised altar that supported a carved marble relief of a young man sacrificing a bull. To the left hand side of the altar stood a font, and running along either side of the nave was a row of reliquaries containing a series of carved divinities.

"Mal, the layout of this building - you thinking what I'm thinking?"

"Christian church?"

"There's even an apse behind the altar."

"Silence," whispered Titus Pontius, "the ceremony is starting."

99

At the far end of the temple, in front of a raised tribune, a priest began to intone loudly:

> *"Give ear to me, hearken to me, O Lord Helios Mithras, you who have bound together with your breath the fiery bars of the fourfold root. Hail, O guardian of the pivot, O sacred and brave youth, who turns at one command the revolving axis of the vault of heaven, who sends out thunder and lightning and jolts of earthquakes and thunderbolts against the nations of impious people, but to me, who is pious and god-fearing, you send health and soundness of body and acuteness of hearing and seeing, and calmness in the present good hours of this day, O my Lord Mithras!"*

At a signal from the priest, the congregation, numbering some thirty or forty, commenced vocalising an unnerving sequence of hissing and popping sounds. Two eerie figures, one clad in a lion's head and the other dressed as a giant bird, began to perambulate down the nave waving incense-bearing torches. Their shadows danced in mad ecstasy on the roof and walls. At a sign from the priest the congregation responded to his promptings by chanting the names of seven deities.

> *"Hail to you, the first, CHREPSENTHAES!*
> *Hail to you, the second, MENESCHEES!*
> *Hail to you, the third, MECHRAN!*
> *Hail to you, the fourth, ARARMACHES!*
> *Hail to you, the fifth, ECHOMMIE!*
> *Hail to you, the sixth, TICHNONDAES!*
> *Hail to you, the seventh, EROY ROMBRIES!"*

The entire ritual was then repeated once again, but this time with the inclusion of seven new deities and a whole raft of orchestrated vowel utterances from the congregation:

"EEO OEEO IOO OE EEO OE EO IOO OEEE OEE OOE IE EO OO OE."

Rattigan and Crawley were mesmerised by the sound but remained bemused by the rites being enacted.

The longer the ceremony continued, the more Rattigan found himself intrigued by the rituals. Finally, taking advantage of a slight lull in proceedings, he gave vent to his curiosity. "Forgive me, Tite Ponti," he whispered, "but what is the purpose of this ceremony?"

Titus Pontius covered his mouth with his hand before replying. "Mithraeans use astrology and magic to assist the ascent of the individual soul to paradise. We initiates are using the ceremony to invoke a request for immortality."

"So Mithras is a God then?"

"Mithras is half-god and half-man. We believe that when Mithras slayed the primeval bull, the blood that was spilt gave life to the earth and everything that grows upon it. His role is to act as an intermediary between mankind and the gods. He is the redeemer of mankind. His status is semi-divine."

"A bit like Jesus, then?" Rattigan muttered to Crawley.

Crawley shot his comrade a nervous look. He leant in close to Titus Pontius. "So Mithras exists alongside the other Roman Gods?"

"Oh yes, we're not like Christians. We're not fanatics. We respect all local Gods."

"Did you say Christians? You know about Christians?

"Alas, yes."

Rattigan leant in closer to the Roman. "Have you heard of Jesus Christ?" he whispered in a barely audible manner.

"Iesus Christus? He is their god I believe," Titus Pontius responded with a weary sigh. "They are a very troublesome and intolerant sect. There is no place for them in a place like Londinium. We had to drive one of the priests out of the city last year."

"Drive him out - but why?"

"People sometimes accuse Mithraeans of wanting to supress other deities, but compared to the Christians, we are nothing if not tolerant, believe me. Their kind of bigoted religious extremism, viciously denouncing all other gods, is a threat to us all. I distrust any group who are prepared to sacrifice their own lives in order to coerce the general population into adopting their religion. They are a mystery to me. They pose a threat to the very fabric and order of Rome."

Rattigan couldn't contain his surprise. "You really believe this?"

"Indeed, I do. Why, only last week Ateaqab Aqqabai was relaying reports of a Roman centurion, no less, who had sacrificed himself after being accused of promulgating religious discord and sheltering a Christian priest in Verulanium. If these zealots get a foothold then they will see to it that every other god, with the sole exception of their own, is eradicated from this land."

Titus Pontius closed his eyes, covered his face with his hands and began to intone softly.

Rattigan leant over and whispered to Crawley. "You believe what you're hearing? Did you get all that?"

"Not all of it, but enough. Just as well I'm a lapsed Catholic. I wouldn't give much for my chances otherwise. You think that Roman martyr may have been St Alban?"

Rattigan did a double-take. "What are you like, Mal? That's pure myth, you dick-head." He looked around him to ensure they were not being overheard. "Them kind of stories are just an early form of Christian propaganda, you know that. You heard what Titus Pontius said. Christianity's a ruthless religion."

"But I swear Christians are the ones being supressed now."

"You're not wrong there, judging by what he's been saying. I tell you what, though, come back here in a hundred years' time and check this place out then. You just know the Christians will have taken over the temple and hundreds of others like it."

"The price of progress for you."

"Maybe. Or maybe it's just the price of a better class of mumbo-jumbo. Is that progress, swapping tolerance for intolerance? It's a right heavy price to pay, if it is. And I tell you what, it's a price that'll continue to haunt mankind for thousands of years to come."

"Come on, Sarge, lighten up. Christianity's got to be an advance on this stuff," Crawley replied, motioning towards the perambulating figures in animal costumes. "At least it beats putting your faith in magic potions, secret spells and astrology."

"Fair play, but when you boil it down and that, ain't it just amounting to the same old claptrap? It looks like them Christians are only gonna go and nick a whole bunch of ideas and rituals from Mithras. Then they'll head out and eradicate him and his followers."

"It's evolution, Sarge - the survival of the fittest. Make sure you're on the winning side."

"It's all about us mankind adapting to changing conditions." He patted his comrade on the knee. "We're all humans after all - even you bleeding Christians."

"Shh," whispered Titus Pontius. He gave his two inductees a scolding look. "Now is the time for you to invoke the spirit of Mithras personally. As novices, you are invited to repeat the priest's words when he next speaks."

Rattigan and Crawley looked unprepared for such a development. Their attention had begun to drift away from the ritual being enacted in front of them.

The priest raised both his arms in supplication and began to intone the words of a short prayer. The two Brits did their best to repeat the invocation:

"Spirit of spirit, if it be your will, give me over
to immortal birth so that
I may be born again – and the sacred spirit
may breathe in me."

The congregation was ushered forward to receive a form of communion. "The wine represents the blood of the bull sacrificed by Mithras," explained Titus Pontius, "and the bread the bull's flesh." Rattigan and Crawley awaited their turn and followed the rituals as directed by their Roman sponsor.

"What did you think of the ceremony?" enquired Titus Pontius, once proceedings had been brought to a close.

"We liked it very well, Tite Ponti. A thousand thanks for honouring us so generously."

"I'm in your debt, not the other way round. I took a vow, on my return to Londinium, that I'd make an offering of thanks to Mithras for sparing my life through your agency."

Titus Pontius removed a small leather purse from his pocket, unfastened the brass catch and carefully tipped two items into the palm of his right hand. Rattigan and Crawley watched in fascination as he arranged the articles, a pair of ornate black and silver trinkets, for closer scrutiny. The objects appeared identical to each other as they glistened in his hand. They were rectangular, measured just over an inch in length, and possessed exquisite, carved surfaces.

"What are they, Tite Ponti?"

"They are amulets, one for each of you. They will help ward off evil spirits."

"They are beautiful. What are they made of?"

"The black inner stone is hematite and the mount is silver, made by my own hand these past two weeks."

The silversmith presented Rattigan and Crawley with an amulet each. They stared at them in wonderment.

"They are magnificent. But these carvings on the amulets, what do they mean?" asked Rattigan. He screwed his eyes up to get a better look.

"This scene represents the Tauroctony, the sacrifice of the primeval white bull by Mithras. He is flanked by his two attendants, Cautes and Cautopates, and there you can see the accompanying figures of a dog, raven, scorpion and snake."

"It's beautiful," said Rattigan. "Is this scene the moment of creation?"

"Yes, at the very instant he performs the sacrifice, the bull transforms into the moon, and Mithras's cloak becomes the sky, stars and planets."

"Wonderful. Now we are in your debt, Tite Ponti. We will wear these amulets with pride."

"They are yours to keep with my blessing."

"Thank you, my dear friend," added Crawley.

"I have another gift for you, one that has served me well for many years. But this offering has a condition attached."

Titus Pontius unwrapped a second leather cloth to reveal a superb cylindrical silver container, complete with a matching circular lid. Every inch of the object was decorated with a series of flowing ritualised scenes of humans and beasts.

He prised open the lid to reveal inside a delicate silver cup with a perforated bottom.

"It's a tea strainer," Crawley whispered to Rattigan.

"It's wonderful, but what is it, Tite Ponti?"

"It is an infuser. It aids the preparation of religious draughts used in the Mithraic initiation rites. It will be my honour to dedicate this cup to Mithras, himself, once both your novitiates are complete and you are fully initiated into the cult."

"You said there was a condition, Tite Ponti?"

"Alas, there is," he replied, with a tone of exaggerated regret. "Being called upon to join the Mithraic cult is a very great honour, and every honour carries with it an element of sacrifice."

Crawley's eyes widened in apprehension.

"What does this sacrifice involve?" Rattigan asked.

"Tiberius Stogdanus."

Crawley recoiled in shock. "Stog? Did he say Stog?" He looked at Titus Pontius. "I don't understand," he responded.

"Tiberius Stogdanus is neither worthy of your friendship, nor of my continued patronage. He is of base character - licentious, ill-mannered and uncouth. Why, only yesterday I caught him dipping his hand into my strongbox."

"We know all this, Tite Ponti. What he has done is truly reprehensible. But despite all his obvious shortcomings and faults he possesses two truly outstanding qualities. He is both loyal and brave beyond measure."

"The Gods don't assign human virtues as if they were dispensing exotic spices from a market stall. After all, anyone with a pinch of common sense can observe that bravery and loyalty are merely two of the qualities that you both possess, and that they naturally complement all the others virtues that are so manifestly embodied in yourselves, and yet are so obviously lacking in your unworthy comrade. No, it's no good, my mind is made up. You will have to forsake your friendship with Tiberius Stogdanus. If you intend to prove yourselves worthy of initiation into the cult of Mithras, and to continue to enjoy my patronage and familiarity, then you will have to do as I ask you. You must sacrifice your worthless friend."

FOURTEEN

Aballava Tablet No. 5, Inventory No 13.24 (Morris Archive)

Caeluibianus, Cohort Tribune and Praepositus of the Company, to Julius Rufinus, Tribunus Laticlavius and commander-in-chief, I send my greetings. In the matter of determining the fate of Galla Placidia (undertaken in the utmost secrecy as directed) I have done so in full accordance with your wishes and have set out my findings below. By the Gods, I have some juicy news to report. We are back on the track of the she-devil! Following my recent fortuitous meeting with our Syrian friend, Ateaqab Aqqabai, and determining to pursue the intelligence he so generously divulged under Bacchus' influence, I was able to track down the whereabouts of her three acolytes to Londinium, to the shop of a certain silversmith, Titus Pontius, a man, if local gossips are to be believed, of no little wealth and even greater self-esteem. At any event, his self-esteem took quite a battering at the hands of Bostar. The silversmith proved unresponsive to initial prompts for information about the trio in question, and there being no obvious sign of them about the premises, we were obliged to ensure his full cooperation by the use of force. Thenceforth, it required little coaxing to extract the required information. I must say, my Lord, that Bostar has proved a most dutiful and diligent disciple, especially when it comes to the application of torture techniques. He applies himself to his commission with a scientific rigour and is proving to be a fast learner. And what information he has extracted. By the silversmith's own account, the rebels confided in him that Galla Placidia, whose name was unknown to him, but whose legend was not, is currently bound by sea for Volubilis, the recruitment centre for our auxiliaries, the *Maurorum Aurelianorum Numerus*. Volubilis, my Lord, our cohort's spiritual home! The men themselves have departed Londinium for the same destination, but in their case, he thought, by overland route through Gaul and Hispania. He attested that bad blood had erupted between himself and one of the three rebels in question, a low-bred reprobate by the name of Tiberius Stogdanus, who he had found rifling through his strong box and had promptly banished from his employment. While cursing him to us for an immoral son of a dog, he professed to still hold his two other comrades in the highest possible esteem. Sad to report, a warrant for their immediate custody has been issued by the provincial governor in connection with the slaying of the very same Titus Pontius - poor man! Alas for them, every rumour, particularly one spread by a company Praepositus, is believed when directed against the unfortunate! We will leave it to the implements of law and order to apprehend these three rogues. Meanwhile, by the time you receive this report, we will be making all haste to Volubilis by sea. I will write as soon as I have further intelligence to impart. May I not shrink from my purpose, my Lord. I will do what I am ordered and at every command I will be ready.

FIFTEEN

Location: Jbel Dar Chaoui, Mauretania Tingitana
Coordinates: 35°33'00" N and 5°43'48" W

Time and Date: 17.00, 8th August, 258 C.E.

Only two Roman roads run south through the African province
of Mauretania Tingitana. Both extend for two hundred miles or
so. To the novice map reader, they may appear to hang like a
pair of untied shoelaces, one hugging the north-west Atlantic
coast and the other heading off into the foothills of the
towering Atlas Mountains. Neither road, however, is designed
to serve the needs of the native population. They've been
constructed, instead, with another wider purpose in mind: to
satisfy Rome's appetite for an endless supply of cheap grain.
The final destinations of these routes, Sala Colonia and Volubilis,
effectively demarcate the southern frontier of the Roman
Empire, in much the same way as Hadrian's Wall does for its
northern border. Further south lie the Atlas Mountains and
beyond that the Sahara Desert.

A modern-day traveller would be hard pressed to recognise
the scenery and vegetation as it existed two thousand years ago.
During the Roman era, the landscape was covered in endless
forests of cork oak, cedar, fir and pine. The ecosystem
contained a huge biodiversity of plant species and endemic
fauna unique to the Maghreb. There was little or no evidence
of the soil erosion, the deforestation, the meagre scrubland and
the low bushes that would later disfigure the topography. Wild
figs and olives grew profusely and the land echoed to the sound
of abundant insects and wildlife. Of ubiquitous herds of grazing
goats and sheep there were no sign.

However, reality is rarely stratified in so orderly and convenient a manner. Often the truth is harder to excavate. As Birch and Ojokwu were reminded by Sands, thing aren't necessarily what they seem. Maybe the early twentieth century French invaders of this land invented this contested description of the classical landscape as justification for its annexation? Alternative histories can sometimes be obscured under layers of topsoil and dust. Proper excavation of the truth demands multifaceted skills of the cultural archaeologist; especially when the substratum is concealed beneath multiple layers of colonial sediment.

In 258 CE, as if to illustrate the point, and running contrary to all laws of logic, physics and nature, it was these three British soldiers who were making their way along one of these North African Roman roads. They'd endured a long and demanding day's ride south from Tingi. And it was twentieth century French colonialism whose evils they had been dissecting at the very moment when Sands' horse had given way beneath her. The unfortunate animal had died before it had hit the roadway. Sands was hurled clear, shocked and winded, but was otherwise unhurt.

After they'd recovered Sands' meagre belongings, Birch and Ojokwu attached ropes to the carcass and hauled it to the kerbside to allow other travellers to pass. They then lay down in the shade. Their options appeared thin. The sun was still beating down and the heat was reflecting back viciously off the cobbled road surface.

"That bastard of a horse dealer," swore Birch. "We've come no more than thirty miles."

"You think he knew?" asked Ojokwu, wiping the endless sweat from his brow.

"Damn right he knew. Look at my mount – he's already going lame."

"We've got no choice. We're going to have to walk," replied Sands. Her back was stiff and sore and her knees were bruised.

"In this heat?" Ojokwu protested.

"The lame horse can carry our lighter provisions, and we can take it in turn to ride the other one."

"But the horses are right done in. Where are we going to camp? We need water and the horses need feeding."

"I know, but we definitely can't stop here."

Their conversation was interrupted by the sound of approaching horses in the distance. They strained their eyes in both directions. "Look - here comes a carriage," Sands said, pointing north. "Maybe they can tell us where the next source of water is."

On the horizon, a cloud of dust and flying hoofs could be seen approaching. The ambient sounds of the countryside were overwhelmed by a cacophony of noise. The carriage's metal wheel rims crashed with a hideous insistence across the hard, pebbled road surface. As the coach drew near, the driver was eyeing them with care, and a piercing face could be seen inspecting them from inside the nearside window. The four-wheeled carriage was a rather grand affair, three metres or so in length, able to accommodate four passengers under cover and in comfort, pulled by four horses abreast, and with a driver sitting outside. The three expectant Britons were impressed.

Sands waved both arms above her head. "Hello, there, slow down, driver, will you?"

"Pull up, Guenfan, there's a good fellow," yelled one of the passengers. He was a middle-aged man, lean and alert and with a deeply lined, affable face. Before the carriage had even come to a complete halt, the passenger opened the door, leapt from his seat with impressive suppleness, and was then followed by a much younger companion, a handsome youth with a bronzed complexion and vivid green eyes. The pair waved a cursory greeting, surveyed the dead horse with a look of dismay, and then addressed some remarks to the Britons in an unintelligible language.

All three looked at a loss. Birch and Ojokwu turned to Sands for a translation.

"Alas, I only speak Latin," Sands told the strangers. She gave an apologetic shrug.

111

The older man smiled. "In that case I will address you in Latin, not Tamazight," he responded. "You've suffered a misfortune, I see." He gestured at the carcass, which, despite their best endeavours, was still partially blocking the roadside.

"Yes, we tried to clear the way for other travellers."

"Don't concern yourselves with such trivialities. Jackals will pick the carcass clean by morning. Do you have far to travel?"

"Volubilis."

The man smiled and exchanged a joke with his companion. "You mean Oualili. Only the Romans call it Volubilis. But that is five days' journey hence; and only then if you are mounted on healthy horses."

"I know, but we just need to find some water for the night, and somewhere to feed our two other horses."

"Yes, they look in a bad way," he replied, shaking his head.

"Is there a well nearby?" she asked.

"Yes, indeed. At least we can help you with that. There is a reliable water supply five miles south of here. Now look, one of your companions can sit up beside my driver. And you, being the smallest of your group, can fit inside with me and my son and daughter. The other fellow, him over there, will have to ride his horse or walk, I'm afraid. I'm not squeezing him in with us. Look at the size of him! Now let's get a move on before night falls."

"Thank you. We are in your debt."

"Don't thank me. It is a Berber tradition to help all travellers in need. It is our pleasure and our duty." He glanced up at the driver. "Now, Guenfan, help our new companions transfer their belongings to the *rheda*. Be quick about it, everyone, please."

Realising that providence was smiling down on them, Birch and Ojokwu leapt into action and transferred the provisions from the lame horse to hooks on the rear of the carriage. When everything was ready, they continued their journey, Ojokwu on horseback and Birch next to the driver.

As Sands ascended the step into the covered *rheda*, the driver delivered a reminder of her continued male disguise. "Mind your head, young fellow," he urged.

"Here, come sit next to me, friend," the older man indicated, patting the cushioned seat. "You'll have to make do with my family's company for the next five miles."

"Oh, father, do stop teasing, and introduce us to your guest, please," replied a striking young woman. She was sitting opposite Sands and beaming with delight.

"Of course, please accept my apologies for being so discourteous. Let me introduce myself. My name is Antalas Alfassi. I am but a humble grain merchant of Oualili, the town that you say you intend to visit. And these two fine young people are my son, Azulay, who you have already met, and my daughter, Tufayyur, who, as well as being the love of my life is also the bane of my existence."

Antalas smiled with pride at the young woman and pinched her knee.

"Oh, hush, father, you risk frightening our guest away with such talk. What is your name, sir?"

"My name? My name is Kalius Placidius. My two companions outside are my brother Sextus Placidius and our friend Titus Ojokwus. We are all from Britannia."

"Well, it's very nice to meet you, Kalius Placidius," replied Azulay, "and for Father to grant us permission to speak to you in Latin."

"You don't normally speak Latin, then?"

"No, Father does not approve," replied Azulay with an admonishing smile.

"It is an imported language," explained Antalas. "We view Latin as the language of our oppressors and prefer to speak Tamazight whenever we can as a matter of pride."

"Father considers speaking Tamazight to be an expression of our self-respect," explained Tufayyur.

"Indeed I do," Antalas nodded. "Latin is not widely spoken among the native population in Oualili, for this very reason, as you will doubtless discover for yourself. In some respects it's as much an expression of our identity as our religion is."

"And what religion is that, sir, if you don't mind me asking?"

"We are Jews."

Sands sat back in surprise. "You are Jewish?"

"We are."

"So you also speak Hebrew?"

"We do, but only at home or in religious observance on the Sabbath day."

"And are there many Jews in Oualili?"

"Not a great number, but a few. We have lived there for many, many generations."

"And are you Jews well treated?"

Antalas pulled a quizzical expression. "Well treated? What a funny question. By the Amazigh? Yes. By the Romans? Let's say we are tolerated."

"Well, it is an honour to meet a Jew. I have a great interest in your religion."

"In that case, the pleasure is mutual."

"And you're travelling on business, sir, or on family matters?"

"A bit of both - we've been visiting some family connections; but they also happen to be eminent gold traders in Sala Colonia."

"Oh, do tell him the truth, Father, I'm sure it's nothing to be ashamed of," prompted Tufayyur with a laugh. "He's trying to marry me off, you know," she confided to Sands in a stage whisper.

"I have to find a suitable husband for this one - a nice Jewish boy from a good family," the father winked at Sands. "It's not an easy job where she's concerned, I can assure you."

"Really? I'm astonished to hear it."

"No, I'm sorry to say this girl doesn't intend to make life easy for her poor father," he replied with a weary shake of his head. "She seems bent on driving me to an early grave." He winked at his daughter.

"She is beautiful, don't you agree, Kalius?" asked Azulay with a playful tickle of his sister's waist.

"Stop, I won't have you hawking me around like some sleazy trader. Look what you've done, Azulay, you've made Kalius blush with embarrassment."

Sands was indeed blushing. From the moment she'd stepped into the carriage she'd felt overwhelmed by the beauty and magnetism of the two siblings sitting opposite her. The stunning daughter, Tufayyur, presented a captivating sight. Her body was decorated from head to toe in multiple layers of densely woven, wildly textured fabrics; on her head she sported a simple white lace shawl and around her neck she wore a complex amalgam of brass, bone, bead and gourd necklaces. But most breath-taking of all were her facial adornments, a range of geometric tattoos the likes of which Sands had never seen before. Her eyelids were tattooed with a solid black colour. Underneath each bottom set of eyelashes was a small five-pronged light-ray shape which emitted a single straight line running down the length of each cheek and ending at the jawline. These strokes had the effect of splitting the face into thirds. The bridge of her nose was decorated with a simple dotted line tattoo, which expanded in width as it continued down the tip of her nose, between her nostrils and across her upper lip. The *piece de resistance* was a solid, thick stroke, which ran from her lower lip to the tip of her chin and was intersected at right-angles by four cross hatchings. Sands was mesmerised by the intricate symmetry of the designs, which had the added benefit of focusing the viewer's full attention on Tufayyur's elliptical mouth and sumptuous lips.

"Anyway, look at Azulay, Kalius," the young woman commanded with a mischievous smirk. She held her brother's face in both palms and manoeuvred his gaze towards Sands. "Don't you think he is the most handsome man you've ever seen? Just look at that face and those eyes."

"They are a beautiful colour."

"Ask him what *Azulay* means in Tamazight," Tufayyur responded. "Go on, ask him."

"Shh, sister, please."

Tufayyur would not be silenced by her brother's plea for discretion. "His name means 'The man with the beautiful eyes'. A perfect description, don't you think, Kalius?"

Now it was Azulay's turn to blush. He looked away. "Stop, Tufayyur," he whispered.

"Yes, daughter, stop teasing your brother. I'm sure you are boring our guest with your nonsense." Antalas cast an apologetic glance in Sands' direction.

"No, not at all, it's nice to be among family members who clearly love one another so much. It's something I've missed dearly." Sands smiled at the two siblings who sat hand in hand. "Tell me, Tufayyur, what is the meaning of *your* name in Tamazight?"

Tufayyur cast her eyes down in mock humility.

"More beautiful than the moon," announced Azulay.

Sands smiled. "Your sister could not have been given a more appropriate name. My compliments go to your parents on their foresight."

Antalas chuckled with delight. "Enough, enough, that young woman has endured more flattery in the past two weeks than is good for her."

Tuffayur beamed at Sands with pleasure.

"Thank you," she mouthed. Although Taffayur's words were delivered with an appreciative nod of her head, she ensured that her eyes never left Sand's admiring gaze for an instant.

Sands felt intoxicated by the warmth of feeling she was experiencing. She'd been taken aback by the directness of Tufayyur's gaze. Her body tingled all over with pleasure and goodwill. She was oblivious to the bone-shaking lack of suspension underneath her seat, the noise of the wheels as they pounded against the gravel and the discomfort of her two British comrades who were enduring the last of the summer sun's scorching rays. She just wanted to bask in the luxurious affection of this small family group, and to find out more about them all.

She next turned her attention to the father. "Tell me, Antalas, as a Jew, have you ever felt the need to make a pilgrimage to Jerusalem?"

"No, and why would I? Do you think God only lives in Syria Palaestina?"

"No, but do Jews not visit the holy places in Jerusalem; the Temple Mount, for example?"

"No more. And not for many generations, I would say. My ancestors left Judaea hundreds of years ago, long before the Romans destroyed the second temple. My family have lived in Volubilis, as you call it, or Oualili, as we call it, for over twenty generations. This is my homeland, remember. Judaea is a strange land to me. I have no need to visit there. When we travel, we travel for the purposes of trade, or for family reasons."

"And do you inter-marry with the local Berber population?"

"Of course, many Imazighen have converted to Judaism over the years. Some prefer to convert to Judaism rather than assimilate into the hated Roman culture. Jewish communities are hardy. Some have penetrated far into the hinterland, throughout the Oufrane region and Tinghir in the Atlas Mountains and, according to some knowledgeable rabbis, along the Draa River Valley and to Tiyumetin on the very edges of the Sahara, even."

"Really? I find that incredible."

"It may sound incredible to you, but you must remember Berbers and Jews are part of the fabric of this land, indivisible, woven together like strands of cotton. You pull on one thread and the whole garment starts to unravel."

"But what are these more isolated communities like?"

"In the Draa Valley? Illiterate, largely, I would imagine. Some say they refuse to recognise the authority of the Talmud. But who knows?"

At that moment, Ojokwu pulled his horse up next to the carriage window and leant in. "Looks like we've made it Kal. The driver says our destination is just ahead. Now we can give these poor horses a proper rest and have some grub." He gave a thumbs-up to the other passengers and flashed a broad smile.

"What language are you speaking, Kalius?" asked Antalas.

"English. But not many people understand it."

"English, you say? It's a strange sounding tongue. Is English the only language your friend Titus, there, speaks?"

"No, no, he can also speak Latin quite well. And I've taught him a bit of Greek. He's an attentive student."

"Very good, Kalius, in that case please ask Titus and your brother to share a meal with us tonight."

"That, I understand," confirmed Ojokwu with a grin. "Many thanks, Antalas Alfassi." He waved and withdrew to relay the message to Birch.

"I have a question for you, Kalius," interjected Tuffayur, "seeing as how you've been so inquisitive about us Amazigh."

"Forgive me my forthrightness. Ask me anything you wish."

"Are all the young men in Britannia as handsome as you?"

Antalas erupted with a guffaw of laughter. "Now look here, girl, enough. My apologies, Kalius, she's being unusually outspoken this evening, even by her standards. Now hush, child, before you offend our guest."

Sands blushed once more.

SIXTEEN

Location: Jbel Dar Chaoui, Mauretania Tingitana
Coordinates: 35°33'00" N and 5°43'48" W

Time and Date: 20.30, 8th August, 258 C.E.

A clear Moroccan sky at night is a spectacle of almost supernatural beauty.

The mystical power of such a phenomenon evokes dreams in all those who experience it. Words of description seem quite inadequate as a means of capturing its capacity to inspire, or its ability to provoke the imagination to soar to unvisited realms. To do that, one is obliged to leave behind the literal constraints of language, even in its most poetic manifestation, and to embrace, instead, the field of metaphysics.

Even blinkered atheists such as Birch, or open-mouthed agnostics like Ojokwu, will find themselves seduced by the power of the universe and be tempted to think the unthinkable, if only for a moment. As a spark of consciousness, as a spiritual being that's undergoing a physical experience, could they not be a part of God? It is often said that God is everywhere and in everything, God is moving through form, into form, and out of form. Maybe God is merely what we mean by energy? When one is overwhelmed by the majesty of a Moroccan night sky, even a clear-headed rationalist like Sands will find that such reflections linger seductively, and, on occasion, may come and go in a mere instant. But there are few people who've not been touched by similar thoughts when exposed to a panorama of such breath-taking intensity.

It was under such a sky, that Antalas Alfassi played host to a feast for Sands, Birch and Ojokwu. On the advice of Guenfan, they had set up camp in a small village that acted as an overnight stop for travellers. Easy access to fresh water was on hand, as were basic provisions and feed and stabling for the horses. After rejecting the unhygienic conditions on offer at the local tavern, the three Britons had jumped at the prospect of sleeping under a mantle of stars.

Later, as they were eating, the group sat cross-legged on embroidered cushions in a circle around the cooking fire. The three Britons stared at the sky in wonderment. The scene, evoking a biblical tableau, was illuminated by a pair of oil lanterns that otherwise adorned the front of the grain merchant's carriage. Further radiance was emitted by the fire's embers, the red light of which danced seductively across the glowing, smiling faces of the diners. They were savouring the last mouthfuls of their communal meal, and loud peals of laughter could be heard punctuating the natural sounds emitted through the still Moroccan air.

Guenfan, the driver, steward and general factotum, had been the source of this feast. To accommodate the needs of the diners, he'd acquired additional ingredients from some nearby traders. With the help of Tufayyur and Ojokwu, he had produced a spread to gladden Antalas' heart and to satisfy the appetite of the hungriest guest. Copious amounts of couscous had been cooked in a large metal steamer, part of an array of cooking implements purloined from under the *rheda's* front seat. Earlier, Guenfan had prepared a Berber variant of ratatouille: fried olives, onions, okra and aubergines. This had been laid down to bake in a fireproof cooking chamber buried in the fire's embers. The meat course was comprised of spicy merguez lamb sausages, hand minced by Guenfan and mixed with a harissa paste of chillies, coriander, caraway, garlic and lemon. The mixture was then stuffed with great skill, and no little help from Ojokwu, into long thin strips of lamb intestine casing. The dense, thin sausages were then grilled for fifteen mouth-watering minutes, hissing, spitting and sizzling above the flames, their provocative aroma drifting far and wide across the camp grounds, and inciting many envious remarks from nearby travellers.

While Guenfan and Ojokwu were preparing the meal, Birch used the pretext of looking for a replacement horse in order to slink off and explore local gambling possibilities. It was recognised by his two companions that Birch's capacity to win wagers was central to their continued travel and subsistence plans. Up till now, they'd been happy to indulge his gambling excesses as long as it kept the money rolling in. Of late, however, Ojokwu had been obliged to extricate his companion from several dangerous encounters. Such incidents were more stressful for Ojokwu than they were for his comrade. In common with most high-rollers who are yet to meet their match, Birch possessed a cool head and an air of insouciance that was expanding to match his self-esteem. But the way that Ojokwu saw it, the guy was riding for a fall. It was just a matter of time.

While the meal was cooking, Azulay had been assiduous in offering medical advice to Sands. He'd managed to lay his hands on a herbal unguent, one that he recommended to his young male friend as being particularly effective in the treatment of cuts and grazes. Sands took little persuading in allowing Azulay to bathe and anoint her skinned, bruised knees with the cooling cream. His touch was both sensitive and restorative, his manner attentive and charming. Sands accepted his ministrations with warm gratitude.

This growing bond between the two was cemented further over dinner as they conversed at length. Antalas, meanwhile, had developed a keen interest in Ojokwu. As a trader of enormous practicality, he had become fascinated by the Briton's resourcefulness and adaptability. Ojokwu, for his part, was anxious to discover more about the potential for growing crops in the region around Volubilis.

"If it's wheat you want to know about, then you're talking to the right man," said Tufayyur. "No one in Mauretania Tingitana knows more about grain than my father."

"Well, in that case, I think a toast is in order," suggested Birch. "Here's to Antalas Alfassi."

121

The others all cheered and downed their wine.

"Music, we need music," shouted Antalas. "Guenfan, where are those travelling musicians? Go bring them here, please."

Within seconds a troupe of half a dozen wandering performers had appeared to provide entertainment for Antalas' guests. The musicians arrived together on cue, singing and carrying an array of instruments. The oldest musician was playing a form of Berber bagpipe, another man plucked a four-stringed instrument the size of a mandolin, and a third player held a long-necked one-stringed bowed instrument. The other three musicians were percussionists and played a variety of metal castanets, cylindrical double sided drums and big hand frame drums. Collectively, they produced a mesmerising sound that, in combination with the Moroccan wine, made the heads of the diners swim with glorious intoxication.

"Dance Tufayyur," pleaded Antalas. "Come on Azulay, get your sister to dance for our guests."

The young woman required no second bidding. Before her brother could respond, she was on her feet and dragging Ojokwu up with her. The musicians picked up the tempo, and spurred on by Tufayyur's exhilarating movement, they ascended to a peak of rapturous abandonment in their playing. Soon the entire party was on its feet and whirling in a state of mad chaos. Azulay grabbed Sands by the arms and swung her around in an ecstasy of euphoria. Finally, at Birch's insistence, all six dancers locked limbs and performed a frenzied hokey cokey, before collapsing on the ground, exhausted and in an uproarious condition.

"Wonderful playing, my friends." Antalas tossed over a few coins in payment. "Many thanks."

Later in the evening, when the mood had become more relaxed and conversational, Antalas decided to extend the hospitality of his table to three new travellers who had been smiling at the party from afar. "Come over and enjoy a glass of wine with us before we go to sleep, my friends."

Two of the new guests were Greek, both hailing from Mycenae in the Peloponnese. The third man, a Syrian, was a refugee from Dura-Europos, a legendary city located on the banks of the Euphrates in the far east of the country. He'd been forced to flee his benighted birthplace the previous summer after its destruction following a Sasanian siege. All three were traders and were searching for new markets for medicinal and herbal products in Mauretania. Sands and Ojokwu spent some time in deep conversation with them, and were quick to exploit their passable familiarity with Greek, a skill that did not pass unnoticed by Antalas.

As the night wore on and the wine continued to flow, Tufayyur started to serenade the guests softly. She sang unaccompanied, a confident, proud and inspiring young woman. The heart of every stranger ached for her. Her brother was wreathed in smiles of affection; her father wept long and openly.

When she had finished, the Syrian prepared a concoction for his clay pipe, lit the contents and handed it around the circle of guests for them to smoke in turn. The inhalation of the smoking fumes created a warm sense of goodwill and relaxation among all of them.

"Hashish?" queried Birch, with his thumbs up in the universal sign of approval.

The Syrian looked blank. He addressed a few words to Sands in Greek.

"Its Arabic name means grass," she explained. "How do you say the name?"

"حشيش," the Syrian shouted in Arabic. "Assis," he repeated, nodding his head with pleasure.

"Assis? I've never come across this before," replied Antalas. "What is Assis?"

"He brought a small supply from Syria. He's never seen it anywhere in Mauretania. He says it comes from the buds and leaves of a plant native to his own country."

"I fear its fumes may be poisonous," responded Antalas, suddenly concerned for the welfare of his children.

"No, it is hashish, alright," confirmed Birch. "It's perfectly safe stuff, nothing to worry about, Antalas."

123

"If you gotta die, hell of a way to go," declared Ojokwu. "Thumbs up, everyone, for our Syrian friend. Refugees welcome here, man."

They all laughed, stuck their thumbs up and cheered.

After a short while, Antalas clapped his hands together in order to bring the evening's proceedings to a close. "Now, my friends, I'd be grateful if you'd grant me your attention for a moment. If we are to have any chance of making it as far as Oualili by the next Sabbath day, then we must attempt to get a few hours' sleep tonight."

His announcement was greeted by a chorus of objections from his son and daughter. "Father, don't be such a stick-in-the-mud," implored Tufayyur. "With the help of our Syrian friend, we can all simply fly back home. We'll have no need to walk. Isn't that so, dearest Kalius?" Her voice was beginning to slur alarmingly.

"Okay, so now I'm beginning to side with your father," laughed Sands. "As much as it pains me to say it, you really need to be getting to bed."

"But, darling man, we may never see each other again." Tufayyur was starting to sway from side to side. "Please say you won't all leave us alone tomorrow."

Sands looked at Antalas for moral support.

The grain merchant guffawed. "So be it!" he cried. "If it suits my daughter to travel in the company of three dishevelled, good-for-nothing strangers, then who am I to object? What say you, Azulay?"

Azulay hurled his arms around Sands. "Please join us, Kalius. Travel with us and I promise you won't regret it. We'll eat and drink like kings every night. Guenfan will see to that, won't you, my dear fellow?"

Guenfan's shoulders sagged.

"Don't worry, Guenfan," interjected Ojokwu, "Tufayyur and I'll help you out, won't we, girl?"

Tufayyur beamed at Ojokwu with delight. "Oh Titus, you are a wonderful man. You're all wonderful men, even you, dear Guenfan! Aren't they, father?"

"Go on, off to bed with you. Our faithful Guenfan has laid out your bed in the privacy of the carriage. Good night to you all, and thank you for your company this evening."

And with that, the lanterns were extinguished, the fire doused and the sleeping mats laid out. Within thirty minutes the campsite was bathed in silence.

Despite the all-encompassing darkness and the stillness, Sands endured a desperate night's sleep. The intensity of the evening's stimulants - the hashish, the wine, the rich food, the brilliance of the night's sky, the wild dancing, the engaging company - all caused her mind to race in circles. She sweated profusely, tossed and turned and suffered wild visions. She seemed to awake at one point but still remain asleep. In this state of purgatory she suffered a hellish revelation about her old British Army comrade, Corporal Crawley.

On first stumbling into the hallucination, Sands felt an overriding sense of alarm. She reacted to Crawley's presence with fear, which greatly surprised her. He was waving to her but there was a malign glint in his eye. In the dream he seemed to conquer and possess the space around him. As Crawley moved towards her he gave the appearance of generating an irresistible force field that spilled out and swallowed up everything contained within its gravitational orbit. Any unfortunate humans, like Sands herself, who happened to be caught within it, were just as much subject to its physical forces as were the surrounding inanimate matter and geographical space. Everything sucked into its field of influence suddenly appeared inert, helpless, and subject to this man's indomitable power.

Now Sands' attention was focused on Crawley's appearance. She was mesmerised by the easy swagger and confident gait with which he approached her. Even when he was within touching distance, and facing the sharp end of her drawn sword, he appeared fearless, invulnerable even, with not a hint of concern for his life. And his physique spoke for itself. Rarely, if ever, could Sands recall having seen a man of such imposing stature. Why had she never noticed it before? Crawley stood a good head taller than her, if not more, and his upper body and arms were immensely developed. She was particularly struck by the thickness of his neck. He really was more like a bull than a human. And when he began to address her, in a language and manner that was both ugly and indecipherable, these brutish characteristics showed even more signs of asserting themselves.

With every step that Crawley advanced towards her, Sands became more convinced that she was about to die, that she would be slain with terrible force and suddenness, and that this anticipation would in no sense lessen the hideous shock of the assault that she was about to endure. As Crawley prepared to strike, quivering in his blocks, readying himself to unleash an explosion of destructive kinetic energy, Sands studied his facial mannerisms with cold fear. In among the tightened cheek muscles, the forehead creases, the sweat stained temples, the wildly flaring nostrils and the squinting eyes there was not a single feature that hinted at a flicker of self-doubt, pity, regret or humanity. In the darkest depths of his eyes was there even the slightest trace of respect for his victim? No, not a hint was detectable, and neither was there any understanding, nor compassion, nor empathy. This assault was going to be one of unscrupulous vindictiveness. Pure carnage was about to be visited upon her by a conscienceless murderer who neither valued nor honoured the meaning of death or life. How pitiable to be executed at the hands of a man such as this, Sands found himself reflecting, even as the assassin's blade was beginning its long, slow, bullying journey towards her through the cool night air.

It was a tiny flash of light reflecting off Crawley's knife that kick-started a different set of emotions in Sands. She watched, transfixed, as the reflection passed, millimetre by millimetre, along the edge of the blade. But it was the long-dormant feelings that this minute spark of light awoke in her, rather than the blade itself, that terrified and appalled her most. For she was aware in her dream that she was now no longer herself, no longer Kalahari Sands, but instead channelling the fears and regrets of a young Moorish auxiliary, an innocent male victim

126

of Crawley's casual brutality, killed a year earlier after enjoying an evening soak in the Aballava bathhouse.

The long-forgotten smells, sights and sounds of this auxiliary's childhood in Volubilis impaled themselves, one by one, on Sands lacerated mind. Every distant memory seared itself onto her consciousness, agonisingly, as if laced with salt and cordite. For this is how longing and regret present themselves to the dying, not as a balm or as a comfort but as a series of excruciating, intolerable astringents, applied without pity, one after the other, when the human spirit is at its most porous.

And suffer she did. The man's boyhood memories engulfed Sands: the storks nesting year after year on his uncle's roof; his grandmother pouring warmed olive oil into his ear canal to cure his constant ear-aches; the wind blowing through the golden-brown, endless wheat fields; the market in Tingi where ferocious beasts - bears, lions, elephants - were sold for gladiatorial combat; warm evenings spent sleeping under the stars with his countless brothers and sisters; and the tastes of his childhood, the dates, the olives, the spices, the almonds, even the occasional sip of wine when his parents were being indulgent. But most painful of all were the memories of people this young Berber had known as a boy and a teenager: his immediate family, of course, his grandparents, parents, uncles, aunts, in-laws, brothers and sisters, cousins (so many cousins), but also his childhood school friends and occasional sweethearts. The sadness he'd experiences at leaving Mauretania Tingitana as an eighteen year old was assuaged by his promise to return home one day, but this time as a proud land-owning Roman citizen. He'd make a fine catch for a young wife. He'd cultivate his own olive groves and spend the second half of his life basking in the respect of his extended, loving family. Or so he'd planned. These dreams would now come to nothing. They were being extinguished one by one, his ambitions stymied by an off-duty encounter with a capricious psychopath who'd crossed his path during an evening stroll to the bathhouse.

In the morning, Sands, still haunted by the dream, unburdened herself to Ojokwu. He, at least, knew Crawley well;

unlike Birch, who still took pride in distancing himself from the lower ranks.

Ojokwu applied himself to every detail of her account. When Sands had finished, she stared at him in trembling expectation. "It's a question of proximity," he responded.

"Proximity? What does that mean?"

"Why do you think you had that nightmare last night?"

"It wasn't a nightmare, really; more a revelation, a vision."

"Ok, listen to me. What I'm trying to get at is that yesterday evening you experienced proximity to Azulay, right? He's a young Berber, just like the soldier whose memories you inhabited in your 'vision', if that's how you prefer to describe it. It struck a deep chord with you, right? So now you're starting to empathise with young men like him. Us soldiers are forced to trample on guys like him like they ain't even human, you get me? Now you're beginning to see guys like Crawley through new eyes, like the enemy does. The meaning's straight forward, no question of that. You get what I'm saying, yeah?"

"But I like Crawley."

"Liking him don't come in to it, Kal. Crawley's a good guy alright – but only if you know him. No one's saying he ain't. But he's got another side too. He's a cold-hearted killer, I told you that already, just like Stogdon. If you're wearing the wrong colour uniform, I'm telling you now, man, they gonna kill you just as soon as look at you, trust me. It's been trained into them. They're programmed. But they ain't the ones to blame."

"Jesus, Ojo, are you the same?"

"What you think? You think I'm the same as them two guys? The same as Crawley and Stog? No man, I'm sewn from different cloth. Cut me and I bleed African blood. I don't fear proximity to no 'other', man, I embrace it. I am the 'other', you get what I'm telling you?"

SEVENTEEN

Aballava Tablet No. 6, Inventory No 13.25 (Morris Archive)

Caeluibianus, Cohort Tribune and Praepositus of the Company, to Julius Rufinus, Tribunus Laticlavius and commander-in-chief, I send my greetings. In the matter of determining the fate of Galla Placidia (undertaken in the utmost secrecy as directed) I have done so in full accordance with your wishes and have set out my findings below. I give thanks to the Gods that Fortuna and the Venti have conspired to give us wings to fly, my Lord! For the last ten days we have been transported south by the seven oxen of Septentrio. Since embarking at Durnonavaria, our progress towards our final goal has been steadfast and unremitting. Last evening we disembarked briefly at Falvium Brigantium on the north-west tip of Hispania, having received reliable reports of a possible sighting of our prey there. The winds have been so lively that I was forced to confine the loathsome Bostar to the sick bay for four days while we crossed the Mare Gallaecum. The sight of his livid green complexion could not be endured, my Lord. He whimpered like a puppy with every pitch of the cortiba. Sometimes I despair of that wretch, I really do. I know I can count on your every sympathy, my Lord, when I confess, that if I hadn't had urgent need of his services, I'd have gladly flung him overboard myself in order to be spared his constant mewling. However, this sorry tale has an improbable ending, or, as the Greek dramatists would have it, a *deus ex machina* contrivance with Bostar featuring as the unlikely hero. Indulge me momentarily, my Lord, while I explain the circumstances thus. You'll recall that Galla Placidia claimed to hail from Eboracum, which lies in the heart of the territory dominated by the Brigantes tribe. Her influence can therefore be assumed to extend out from that location, and logic would dictate that it would naturally spread to other territories where her tribes shares kinship connections. As your Lordship would be only too aware, the Brigantes trade far and wide around the western shores of Britannia and coastal Hibernia, and as far south as Armorica in Gaul and Gallaecia in north-west Hispania. The port of Flavium Brigantium, as is implied by its name, bears historic kinship ties with Galla Placidia's tribe in Britannia. It was with this understanding that we initially and fruitlessly scoured both the harbourside and radiating streets for evidence of the Placidian cult. We were on the cusp of terminating our futile quest, when fortune, as is her wont, smiled down in the most capricious manner. It began with a trifling remark, my Lord, brought on by a moment of understandable frustration at our failure to uncover any sign of our prey during our hunting expedition. "May the God's damn Galla Placidia to all eternity and back", said I in earshot of a gang of local ruffians. To my astonishment several of their number leapt to her defence and roundly abused me for my pains, upbraiding me for insulting her name on the very day that a shrine dedicated to her veneration is to be consecrated. May Jupiter curse you for a pack of lying curs, said I. Are we now obliged to add sacrilege to her many crimes against the state? Where does this shrine lie, you blasphemous scoundrels, you impious idolaters? Bostar made haste to intervene in order to save the villains from a savage beating at my hands. Later that evening, however, divine justice was indeed meted out to this sacrilegious cult through the good offices of Bostar in the form a burning brazier dipped in tar and oil. As we cast off from the harbour on board the cortiba, the sky was emblazoned and aflame with the orange glow of Galla Placidia's shrine immolating in the distance. The screams and wails of her followers, echoing out across the water as we slipped from view, will serve as a small foretaste of the vengeance of hell that will pour down upon her head and the heads of all those who have offered her assistance; this I, Caeluibianus, in the name of Julius Rufinus, Tribunus Laticlavius and commander-in-chief, will personally guarantee.

I will write as soon as I have further intelligence to impart. May I not shrink from my purpose, my Lord. I will do what I am ordered and at every command I will be ready.

EIGHTEEN

Location: Volubilis, Mauretania Tingitana
Coordinates: 34° 03' 36" N and 5° 33' 00" W

Time and Date: 14.00, 13th August, 258 C.E.

"That's one helluva sight, Sands. Civilization at last."

Birch was looking down from the coach driver's perch next to Guenfan. From his elevated spot, basking in the early morning sunshine, he was able to gaze for miles across a magnificent broad green valley. This fertile plain, criss-crossed by centuries of agricultural activity, was edged by a high range of jagged mountains, their silhouettes etched hard against the saturated sky. The panorama appeared as a perfect pastoral backdrop to the great walled city looming five miles ahead of them.

Sands wore a rapturous smile.

"So this is Volubilis."

After a tough, uncomfortable, five-day journey they had reached their final destination. They had ridden under a merciless sun for two hundred and thirty kilometres. Their supporting caravan, dragging along behind them for tens of miles, contained untold millions of subscribers. And every time the convoy passed through a township, the numbers would decline as individual gamers decamped to explore the surrounding countryside. From the village of Ad Novas in the north to Aquae Dacicae in the south, via the townships of Oppidum Novum, Tremuli, Vopisciana and Gilda in-between, the opportunities for exploration and adventure were endless.

However, as far as the three Britons and their Berber fellow-travellers were concerned, this moment represented the end of the line. And the surrounding environment, as if to mark their achievement, had assembled a suitable welcoming committee.

The sky was of an intense, ecstatic blue; the air was calm, warm and fresh; and the wind, or what little breeze there was, was sufficiently strong to transport the pungent aroma of wild herbs, the sweet scent of pomegranate bushes and the light fragrance of jasmine and oleander flowers to their nostrils. The overall effect was quite scintillating.

Azulay was standing with his left arm casually propped on Sands shoulder. "Kalius, I must correct you: the city is properly called Oualili, not Volubilis. In the Tamazight language we always use the name Oualili."

"Whatever you call it, it looks magnificent in any language. Look at the mountain range over there. And the city, itself; how beautiful is that, Ojo?"

"Come on, what do you say, Titus?" Antalas prompted. "Do you like what you see?"

"I like it very well."

Ojokwu was transfixed. "It looks a beautiful city. But, tell me, where do your olive groves and wheat fields lie?"

Antalas turned to address Sands. "We show him stone and mortar, and he demands soil and crops. I can see it doesn't take Titus long to get down to the nitty-gritty." He laughed and pointed to the distant horizon. "Far to the south west of the city, can you see the green plain over there? Look, beyond the river, stretching as far as the eye can see, everything out there is highly fertile land. It is the source of the city's wealth and wellbeing."

Ojokwu strained his eyes to stare into the distance.

"It's also the source of Rome's full stomach," added Azulay.

"That, I cannot deny," his father replied.

"Antalas, there's something I've been meaning to ask you," interjected Sands. "Titus and I once met a native of these parts who told us that Oualili was famous for possessing a hundred olive presses."

"In the bathhouse at Aballava," nodded Ojokwu. "That was one weird night."

"One hundred olive presses in Oualili? Oh, yes, at least a hundred. There's scarcely a family in the town who doesn't operate an olive press within their own property. Why, we have one, ourselves. It's Tufayyur's pride and joy, isn't that so, my darling?"

Tufayyur shot her father a reprimanding glance. "Mother may take issue with you on that score, Father. It's under *her* eagle eye, not mine, that our press produces the best olive oil in all of Mauretania Tingitana." Tufayyur turned to address the three Britons. "You must judge its quality tonight when you dine with us. Mother will be delighted to meet you all. Isn't that so, Father?"

"You presume to know your mother better than she knows herself, my dear. Let us reflect for a minute. At the very least, let us permit her the honour of issuing her own dinner invitations. After all, she won't have laid eyes on her darling children for over a month now."

Tufayyur shook her head. "He's always like this when we've been away travelling without Mother," she explained to the Britons. "He feels guilty," she said with a smile. "Look Father, Matrona won't be wanting to miss out on the fun of meeting new people, believe me."

"It's true, Father, you know it is," confirmed Azulay. "Why would we deny her the pleasure of our new friends' delightful company at dinner?"

Antalas conceded defeat with all the mock reluctance of a bridegroom being dragged to his matrimonial bed by his ushers. "Oh, well, it appears as if I may be outnumbered. There's nothing else for it then." He turned towards the Britons. "It would be our great pleasure if tonight you would dine with us - at the invitation of my wife, you understand."

"Of course," the three Britons concurred in unison.

"Good, well that's settled, then," he confirmed with a gratified nod to Azulay and Tufayyur. "Now let's get along home before the mid-day sun hits us."

"If it's all the same to you, Antalas," said Sands, "I think I'd like to walk the last few miles to the city gates."

"I'll walk with you, Kalius," Tufayyur said, grabbing Sands' arm and pulling her along. "Azulay has monopolised you quite enough already."

"Bad luck, young man," shouted Antalas to Sands as he climbed back into his carriage. "You can't expect Azulay to protect you from Tufayyur all the time." He looked down at Ojokwu and offered him his hand. "Come on, Titus, there's room up here for you with the two of us. There's much I want to talk to you about."

Tufayyur smiled to herself. She whispered to Sands as they walked. "Father is greatly taken with Titus, you know."

"I can see that. The admiration seems mutual."

"He wants to ask Titus to work for him. Do you think he'd accept such an offer?"

Sands looked surprised. "I really have no idea. What does he want him to do?"

"He needs an agent, a factor, someone who he can depend on to protect his financial interests when he's not around."

"What about Azulay?"

"He's too young and inexperienced to deal with some of the crooks around here. And Father is growing too old to undertake long trips to the coast. Titus is a very capable man and he appears so honest and trustworthy. And he has been so kind to me."

"Has he now?"

"As have you dear Kalius. And as has your brother, Sextus."

"We're all very fond of you and your family. I have to say I hold Titus in the highest esteem. If ever a man merited your father's trust and confidence it is he."

"But do you think he'd accept such an offer? Say he will."

Sands laughed. "Be fair, Tufayyur, I have no more right to speak for Titus than you do for your mother. All I can say is this, if he doesn't accept an offer from so honourable a man as Antalas Alfassi, then he must've had his wits scrambled by the Mauretanian sun."

"Oh, thank you. I do love talking to you. You say the nicest things."

Sands returned her smile. "I love talking to you too."

"Kalius?"

"Yes."

"Do you mind if I say something to you?"

"Not in the slightest. Feel free to say whatever you want."

"Are you sure?"

"Of course."

"You're really like no other man I've met." Tufayyur stopped in her tracks. "There, I've said it and I can't take it back."

"Really, in what way do you mean?"

"You're so kind and gentle to me, and yet so strong and confident. Compared to you, Kalius, other men seem to behave like overgrown schoolboys, arrogant and disdainful of women." Tufayyur's expression reflected the open distaste with which she summoned up the comparison. "I hate most of the men I'm obliged to come into contact with. Why would I agree to be dominated by such a person, by someone who's not worthy of me? Tell me that."

"Clearly, you shouldn't have to. That's one of the things I admire most about you, Tufayyur. You'll only do what feels right for you. You're like me in that respect."

"I think so, too, Kalius. We *are* alike, you and me, except for one thing. You, being a male, are free to make your own way in the world, while I'm not. My fate is to be tied to whichever strutting peacock I'm married off to."

As she pondered her fate, a hint of sadness was evident in Tufayyur's voice. Sands felt a flash of shame, a pang of regret at her duplicity in disguising her gender. This subterfuge, adopted in a desperate attempt to evade capture, was threatening to brand her as an unconscionable liar.

"I don't really feel worthy of your admiration. There's a lot that you don't know about me."

"Don't be silly, dear Kalius. You're the very best of men. Nothing you could say could dissuade me from that opinion."

"I'd be very happy if that were true. However, I'm not the paragon of virtue you take me for."

"What do you mean? I have no reason to doubt you, do I?"

"Doubt me? No, of course not. At least not in the way I think you mean."

"Are you married or betrothed to anyone?"

"No."

"You see, I knew it. I could tell you are an honourable man."

Sands could feel her resolve weakening. Surely this young woman deserved to know the truth? "Is there anything else about me that you'd like to ask? Anything about me that puzzles you?"

Tufayyur pondered as they strolled behind the carriage.

"Yes, there is something odd I've noticed. Your brother, Sextus, calls you 'Sands' in a brusque manner from time to time. You don't seem to have a close relationship with him like I do with Azulay. Why is that?"

"Wish I knew. We've never been close. He's protective towards me and he's a dutiful big brother, but that's as far as it goes. We just see the world differently, I guess."

Tufayyur nodded her head. She contemplated Sands' response before asking another question. She looked tense.

"I've also noticed that you look at me differently from the way other men do - I mean all men, including Titus."

Sands reddened.

"Why is that, Kalius?"

Sands was unprepared for the directness of Tufayyur's question. She could sense herself blushing. "I really have no idea. I feel shy when I look at you. You're really very beautiful."

"All men seem to think I'm beautiful. At least, that's what they insist on telling me when Father's attention wanders." Tufayyur stopped and inspected Sands for a moment. "No, that's not it. With you, there's more than that - I can feel it."

"What do you think it is then? You tell me."

"I feel you inhabit me when you look at me. Other men just gaze at me. You seem to understand me; they just admire me. It is very draining to be continuously admired like some object on a sideboard. Can you understand that?"

Sands nodded. She could feel her face burning with the enchantment of Tufayyur's words. She felt like a fish on a line, being carefully reeled in, foot by foot, inch by inch. "And how does it make you feel when *I* look at you?" Sands asked.

"When you look at me I feel replenished, not consumed," said Tufayyur. "It makes me feel alive, like I want to scream and shout and laugh. Sometimes when you look at me, you make my skin shiver, Kalius. That's the effect you have on me."

Sands recognised the symptoms. During the previous five days, she'd experienced the same vivid sensations described by Tufayyur. Now, as she gazed in turmoil at the young Berber woman, she struggled to manufacture a plausible explanation for her condition. "That's because we've become close friends, Tufayyur, you and me. This is how good friends feel in each other's company, when they talk together warmly, or go to the bathhouse together, or share a meal together."

"Really, is that how you and Titus feel when you spend time together at the bathhouse?"

Sands nodded in the affirmative, relieved that she was able to respond more or less truthfully to one of Tufayyur's question. "Titus and I are very close. And have been for a long time."

"But Titus is a man and I'm a woman. Doesn't that make a difference to how you feel about us?"

"Sometimes there are no easy answers to questions like that. In my experience, the more straightforward the question, the more complicated the response is likely to be."

"Don't say that, Kalius. Why can't life just be simple for once?"

Sands shrugged. What else could she do? How could she continue without revealing more than was prudent?

"I don't know what to say to you, Tufayyur."

The young Berber sensed Sands' sudden unease. She attempted a smile.

"Forgive me, I've talked too personally. Come, let's walk more quickly. Let's see how Titus is getting on with Father."

They ran to catch up with the carriage, kicking their way through the dust on the road.

They spent the next few miles chatting about the delights of Oualili and the neighbouring countryside, and, such was their level of mutual-absorption, that the group had passed through the north-east gate of the city and was proceeding up the main street before they'd even had a chance to register the fact.

"Look we're here, Kalius, my home city, the most wonderful place in the world!"

Sands laughed with undisguised pleasure. "Hurray for Oualili." She ran up to the carriage and banged on the door. "Ojo, we made it. Come out and have a look."

"I can see fine from in here. I got me my own tour guide in here," he replied, grinning at Antalas.

"Just look at this street, Sands," Birch exclaimed. "Keep your eyes peeled for gambling houses, there's a good girl."

"If you want to patronise me, you could at least try getting my gender right." Not even Birch could spoil her good humour on such a morning.

"Dammit, Sands, my apologies! I thought I was just being sexist. I didn't realised I was being patronising too. Bloody typical, that's a double-whammy right there. Years of training and I hadn't even clocked it. I must be losing my touch, Sands."

"We live in hope, Birch," she yelled back, but her remark was lost in the din of the wheels as they bounced over the cobbled stone surface of the main road. It made no difference, in any event. Captain Birch, true to form, had already checked out of their exchange and was focused on scouring for gambling activity along the main thoroughfare.

The first five hundred metres of this street, the *Decumanus Maximus,* was composed of continuous arched porticoes that enclosed both sides of the street. The shops behind the arches were open for business and the air was throbbing with activity. The porticoes provided shaded walkways to pedestrians as well as to shoppers and helped keep the street clear for carriages and horses.

"Come on, Kalius, off the street before you get killed!" yelled Tufayyur. She was skittish with delight. "Guenfan, tell Father, the two of us are going to walk home."

"We'll await you at the fountain, while we water the horses."

"Okay, see you later. Over here, Kalius."

Tufayyur grabbed Sands' arm and yanked her off the street.

"Tufayyur, this is so exciting. I love shopping. I can't wait."

"Well, you've found the right companion, dear friend. Come on, then, they won't mind waiting for us."

"Yes, we'll just be a couple of minutes." Sands' head was swivelling in anticipation. "They won't mind."

"Kalius, no wonder I like you so much. You think like me."

The next hour counted among the most pleasurable that Sands could recall. She passed from one shop to another in a state of total and utter captivation. Purveyors of houseware and pottery; sellers of writing equipment and papyrus; apothecaries stuffed full of mysterious tinctures and remedies; vendors of foodstuffs, weaponry, furniture, and wine: all were of as great an interest to her as the shoe shops, jewellers and clothes emporiums of her twenty-first century experience. Tufayyur was enthralled by Sands' open-mouthed stupefaction at the range and variety of goods on sale.

"Look in that shop over there," Sands yelled at one point. "Over there, Tufayyur, look – are those lion cubs?"

"Where do you mean? Oh yes, aren't they sweet? They're Barbary Lions, caught in the Atlas Mountains."

"I don't believe it. They're so small. Who buys them?"

"They're sold here as pets for the amusement of local patricians. It's a horrible thing to do, separating them from their mothers like that."

"Horrible. And what happens to the parents. Are they killed?"

"Oh no, they are far too valuable. They are sold on to the wild beast market at Tingi and then shipped by boat to Rome for the gladiatorial contests at the Colosseum. My father has witnessed such combat himself."

"I had no idea you could hunt lions this far north. What other animals get sold here?"

"Leopards, naturally. Brown bears are a great favourite, of course. The Romans say they are very fierce and put up a good fight. Oh, and elephants, how could I forget them?"

"Really, you have elephants in Mauretania Tingitana?"

"Oh, yes, our Mauretanian elephants are very famous. Where do you think Hannibal son of Hamilcar got his war elephants from?"

Sands grimaced. For the first time she was losing her appetite for shopping.

"Look, here we are," said Tufayyur, pointing across the street. "There's Guenfan waiting for us."

"Oh dear, your father doesn't look well pleased. We have been rather a long time."

"Leave him to me. Wait till he sees the ornamental carp I got him for his fish pond. He'll be overcome with delight, you'll see." She waved to Antalas and skipped across the road with her present. "Father, look what I've got you!"

Tufayyur's prognosis was correct. Her father's ire melted as soon as he laid eyes on her gift, and by the time they were ready to continue to the house he was once again proclaiming his daughter's qualities.

"Look, my friends," he pointed out, "to your left is the northern bathhouse, and straight ahead lies the Arch of Caracalla. What a waste of tax payers' money that was."

The monument in question was a squat, grandiose affair, impressive in stature but, as far as Antalas was concerned, of precious little civic value or significance.

"I was a one-year-old when the Romans put that damned thing up. My father was forced to pay through the nose for the privilege of observing that monstrosity for the rest of his life. He insisted on moving so that it couldn't overlook the house. It was the only way he felt he could register his disgust. I, at least, can express it out loud. Come on, we're nearly there."

Antalas' house sat one street west of the *Decumanus Maximus*. It was evident to his guests that the scale of the property reflected their host's prominent status in the community. The three Britons vocalised their appreciation.

Antalas beamed with pride. "Welcome to the House of Oleanders. You're all very welcome. Now, where's my wife? Come on children, let's go find her."

As soon as he spoke, the door burst opened and an avalanche of bodies came pouring forth to welcome and embrace Antalas and his children. The sounds of joy and laughter echoed through the street. The three Britons looked on, not knowing how to respond, but began to take stock of their surroundings. The house lay hidden behind a seven-arched portico, with the main grand entrance to the house's atrium being flanked by a row of shops on either side. The façade rose to two stories, the upper floor containing small windows that overlooked the main street. The roofs of the upper storey and the portico below it were dressed in warm terracotta tiles. They were just able to discern the semi-circular towers of the city's south-west gate about one hundred metres behind the house. The property's compound appeared to extend back for over seventy metres and was enclosed within a windowless wall on the longer side. The visitors couldn't wait to have a nose around inside.

"Come in, come in," laughed Antalas above the din. "Come in off the street and meet my family. Then we can take some refreshment. Guenfan, tell the cook to prepare something before you stable the horses, there's a good fellow."

Sands, Birch and Ojukwu were ushered through the front entrance and into a large airy atrium, where Antalas introduced his new friends, one by one. There was great excitement and a shouting of greetings. Once the first part of the introductions was complete, he then attempted to affect the second half.

"Now, let me see if I can remember who everyone is," he joked to general merriment. "It's been so long since I've seen you all. Now, this one I'm not so sure about," he said, rubbing his chin and looking at his wife with a mischievous grin. "Ah, yes, if I'm not very much mistaken, this must be my wife, Matrona."

"Welcome to my humble house, and please forgive my husband for his terrible sense of humour and his appalling manners in not introducing us earlier. Shame on you, Antalas. He tries to lock me away from all society, you know."

"Enough, enough, Matrona, my sweet - my reputation cannot survive another public reprimand." He kissed his wife on the hand and she favoured him with a radiant smile.

"Next, it gives me great pleasure to introduce you to my father-in-law, Rabbi Yehuda, a very distinguished scholar and religious leader."

A grey bearded gentleman, of sixty or so, stepped forward and welcomed each Briton in turn with a firm arm-shake and a warm, inquisitive smile. He scrutinised each guest at close quarters. He was weighing up each of these strangers.

"Now, who have we got next? Ah yes, here is my widowed sister-in-law, Tamalut, and her three children, who are, of course, the younger cousins of Azulay and Tufayyur. So, from left to right we have my niece, Ultafa, who is now aged what, my love?"

"Twelve, Uncle."

"Just checking you remembered," Antalas teased. "And next to her is my splendid young nephew, Solomon, who is now how old?"

"Fourteen"

"Correct. And, finally, Hananiyah, who I can definitely say is seventeen."

"Sixteen!"

"Are you sure, my boy? I've never been wrong before."

"Stop teasing him, Father, and let's offer our guests some refreshment. I must put this poor fish in the pond or we'll all be dining on it tonight."

"Oh, talking of which, did I mention, my love, that you and I have invited these three splendid young fellows to share our humble table this evening?"

"I did hear of it, Antalas, but not from you; your son beat you to it. I am greatly honoured that our guests have accepted my invitation," she said to a great roar of approval. "Please forgive my husband's clumsiness in these matters. Come through into the courtyard. It is shady and cool out there."

Azulay slapped Sands on the back. "A quick drink, a light bite to eat, and then I think a trip to the bathhouse is in order. What do you say, lads?"

Sands appeared to be disconcerted by the suggestion. "I'm not sure I can…"

"Why ever not, Kalius? You can't have bathed properly in over a week. I know I haven't."

"Ah… my religion forbids me from engaging in communal bathing. It requires me to…I am required to retain my modesty at all times."

"Really, however do you cope?" asked Antalas in astonishment.

"It's not that unusual," interjected Rabbi Yehuda. "Feel free to use my private toilet if it suits your religious requirements."

"You have a private toilet? Would that be acceptable to you, sir, if I was to use it?"

"Of course it's acceptable, young man. There are strict religious rules regarding the privacy of religious elders in Judaism. The act of defecation should not be seen by the eyes of God. Like you, I am required to maintain my modesty in all matters relating to my personal ablutions."

"I see."

"Good, that's settled, then. You'll find it beyond the *tablinum* at the rear of the house," added Antalas. "Now, what do make of my courtyard?"

While talking, they had wandered through into the inner *peristyle*, a delightful open courtyard that was surrounded on all sides by columned porticoes providing welcome shade from the late morning sun. It appeared to take up almost a fifth of the entire ground floor area of the property. In the centre of the *peristyle* sat two rectangular ornamental ponds, one containing a small fountain and the other a collection of exotically patterned fish. Tufayyur carefully poured her father's carp into this latter pond and watched it as the fish adjusted to the sudden change in water temperature. Around the edge of the ponds were arrayed a collection of large terracotta pots, each containing a flowering oleander bush. At the far end, nearest the back wall, where one might ordinarily expect to see a statue of a Roman god, a large menorah, a nine branched Jewish candelabrum, was positioned.

"Now, I should remind our guests that tomorrow is our holy Sabbath day," said Antalas, "so we will be spending the day at home or at the temple. You will be very welcome to stay with us and you are not obliged to follow our customs."

"No, no, that's very kind of you, Antalas," replied Sands. "We will not impose on your hospitality further. Is there anywhere you could suggest where we could find suitable lodgings?"

"Could we not make space here, my dear?" asked Matrona.

"I don't see why not, if that's agreeable to you gentlemen. Guenfan has said he can squeeze a couple of you into the servants quarters if that is acceptable to you. We have many rooms here, as you can see." Antalas gestured around the perimeter of the peristyle to five separate doors, each one of which led on to a bedroom. "However, we have a full household at the moment and not much space to spare for additional guests."

"How about my room on the second floor, Father?" said Azulay. "I have plenty of space in there for a roommate. Why doesn't Kalius move in with me for a few days?"

"That's a very generous offer, my boy. That would take care of all three of them. Would that be acceptable to you, Kalius? Do you mind bunking up with young Azulay over there?"

"Not at all, sir; that is indeed a very kind and generous offer."

NINETEEN

Aballava Tablet No. 7, Inventory No 13.26 (Morris Archive)

Caeluibianus, Cohort Tribune and Praepositus of the Company, to Julius Rufinus, Tribunus Laticlavius and commander-in-chief, I send my greetings. In the matter of determining the fate of Galla Placidia (undertaken in the utmost secrecy as directed) I have done so in full accordance with your wishes and have set out my findings below. I am going to speak frankly, my Lord, and, if I do so, it is provoked out of two mutually powerful motive forces; the first being the manifest love and fraternal esteem that I hold for you as my commander-in-chief, and the second being the hate I carry in my bosom for that traitorous bitch whose name I can no longer bring myself to inscribe in these reports. At times, my Lord, my desire for retribution so overwhelms me that I fear it will unhinge all capacity for reasoned thought. Even Bostar looks at me now with a wary eye, the rogue, although the God's will attest how sorely provoked I have been by his surly and disobliging manner. Life would be easier for me if I was to slit his throat when he sleeps and slip his body overboard. His continual grumbles and complaints would test the patience of Jupiter himself, and, unless his humour improves markedly, I wouldn't wager a single denarius on his chances of arriving in Volubilis in one piece. Mention of Volubilis, my Lord, reminds me that I am presently many leagues closer to our final destination than I am to Aballava, and that, consequently, with every shift of the wind I am moving further out with your orbit of command. The certain knowledge that any orders issued by my Lord, particularly those that are intended to countermand any actions of mine, will take many weeks to arrive, grants me fresh licence to speak in a forthright and, I trust, honest manner. From this moment on, my Lord, circumstances dictate that I will be forced to act entirely on my own cognisance. Any efforts to exhort, restrain or upbraid me will fall on deaf ears until the Ides of September at the earliest, by which time I intend to have fully contracted our business, given sacrificial thanks to Jupiter, and commenced my return home. Any further reports received from me, my Lord, will be purely to inform you of actions taken rather than to request guidance or permission to act in accordance with your wishes. I will despatch this tablet from Olisipo when we disembark there shortly. I will then write as soon as I have further intelligence to impart on my arrival in Volubilis. May I not shrink from my purpose, my Lord. I will do whatever conscience and good sense dictates and at every moment of decision you can depend on me to be ready.

TWENTY

Location: Volubilis, Mauretania Tingitana
Coordinates: 34° 03' 36" N and 5° 33' 00" W

Time and Date: 09.30, 14th August, 258 C.E.

It was nine thirty on the morning of the Jewish Shabbat. Sands, Birch and Ojokwu were taking a stroll through the teeming streets of their newly-adopted hometown. The temperature was hovering just the right side of comfortable, the sky appeared a delectable shade of blue and the light possessed a crystalline clarity.

"So how was your night with lover boy?" Ojokwu enquired.

Sands shot him an outraged glance.

"Don't give me that big, wide-eyed look," he taunted. "You know what I'm talking about. I mean that fit young Berber you're bunked up with. He's got a proper thing about you, I'm telling you, man."

"You don't half chat some shit sometimes. I'm not bunked up with anyone. Azulay and I are just two mates sharing a room - and I'm sleeping in my own camp bed. Sorry to disabuse you."

"You know what I mean. He's got a crush on you, that lad."

"Fuck off."

"Just like his sister. I don't know how you do it, Kal. She's one beautiful looking girl, trust me."

"Gimme a break, Ojo. You need to stop fixating on my non-existent sex life." The unexpected nature of the conversation caused Sand's heart to thump wildly in her chest.

"Don't you think she's beautiful?" Ojokwu persisted.

"She is. She's very beautiful."

The Britons began their walk by retracing their steps from the day before. As they promenaded it was hard to believe that it was less than eighteen hours since their arrival in the city. Suddenly the world was opening up and promising them a number of tantalising prospects. In a dream-like state, they made their way back past the massive triumphal arch of Caracalla, every nook and cranny of which was colonised by nesting storks. They then crossed over the *Decumanus Maximus*, stopped for a refreshing drink at the fountain behind the giant northern *thermes* and pondered over the purpose of the giant circular earthwork mound that lay adjacent to it. They clambered to the top of the structure to get a panoramic view of the beautiful city below. "It's a form of tumulus," Sands decreed. "It's where generations of Berbers have buried their dead."

Birch stamped his feet on the ground as if to test Sands' assertion. "A burial ground? What kind of religion are they? Islam isn't on the menu for another five centuries."

"A bit of this, a bit of that," Sands replied. "Antalas says that the Berbers have adopted a number of Roman gods. But there's a big cult around Saturn. They're long-standing sun worshippers and it fits with local traditions."

"Seems a tad pick-and-mix to me. I'd have thought the Romans would find that approach a bit sacrilegious."

"Surprisingly not - the Romans are very flexible when it comes to religion. As long as the locals toe the line politically, they can pretty much worship who and what they like. There's a bit of ancestor-worship, ancestors as gods, that sort of thing. The Berbers believe that deceased relatives respond to their requests by communicating with them through their dreams."

"That ain't such a bad way to channel the dead," said Ojokwu. "Better than an annual pilgrimage to the cemetery." He pointed south to a nearby precinct from which a cacophony of voices could be detected. "Now, who's up for joining me down there, where all the action is?"

Ojokwu was pointing to the main campus of civic buildings. From their vantage point atop the tumulus, Ojokwu and his two companions could see an impressive array of classical structures centred round the city's forum. Even here, in the heart of official Volubilis, every elevation was ornamented with a stork's nest.

"The big building nearest us, the one that looks like an early medieval church, that's the basilica," said Sands. "It's the centre of government and the courts. The columned building behind it is a temple, to Jupiter most likely. The rest are made up of sanctuaries, other official civic buildings and over there is another bath house."

"Come on, Sands, enough of the bloody commentary," interrupted Birch. "Let's get down there. I'm in the mood to sit in the shade and watch the world go by."

Together they scrambled down the side of the tumulus, whooping with delight as they slipped and slid to the bottom. Within minutes they'd found themselves mingling with a throng of locals in the forum. The atmosphere was breathtaking. The market was bathed in equal measures of sunlight, smoke and steam. The boiling water from dozens of copper urns coalesced with the smoke from a multitude of spitting charcoal braziers to create a cloud of sweet-smelling vapour. Brilliant shafts of sunlight cut through the dense haze to blend a latticework of jostling patterns across the piles of earthenware pots, flat-woven carpets and multi-hued fruit and vegetables.

"Let's grab a drink," Birch shouted above the hubbub. "This is much more like it. You two find somewhere cool to perch, and I'll get the refreshments."

Ojokwu stared at Sands in bemusement. "Birch is in a right good mood? What the hell's got into him?"

"He's human, isn't he? Just make the most of it while it lasts. Here we go, grab a seat in the shade."

They sat down on a low stone wall and surveyed the vibrant scene in front of them. Ojokwu stretched his legs and emitted a sigh of pleasure.

"You know something amazing?" Sands said. "This is the first time since we've been here that I haven't woken up and been desperate to get back to the twenty-first century."

"Same here, man. Would you just look at that view?"

Sands smiled at her friend. "You like the look of what you see, then?"

"What's not to like? Look around. You see many Europeans?"

"Nope."

"Neither do I. Ain't it brilliant?"

"Yep."

"No offence, Kal, but you're in a minority here. I ain't. Do you hear much Latin being spoke? I don't. It's pretty much a melting pot of African languages. It's like I'm back home in Ridley Road market."

Sands smiled. Ojokwu was in his element.

"Look at them Tuareg tribesmen over there, Kal. Look at the colour of them indigo robes and scarves they're wearing, man. They're electric blue. They're amazing. I'm gonna get myself one, I'm telling you. And, hey, look over there, ain't that the Syrian dude we met a week ago on the road? You know, the guy with the cannabis - and there's his two Greek mates. Hey, boys!"

Sands peered through the crowd before spotting them on the far side. She leapt to her feet.

"What's their names?" said Ojokwu. "Wave to 'em, Kal."

"Χαίρετε!" Sands yelled in Greek. "Τί πράττετε?"

The three men looked around in surprise and scanned the surrounding crowd. They saw her waving from the edge of the forum and beamed back in acknowledgement. "Πάντ' ἀγαθὰ πράττω, ὦ φίλε," they shouted in unison. "Καιρὸς δέ!"

"They've seen us. They're coming over!"

The three men pushed their way through a jostling horde of traders, merchants and buyers, their progress slowed by the obligation to greet fellow vendors en route.

"Welcome friends," shouted Ojokwu in Latin. The five travellers exchanged arm shakes and warm smiles. Sands swapped news with one of the Greeks.

"You hear what he said, Ojo? They're going to stay in Volubilis. They're going to be selling their goods in the forum every day. Their stall is over there on the far side near the rostrum."

"That's so cool, guys. *They're* gonna stay in Volubilis, *we're* gonna stay in Volubilis! Now we can become real pals. Man, I'm starting to proper like this town."

A few moments after the three visitors had headed back to their market stand, Birch reappeared with hot drinks.

"Cups of tea all round," Ojokwu chimed.

"I've got something better than that, my old chum. Strictly speaking, these are tisanes."

"What you got then? They look wild."

"Boiled mint, lavender and honey. If that doesn't float your boat, boiled hibiscus flower petals and honey. Take your pick."

"I'll take the hibiscus and honey," replied Sands. "It'll complement my personality."

Birch sat down, stretched out his long legs and beamed. "Isn't this wonderful," he said, surveying the scene with a calculating eye.

"You know who we met just now?" asked Ojokwu.

"Indeed I do: our friends from the other night. I spotted them when I was getting the drinks. I must pop over and have a word with the Syrian in a minute. It might open certain commercial possibilities for the future."

Ojokwu laughed. "You referring to drugs or gambling now?"

"Both, as it so happens."

"Birch, you need to diversify, man," said Ojokwu.

"I agree - gambling's become too risky. Some drunken Roman squaddie's going to finish me off before you can save my hide. I can see it coming."

"Hallelujah, Birch - about bloody time. So what's the alternative if you ain't gonna to stick with gambling?"

"After a great deal of thought, Ojo, old man, I've been forced to one inescapable conclusion."

"Which is what?"

"That there are great commercial opportunities opening up in the field of medicinal imports."

Sands laughed. "You serious? Are you really talking about the cannabis trade?"

"Indeed I am, and why not? It's legal, there's a huge untapped demand, absolutely no competition and, most importantly of all, the product is of impeccable quality." Birch kissed the tips of his fingers to emphasise his point.

Sands shook her head in exasperation. "That's all very well, you prat, but you haven't considered the logistics. You'll have to import the stuff all the way from Syria."

"To begin with, yes, but once we get organised we can start cultivating the plants and harvesting the crop on our own doorstep. That green valley out there contains some of the most fertile arable land in the empire."

"Are you serious? I can never tell if you're taking the piss."

"I'm being perfectly serious. Think of it like this: in the next year we can corner world production of a pure, natural product with an unsurpassed record of customer satisfaction and market penetration. If we base the cultivation here then we can tap into a series of trade routes that spread all the way to Rome and beyond. As a business plan it's a no-brainer. And the beauty is that it'll be no more illegal than if we were harvesting olives. Come on guys, admit it, we can't lose."

Ojokwu had been listening to Birch's pitch with mounting enthusiasm. "Dammit if he don't have a point, Kal."

"I hate to admit it, but there is a perversely compelling logic to it," she concurred. "This brainwave could secure our future. You think you can you get the Syrian on board?"

"I'll have to cut him in, of course. But let's take this one step at a time. I've got to get you two onside first. There's one thing that wouldn't harm our chances, though."

"What's that?"

"Ojo's got to take that job with Antalas. We're going to need an insider with access to his international trading contacts."

"I'm so all over that, Birch, don't worry, man. He's gonna have to fight me off. I ain't never wanted something so bad in all my life. First, though, I gotta get my Latin better and I need to learn some Imazight proper quick."

"There's a simple solution," said Sands. "We need to stop speaking English. Total language immersion is the only way."

"Agreed," said Birch. "We need to totally assimilate."

"We start now then, yeah?" said Ojokwu. "Only Latin, Greek and Imazight from now on."

Sands nodded her head. "Μία γλῶττα οὐδεπώποτε ἱκανή."

Ojokwu stared at her blankly.

"An old Greek adage. *One language is never enough.*"

"Hear, hear," replied Birch. He held up his cup to toast the undertaking. "Here's to the future, one language at a time. But how about we start the whole immersion thing tomorrow?"

Sands and Ojokwu smiled and joined their comrade in his toast: "To the future," they repeated in unison, "one language at a time, but starting tomorrow."

Their conversation was interrupted by the sight of a stork flying low overhead and landing on its nest atop the adjacent building. They watched, fascinated, as it fed its ravenous nestlings.

Sands' brow furrowed. It was a look that had become familiar to her two comrades. She leaned forward and frowned. "Is it me, or does anyone else think there's something odd about all these storks' nests?"

"How do you mean?"

"It's mid-August, more or less, am I right?"

Birch performed a little mental arithmetic. "Yeah, I make it the fourteenth."

"So why are we looking at hundreds of nesting storks? I know it all appears very picturesque, but I'd have thought these chicks would've fully fledged and left the nest a month ago, maybe two? They should be migrating south by now. What do you think?"

Birch cast a 'so what?' glance at Sands.

"I'll tell you what, yeah, she's not wrong, you know," replied Ojokwu. "Remember that NATO exercise in eastern Poland a few years back? There was thousands of storks raising chicks everywhere, and that was in like mid-June."

Birch looked unconvinced. "Maybe migrating cycles, like climates, have changed over the centuries."

"Maybe they have," conceded Sands, "but haven't you noticed any incongruities in the natural environment?"

Birch shifted in his seat. He sported the uneasy demeanour of a man reversing down a one-way street. "Okay, I wasn't going to mention this, but there is something that's been nagging away at me since we got here."

"What's that then?"

"It's a trivial example really. It's hardly worth mentioning."

"Go on, Birch, spit it out, for God's sake."

"Look, I've been coarse fishing all over Europe…"

"Wow, all over Europe? You want a medal?" asked Ojokwu.

Birch cast a disdainful glance at Ojokwu before finishing his sentence. "… and I'm quite happy to believe that Moroccan freshwater lakes are full of wild carp. But I'm also damn sure that ornamental varieties didn't exist in the ancient world. All the natural varieties of carp that I've ever seen have been muddy green or silver in colour."

"But the fish in Antalas' fishpond are all red and white."

"My point exactly. I'd swear blind that these selectively-bred ornamental varieties only started coming out of Japan in the nineteenth century."

"Are you certain?"

"I'd stake my life on it."

"So what's going on?" asked Sands. "Are we just imagining things? Have you noticed anything odd, Ojo?"

"What, since we've been in Volubilis? Yeah, just a bit."

"Like what?"

"I noticed something proper weird yesterday when we arrived at the House of Oleanders."

"Yesterday? Apart from Antalas' alarming father-in-law, I wasn't aware of anything out of the ordinary."

"Okay, so answer me this question, then. Why would you have oleander plants all round your courtyard? Ain't there something strange about that?"

Birch looked bemused. "You've lost me. Something strange about oleanders? No, not really, they're indigenous plants, aren't they? It's the name of the house, I suppose. No, I don't get the question. What's so weird about wanting to decorate a house with house plants?"

"What's so weird about it? The whole damn plant is toxic from root to tip – flowers, leaves, branches, stem - that's what. Why would you have poisonous flowers around the house when there are kids running everywhere? It don't make no sense. Not to me, at any rate."

"Poisonous? Are you sure?"

"You think I'm making it up?"

"Just checking."

"Just checking? Check this: Session 1, Day 2 of *"Uses, Side-effects and Interactions of Natural Toxins Survival Training"*, Brecon Beacons, 22-29 October 2012." He cast a withering look at Sands. "You satisfied?"

"Okay, I get it, you're an expert. So is the plant toxic enough to be fatal?"

"Big time. Four grams of leaves would do it."

"What's that in real terms?"

Ojokwu made a small circular motion on the palm of his outstretched hand. "Four grams - the contents of a teabag."

"A teabag? That courtyard's a poisoner's playground."

"That's what I've been trying to say. It don't make no sense what they're up to in that house. You should double-check the contents of your salad bowl in future, I'm telling you, man."

Sands reeled at the bluntness of Ojokwu's forewarning. "Wait a minute, what are we saying here? None of these instances appear to make any sense. There's no rational explanation for these aberrations."

"There's none that's obvious to me," replied Birch.

"But why is all the natural history stuff off-kilter? Everything appears okay on the surface. It's only when you look closer that the discrepancies become obvious."

"But only when the details involve flora and fauna," Ojokwu emphasised. "Birds, fish and plants - why's that?"

"Maybe we just get used to accepting inconsistencies in human behaviour and customs. We're highly adaptable. We make allowances for human variation and diversity. When it comes to the laws of nature, however, we consider the natural world to be immutable. We spot any irregularities immediately."

"I think you're on to something there," said Birch, nodding towards the bird nests on the rooftops. "The more I watch them, the more I'm convinced those storks are purely ornamental."

"That's it," replied Sands. "You've put your finger on it, Birch. The natural world is pure ornamentation. We're surrounded by replicas, simulations, fakes."

"But it looks and feels proper real," said Ojokwu, surveying the scene around him for confirmation.

Sands was struggling to make sense of it all. She leaned forward. "Here's the only way I can explain it," she began.

"Oh, good, it's been a while since you've favoured us with one of your explanations."

Sands threw Birch a withering look. He never wasted an opportunity to ridicule her more didactic tendencies.

"It's like when I was in Austria a few years back. I was staying in a small village near Salzburg. It's picture-perfect, built on a lake with gorgeous old buildings. They have thousands of visitors annually, including, when I was there, a large party of Chinese tourists who were taking great interest in all architectural aspects of the village. When they checked out of their hotel, one of the chambermaids found something left behind in a desk drawer in one of the Chinese guests' rooms. She showed it to her manager, who, in turn, showed it to the town mayor. You know what it was?"

Birch shrugged. "A bar of Toblerone?"

"It was a scaled set of orthographic drawings of one of the village's most picturesque buildings. Alarm bells started ringing in the mayor's head. Their beautiful little village, so unique and so idyllic, was being Xeroxed without their knowledge for exact replication, brick by brick, building by building, by a mining company back in China."

"Are you serious?"

"It's forty miles north of Hong Kong, in Guangdong province. They're still building it. It's real, but it's a simulation."

Ojokwu nodded his headed begrudgingly. "Like this place?"

"Could be."

"So if this is a simulation, what does that make us?"

Complete silence. The three comrades stared one to the other.

There, as easily as that, it had finally been said. Someone, and they weren't entirely sure who, had articulated the most terrifying question of all.

Suddenly, Sands felt as if she was attracting the attention of casual passers-by. One or two appeared to be scrutinizing her in a most inconsiderate and intrusive manner. They were staring at her, very closely. What was their problem?

One individual, a grey-haired lady in her sixties, approached closer than the others and peered at her, almost as if she was examining a specimen in a museum. Sands decided to return the lady's gaze. "Excuse me, but would you mind fucking off out of my space?"

The woman recoiled in utter astonishment, the look on her face registering a shock of seismic proportions. "I'm so sorry," she blurted out in English. "I didn't think you could see me." Her face froze in an agony of indecision, desperate for outside intervention. As her will struggled to assert itself, the woman's outward appearance shuddered and then corrupted into kaleidoscope of multi-hued pixels before disappearing in a sandstorm of digital interference.

Sands' head was swimming. "What the hell happened there? Did you see that?"

"She spoke English. She definitely spoke English," repeated Ojokwu.

"She was as close to me as I am to you. And she looked as real as you do. I could have reached out and touched her."

Birch had leapt from his recumbent position and was jostling innocent bystanders, hunting the vicinity for any clues as to what had happened. "Can you see her anywhere?" he shouted. "She's just disappeared into thin air. She definitely spoke to us in English. Where the hell's she gone?"

"Who was she? Either of you seen her before?" asked Ojokwu.

"Nobody else seems to have noticed anything. Nobody else even reacted," yelled Birch, pointing towards the surrounding throng. "Did you not realise that?" He was wandering in circles now.

"It was like a mirage. She was there one minute, gone the next. What was it – a hologram?"

"How the hell am I supposed to know?" replied Birch. "Was she the only one? Did either of you see anyone else?"

Sands hadn't seen Birch in such a disconcerted state since the night the helicopter had gone down.

"Come on, Birch, calm down. Stay focused, think rationally. There has to be some kind of explanation, no matter how outlandish."

Birch's mind was whirring. "It must be the key to why we're stuck eighteen hundred years from home, it must be. She was watching us." His head swivelled round again. "But why?"

"And why did she assume we couldn't see her?" asked Sands.

"She was suffering some form of malfunction."

"Which implies what?"

"Don't ask me. I ain't got a clue," said Ojokwu.

Birch had retaken his seat. He was showing signs of regaining his equilibrium. "Maybe that we, at least, are functioning properly?" he suggested.

"But as what?"

"Okay, now we're getting down to the real question," Birch declared with reluctance. "I hate to be the one to ask, but what the hell are we here for? Why are we here?"

A look of defeat passed over Sands' face. She shook her head. "Don't ask me. I'm a fucking cocktail of angst. I'm not the best person to ask."

"Come on, Kal, what's going on, man? What's happening to us?" urged Ojokwu.

"How am I supposed to know? What makes you think I've got the answer?"

"Fucking hell, Sands!" cried Birch. "Don't try and duck out. This is no time to disenfranchise yourself. What the hell's going on? Someone was watching us. You saw her. We saw her. And they were speaking sodding English!"

"So after twelve months, you finally want to talk about it?"

"Yeah, I finally want to talk about it," Birch nodded. He gestured towards the forum. "What was that all about? Why are we here?"

"You want to know what I think?"

"Yeah. I want to know what you think. Why've you suddenly gone all silent?"

Sands took a deep breath. "Okay, here's what I think. I'm not a free agent. I'm being manipulated by forces outside of my control."

She looked up at her two comrades. "There, I've admitted it. Oh yeah, and I often hear voices telling me what to do. So there you go. Do either of you know what the hell I'm talking about?"

"Welcome to my world," replied Ojokwu. "I think we must live on the same street."

"Really, Ojo - you too?"

"You and me both."

"I've spent the whole time denying what's happening to me."

"Tell me about it. I should've been more honest. We could've helped each other."

"Oh, shit, I've been weak," Sands groaned. "I've refused to face my anxieties. I thought it would keep me strong." She directed a broad gesture to the world around her. "I assumed this fraudulent situation simply bred paranoid tendencies. If I was to acknowledge them I'd risk being consumed by them."

"You should've talked about it. I should've said something," nodded Ojokwu.

"I've missed not having another woman to confide in. It's been tough."

"We've all let you down, Kal," replied Ojokwu. "We've totally depended on your sense of purpose to pull us through. None of us could have survived without you. Them lot, Stogdon and his crew, would have sunk like a stone without your leadership. I'm telling you, for sure, they'd have ended up getting each other killed, and taken us down too."

"He's right, Sands," added Birch. "Chin up, you've got nothing to berate yourself for. You've got more guts in your little finger than I have in my entire body."

"Not sure I buy that."

"I mean it all the same."

Sands looked unconvinced.

"But, at the risk of appearing insensitive," Birch continued, "can I suggest we stop feeling sorry for ourselves and start asserting control over the one thing we can?"

"Which is what?" asked Ojokwu.

"The future. We've got to look forward, not mull over things that can't be changed."

"Spoken like a true bloke," said Sands, pulling herself together. "I gotta tell you, Birch, you men are all so bloody predictable."

"There you go. That's more like the Sands I know."

"The problem with you, Birch, is that all you want to do is move things along, rather than risk addressing the real issue. You're like the proverbial policeman shooing ladies away from a roadside accident in case one of them gets a fit of the vapours."

Birch looked hurt, but still rose to her provocation. "You know me, Sands. I never fail to live down to your lowest expectations. I'm a man, after all; what else can I do? I mean, I try my best, I really do, but I'm hard-wired to fix problems, not agonise over them."

"So we women agonise and you men analyse, is that it?"

"Why are you arguing about this?" interjected Ojokwu

"No need to pick a fight, Sands. I'm just saying let's look forwards, not backwards."

She shook her head in apparent despair. "I hate having to behave like you guys - like a man. As far as I can see the costs far outweigh the benefits. No way do I want to start thinking like you guys too."

"It's only a disguise, Kal, it ain't permanent. You can swap back any time you feel safe," replied Ojokwu. "You don't have to become like us. Anyway, look at us, Birch and me, we ain't the same, never will be. Trust me, I don't want to start thinking like him any more than you do."

"Not being true to yourself fucks you up," she replied.

"Tell me 'bout it. Just wait a little till the heat dies down."

"But everyone will think I'm male by then. No way will they accept my gender reassignment. What's Tufayyur going to think, and Antalas? They'll feel I've betrayed them."

Sands put her head in her hands.

"It'll blow over soon enough, you'll see," replied Birch.

"Fucking hell, how come *you've* got so much faith in the future?"

"You've only got yourself to blame. You've turned me into an eternal optimist. After all, the future's all we've got to look forward to. Isn't that what you're always saying?"

TWENTY-ONE

Location: Volubilis, Mauretania Tingitana
Coordinates: 34° 03' 36" N and 5° 33' 00" W

Time and Date: 22.30, 14th August, 258 C.E.

The layout of Antalas Alfassi's house followed the classic Roman model. From the front door the eye was drawn through the atrium, across the *peristyle* with its fishpond and fountain, and then led to the ornately mosaiced *tablinum*, the main lounge and reception room from which the owner could observe all the comings and goings in the household. Tufayyur's bedroom was situated on the ground floor. It lay next to her grandfather's office. As one passed from the entrance, through the atrium and into the colonnaded inner courtyard, the door to her room could be found to the immediate right. Its proximity to the atrium also meant that her bedroom lay nearest the steps leading to the upper storey where Sands was sleeping. When the curtains to the *tablinum* were drawn, it meant that a swift, unobserved ascension was on the cards.

After dinner, Tufayyur had withdrawn early to her bedroom. From there she was able to monitor the activities of the younger members of the household as they were put to sleep. After what seemed an eternity, Sands, Birch and Ojokwu bade good night to their hosts, leaving Tufayyur's parents, brother and grandfather still conversing in the *tablinum*. She heard Sands making her way past her bedroom door and up the stairs to her sleeping quarters. Seizing her opportunity, Tufayyur slipped off her footwear, tiptoed out of her room and followed the young Briton upstairs. At the top of the steps she turned right into a warmly-lit, whitewashed corridor with a sloping, wood-beamed ceiling.

"Kalius please wait. I need to talk to you."

Sands turned around in surprise as Tufayyur approached. "What are you doing up here? Your brother will be coming to bed any moment."

"I wanted to talk to you. You've not been yourself, Kalius. Is anything troubling you?" She placed her hand on Sands' arm.

Despite her tiredness, Sands felt a warm tingle of emotion. Her face was starting to flush.

"It's kind of you to worry about me, but I'm fine, really. It's just that sometimes…"

Sands hesitated.

"Yes," urged Tufayyur, "sometimes what? What is it that is upsetting you? I know there's something."

"It's hard to truly be yourself in a strange country."

"You can be yourself with me, you know. I want you to feel you can trust me."

She was gazing into Sands' eyes, and the emotion she was transmitting was palpable. Sands could feel herself being drawn closer and closer to the captivating young woman who faced her in such a receptive mood. Sands glanced over her shoulder in an effort to break the spell. By the time she looked back it was too late to save herself. Tufayyur had succumbed to a spontaneous, uncontrollable urge to kiss the glorious young man who had turned her emotions upside down. Suddenly Sands could feel a surge of electricity jolting through her body as Tufayyur's soft lips met her own. Neither woman breathed for ten seconds as if suspended in a freeze-frame ecstasy of stillness. Their lips trembled and tingled. But otherwise there was an overpowering sense of disembodied motionlessness. Finally, as if deflated by the application of an external force, both parties expelled their long-held breaths in unison.

"Tufayyur, I…"

"Shh," interrupted the young Berber, embarrassed, "don't say anything."

Before Sands could regain her senses, Tufayyur was gone, silently, as if she had never been there. All that lingered was the scent of her fragrance - light, ethereal and elusive.

Suddenly, without warning, another figure appeared at the end of the corridor. It was a grinning, intoxicated Azulay, fresh from polishing off his father's wine.

"What's been going on up here, Kalius?" he asked, laughing. "I just passed Tufayyur on the stairs. Have you been trying to seduce my sister?"

"I'm not much of a one for the ladies, as I'm sure you've noticed. Come on, Azulay, it's time for bed, don't you agree?"

The young Berber slapped Sands on the back. "You're a man after my own heart, dear Kalius," he replied with a laugh. "To bed, my friend, to bed!"

A few minutes later, having prepared for sleep by changing in the ante chamber adjoining the bedroom, Sands lay on her camp bed and pulled the soft cotton sheet up under her chin. Her thoughts and emotions were tumbling in confusion. The events of the day and the effect of the mid-summer sun, combined with the evening's alcohol and her recent enthralling encounter with Tufayyur, had left her breathless and defenceless. And now she lay still, mesmerised by the sight of Azulay as he disrobed in front of her.

"So, you haven't experienced the delights of the female sex, is that right?" Azulay enquired.

"I am greatly familiar with the ways of women, but not in the sense you mean, I suspect."

"You mean not in the carnal sense?"

"No, not in the carnal sense."

"Tell me, Kalius, why do you never bare yourself in front of me? We are good friends after all, are we not?"

"Modesty forbids that I should expose myself in front of anyone other than God."

Azulay flashed a coquettish smile. "Thankfully, dear friend, the Jewish and Roman religions impose no such prohibition on young men, especially, when they are merely seeking to enjoy the intimate familiarity of their closest companions. I hope you will not be offended if I fully disrobe in your presence?"

"No, not at all," she mumbled.

Sands could feel herself becoming aroused and infected by Azulay's provocative manner. "Feel free to do as you see fit." The sound of the words tumbling out of her mouth caused her to bite her lip in anticipation.

Sands watched in breathless admiration as the warm light of the oil lamps trembled over the perfect dimensions of Azulay's physique. His flawless skin burned with a golden hue, wrapping itself over a complex scaffolding of sinews, tendons and muscles that stretched and relaxed with beguiling efficiency as he shed his clothing. She tried not to stare but it was a hopeless mission It was one that she could never win on a night like this, not even if she wanted to, not even if she was to live for a further eighteen hundred years. "Is this what it feels like to be the subject, rather than the object of the male gaze?" she wondered. She was deriving immense sexual gratification from the consumption of Azulay's faultless nakedness. He posed with a relaxed, casual expertise, transparently proud of his physical attributes. He lingered beguilingly in the shadows, like an exquisitely carved heroic sculpture, allowing Sands ample opportunity to admire his overwhelming beauty and perfect physical proportions. Her eyes drank in the sweeping contours of his back, the mellow undulations of his abdomen, the gently engorged penis, the savage musculature of his thighs and calves. Her heightened state of arousal caused her face to flush with a wave of warmth and her sexual organs to tingle at the anticipation of the forthcoming erotic encounter. Her heart was pounding so hard she was finding it difficult to catch her breath. "What is happening? First Tufayyur, and now this?" she wondered, but she was already rendered inert to any reason or rational intervention. She didn't care. She wanted this young man. And she wanted him tonight. Tonight would be the night when she would fully reclaim her sense of self.

Once he had disrobed and cleansed his skin with a strigil, Azulay pulled on a lightweight white cotton nightshirt and sat down on the edge of Sands' camp bed.

"You seem tense this evening, my friend," he whispered. "Come, let me massage your shoulders so you can relax and sleep well."

She nodded at her room-mate. "That would be nice for a few minutes."

"Come over into my bed, then, it's much bigger and more comfortable. You can move back later when we're finished."

Sands slipped between the sweet smelling sheets on Azulay's bed. She was defenceless in the face of this blatant seduction, and she felt no inclination to even try and resist.

"Here, let me pull your up nightshirt, Kalius. Then I can massage your back properly."

Sands did as instructed, while remaining face down on the mattress. Azulay then pulled down the sheet to reveal her torso, buttocks and upper thighs. She heard with pleasure the sound of a sudden, appreciative intake of breath as the back half of her naked body revealed itself to his view. He gazed at her physique. She lay with her eyes shut, poised in anticipation, her expectant body awaiting the first gentle caress of his fingers.

"Your skin is so soft." He traced the defined contours of her back and spine. "Your body feels lean and yet so strong, more like a youth than a man." Now he was applying greater pressure to the small of her back, forcing her to gently exhale as he leant more weight on her. As his hands started to knead the flesh on either side of the base of her spine, Sands groaned.

"Are you enjoying this, Kalius?"

"Very much, Azulay, I beg you not to stop."

"Let me sit astride you, then, to better control my movements."

"Whatever you wish, Azulay. Please do as your instincts dictate. I'm in your hands."

As he sat astride her buttocks, Sands could feel the weight of his body straining above her. He leaned forward and massaged her shoulders, causing her to groan involuntarily. With every rhythmic sweep of his hands she could detect his rising excitement. As he swayed backwards and forwards she could feel unmistakable and pleasurable signs of his growing arousal.

Sands adjusted her position to allow Azulay greater freedom of access to her body, and to relay indications of her mounting receptiveness.

She held her breath as the young man's fleshy lips and sandpaper stubble pass across the skin between her shoulder blades. Now his groin was making unambiguous sexual contact with her rump and was pressing hard up against her. He leaned his mouth against her ear, bit her earlobe and whispered to her.

"Seriously, Kalius, what were you up to with my sister earlier?"

"Nothing, Azulay, I promise."

"Are you sure you wouldn't rather being doing to her what I'm doing to you know?"

Sands' excitement mounted with each new provocation.

"And what do you plan to do to me?"

"I intend to explore your hidden temple, your holy of holies. Is that not what you would wish of me?" he replied, nuzzling her ear. "Just tell me to stop, and it is done."

"Don't stop, Azulay. Don't you dare stop."

Azulay freed himself from the constraints of his nightshirt and began to rub himself freely along the cleavage between Sand's buttocks. She eased her thighs apart to assist his exploration of her body. Now she could feel his fingers searching around the front of her hips in vain. This was the moment for her to intervene.

She moved her left hand behind her and grasped Azulay's erection.

"No," she said guiding his aim, "not there. Put it in here."

Azulay gasped in confusion, but it was too late to back-pedal. Guided by Sands, his penis eased smoothly into her vagina.

"I'm a woman, Azulay," she exclaimed. "As you can see."

Sands accepted his erection with an ecstatic abandon that overwhelmed her young lover. He responded with a euphoric cry of surprise, half shock, half delight. "Push deeper, Azulay, deeper."

"Oh, Kalius, what are you doing to me?"

"Don't stop, please don't stop. Come on, Azulay, show me what you'd like to do to me now that you have the chance."

The young Berber responded with relish. He penetrated her with long, powerful strokes. "God you smell good. No wonder your skin is so soft. You're a woman! I've never seen anyone so beautiful and enticing. Now it makes sense."

"I'm a woman."

"You're a woman, Kalius, a woman! And I'm a fool. I knew there was something about you the moment I laid eyes on you at that roadside."

"Don't stop - I can't help myself." Her excitement was mounting in proportion to Azulay's. Sands had now raised herself on to her knees to aid greater penile penetration and her groans grew accordingly. "That is so good," she exhaled. She could feel Azulay's cool hands encasing her breasts and squeezing her nipples. She closed her eyes and separated her labia to allow unfettered incursion to his frantic thrusts. He grimaced with unalloyed pleasure, each penetration bringing him closer to a pitch of ecstasy. Sensing his impending orgasm, Sands acted quickly. "Now, Azulay, on your back, let me mount you. Quickly, Azulay, quickly."

She flipped herself over and bore down on his erection with all her weight and determination. He groaned with a stupefied grin, eyes half closed, biting his lips in euphoria. "Come on, Kalius, fuck me, fuck me."

Sands was now in a frantic world of her own, immune to her partner's urgings. She gave in to a shuddering orgasm while Azulay writhed beneath her in an uncontained frenzy. He wore a look of tortured rapture. Sands could feel the blood in her body circulating from her head to her toes in crimson waves of rapture. She'd rarely experienced an orgasm so intense. Her torso shuddered again and again in unison with the young lover lying spread-eagled beneath her.

"What joy, what bliss," he intoned again and again, as if in a drug-induced trance.

Sands continued to dredge every last ounce of convulsing pleasure from her orgasm. Finally, after what seemed an age, satiated and quenched, she disentangled herself from the act of copulation and subsided onto the bed, and there she lay spent, panting in a heap next to Azulay.

They unwound together for the next few minutes, the breathing of each slowly adjusting to the tempo of the other until they inhaled in perfect unison. They gazed at each other and smiled.

"Will you hold me, Azulay?"

"Why have you disguised your gender?" he asked.

Sands luxuriated in the comfort of his warm embrace. She didn't really want to talk, but she owed Azulay some form of explanation.

"I've been forced to hide the fact that I am a woman," she replied, picking her words with immense care. "I have enemies who are determined to do me harm. I had to flee my own country in order to save my life."

Azulay was unable to disguise his bewilderment at this news. "But who would want to kill a young woman like you?"

Sands hesitated, unsure of how much information she could safely reveal. "There's one person, in particular, who wants me dead. He's a powerful and influential member of the senatorial class, a *Tribunus Laticlavius*. He has every interest in killing me."

"But for what reason?"

"Revenge - the very best of reasons, I fear. His honour was impugned by me, or so he feels. And for that transgression, I am required to suffer the ultimate sacrifice."

"But who knows you are here in Oualili? Only my family and your friends do. You are protected here, Kalius. Surely, you are safe now?"

"All logic dictates that it must be so," she agreed with a sigh of relief. "I have traversed the entire length of the Roman Empire. There's no plausible way in which my current whereabouts could be known to him."

Sands hesitated, her natural caution reasserting itself.

"And, yet, I still have had to be careful. My name has a certain renown in distant, unexpected quarters."

"And what is your name, if it is not asking too much of you?" His voice betrayed a palpable sense of hurt. He looked much younger once again. "I'd like to know, now that we have become lovers."

"It would be safer for all concerned, especially for you, Azulay, if my real name was to remain buried along with any record of my past history."

"So what should I call you, then? Should I continue to call you by your male name?"

"Call me by my shortened, familiar name, just like Titus Ojokwus and Sextus Placidius do."

"You mean Kal?"

"And what about the rest of your family? Can I tell your sister and father of my true nature?"

Azulay looked alarmed and raised himself up on his elbows. "Tell my sister? That's madness. She'll never forgive you. Tufayyur talks about nothing but you. She's become obsessed with you. She's not a woman that you'd want to get on the wrong side of."

"And your parents?"

"No, no, such a thing is impossible. My parents will feel you've abused their trust and hospitality. It would ruin everything. Surely you can see that?"

"I'm confused. Would they rather you have sex with men than with women?"

"Why wouldn't they? We may be Jewish, but homosexual sex is an entirely honourable Roman tradition, as long as physical relations are conducted in the correct manner, of course. My parents will assume that you're a willing recipient of my desires, as will Tufayyur."

"Really? Are you saying she expects me to have sex with you?"

"Of course she does, secretly. She knows what young men are like. It's the natural thing for you and me to do in our position. My father would probably prefer that I use the services of our slave girls, just like he does. But I rather enjoy the willing participation of my sexual partners, as do you, if tonight's performance is anything to judge by."

Sands shook her head. "I'm amazed. You're all so matter of fact about these things."

"And you are so beautiful, Kal. Let me admire your body."

Sands did as she was bid, reclining on her back, her head supported by her interlocking arms. She felt a thrill of pleasure at being admired with such open appreciation. She trembled at the touch of his hand on her taut stomach, his warm ejaculate still seeping down the inside of her thighs and a reminder of greater pleasures to come.

"You are magnificent," he sighed with delight. "I've never had a lover like you."

She laughed "I've been bottling it up. You happened to be in the right place at the right time. It was just a question of finding the right person to slake my desires on. You are very young, though. I should really know better."

Sands rolled over on her stomach and raised her rump for his delectation.

She threw him an enticing smile over her shoulder. "Now, how about you do to me just what you do to those boyfriends of yours? I'm ready to accept you now, if you're up to it."

Sands ran her fingers between her thighs and, as if to clarify her meaning, anointed her proposed point of entry with her lover's semen. The young Berber's eyes lit up with delight. Sands adjusted her position in anticipation of the intense exertions to come. As the young man readied himself with lubricating oils, Sands lowered her head in preparation for her partner's forceful entry and bit the pillow in order to stifle her cries.

As the two young lovers set about their unbridled acts of carnality, it was clear that the time for constrained behaviour was well and truly over. If anyone out there *was* observing Sands, she was damn well sure she was going to give them more than they'd bargained for.

TWENTY-TWO

"It's like a sodding circus down here, Sterland," *A* shouts.

"If you'd just put the parasol down for a minute we'd be able to see more clearly what you're looking at."

"It's all very well for you to talk, sitting back there in a nice cool office in London. Have you any idea what the temperature is like in Volubilis in mid-August?"

"Warm, I fancy?"

"Warm? The mercury's gone through the roof overnight. We're in an effing heat wave, I'm telling you; seriously, it's pushing forty degrees."

A is standing atop the tumulus from which Sands, Birch and Ojokwu had first viewed the town of Volubilis the day before.

"Is that the spot they were standing on yesterday?" asks Morris. "Jermaine, swing the camera round and show us what *A* can see."

"Bloody hell, Sterland, the poor lad's doing his best, but I'm warning you it's an absolute madhouse at the moment. It's like the *Tour de France* came through town and decided never to leave. It's a fucking horror show, I'm telling you."

"Okay, I get the idea – but what can you see exactly?"

"Hang on, if I can only clear some of these people out the way and Jermaine can get his camera high enough you should be able to see something."

Jermaine's arms are now held carefully above head height, allowing a slow and deliberate rotation through 360 degrees. "How's that, now, can you see anything?" *A* enquires.

The old man squints at the monitor in front of him. "It's not perfect, but I'm getting the gist of things."

A adjusts the volume on the headphones. "You may be in London, but you don't have to yell, Sterland, you're coming through nice and clear. The signal's perfect."

"So what are we looking at now?" he shouts.

"Okay, we're looking north east. That's the *Decumanus Maximus* over there, the main drag they came in on two days ago, and in the distance, at the end of the street, you should be able to make out the north gate through which they entered the city."

"Yes, got it. My God, *A*, just look at all those people. They're overwhelming the place. Why can't they just stay at home and follow the action from the comfort of their own homes?"

Endless streams of game-tourists are swarming down the *Decumanus Maximus*. They begin to proliferate like bacillus spores across the adjoining land.

"They just want to be where the action is. It's hideous, Sterland, I can't begin to describe how bad it is. The place is getting trashed and the authorities can't seem to get a handle on how to control the crowds."

"But it's a historic monument, for God's sake. What's wrong with people? I had no idea it was this bad. Where do they all go at night? They can't all sleep there surely?"

"Wanna bet? This isn't Glastonbury with a bloody dome over the top of it. Anyone who wants to enter illegally can take their pick of places they want to break in."

Jermaine pans the camera right, pointing it towards a mountain range in the south east. He takes up the commentary. "The more affluent game-tourists are finding accommodation in that town over there. Can you see it – sheltered up there in the foothills of the mountains?"

"Where's that?"

"Moulay Idriss," *A* replies. "It didn't exist in the time of the game. Sands and co wouldn't have seen it. It was built about five hundred years later from stone nicked from Volubilis."

"And where's the basilica?" Morris shouts. "Show me the forum where they drank tea yesterday morning."

"Okay, hang on, we'll get there in a second. And Sterland, there's really no need to shout. You're deafening me."

"Okay, message received," he yells. "Now where's that temple to Jupiter?"

"You do realise you could have jumped on a plane yourself, don't you, instead of sending us? You're so exasperating, Sterland. Now, there you go." The temple area starts to fill the viewfinder.

"Wonderful," he bellows, "the remains are simply wonderful. Great pity about the people, though."

"Notice anything that's missing?"

"Apart from image stabilisation?"

"Say what, you cheeky bastard?" replies Jermaine.

"Storks," Morris shouts.

"Exactly."

"The capitals on the columns are all bearing huge empty nests."

"It's the first thing everyone here has been noticing," *A* replies. "We screwed up big time there. Got the migration season wrong."

"It happens," replies Morris. "The game's a simulation, not a replication, we got all the important historical and cultural details right. That's what counts. Now, where's the House of Oleanders?"

Jermaine pans through one hundred and eighty degrees, sweeping past the green fertile plain that lies far in the distance - "That's where Birch plans to cultivate his fortune" – before coming to rest on a familiar scene. "You see the large arch, there, on the left of the screen? Now if you look to the right of it you should be able to make out a large pair of columns adorning a set of steps, yes? You see where all those game-tourists are sitting?"

"Got it."

"Can you see where the crowds are heading around the big walled enclosure? Well, the back of that's where you'll find the remains of Antalas Alfassi's house – the scene of last night's bonk fest. They're crawling all over it, the smutty bastards. And they'll continue to come in their thousands."

"Sadly, it's all over the digital newsfeeds this morning," Morris confirms. "God, those organisations are an abomination. Still, it's not what we really had in mind, I'm afraid, but that's life, I guess. It seems to be what the public wants."

"And, boy, do they want it. It was pretty full-on, I won't lie. I guess you didn't watch it, no?"

"No, of course I didn't. I could see what was coming. Luckily, we managed to issue a public decency warning just in time."

"Still, upsetting for you to hear about it afterwards and hear what people are saying."

"To a certain extent, but she has every right to do what she wants. I respect her privacy, just like I would if she was still living in my own house. People should just have the decency to log out. No one is forced to watch anything they'd rather not."

"But I've been checking out *Digital Screamer*'s news feeds this morning. Their commentators are saying that last night's sex scenes were gratuitously titillating and we're exploiting Kal for pornographic purposes. And they're not alone. Some might say that's a bit harsh."

"I can't comment - you'll have to tell me you think. I didn't watch it. What do you reckon - gratuitous or not?"

A grimaced. "It's a bit of a tricky one to call. It's all that everyone down here is talking about. I liked that she was in control, though. I'll tell you something: I swear she knew what she was up to. She was making a statement last night. Her physical beauty may have been objectified and idealised - but she was definitely expressing something real about herself. Plus, I liked that she got down and dirty with the best of 'em. That was one hell of a message she was sending out to the world last night, you know what I mean?"

"Thankfully, having not witnessed it, I'm not really in a position to say. But she was sending out a message, you say, but to whom? Do you think she's on to us?"

Jermaine leant over to the microphone. "For sure, she's on to something - they all are. That technical fuck-up when that woman's physical information transported into the game didn't help none. That was a complete fucking disaster. All three of them is on real high alert now, trust me."

"So what are we going to do to protect her, Sterland?" *A* asks. "That bastard Caeluibianus is on his way and he ain't planning on delivering flowers."

"Look, *A*, there's nothing more we can do, I keep telling you. The simulation's as fairly weighted in her favour as it can be, without turning it to a complete farce. She's on her own now. Have faith in her."

"She's always been on her own."

"Exactly."

"But how the hell is Caeluibianus always able to track her down? Somebody has to be feeding him information. Just what is in those damn tablets that you're not telling us about?"

"Now's not the time to have this discussion. We don't know who's eavesdropping on our conversation. Everything's perfectly above board. Anyway, you'll find out soon enough. According to his last report, Caeluibianus should be with you in about ten days or so."

"Yeah, but she doesn't realise that, does she? She has no idea what kind of shit-storm is headed her way."

"And neither do we, to be fair. I'd be prepared to back Kal's resourcefulness against any opponent she finds herself stacked up against, wouldn't you?"

"Normally, I'd say yes, you know I would. But normally I'd expect her enemies to confront her face to face when she can see them coming."

A's expression was now filling the screen in close-up. "However, if retribution comes sneaking up behind her in the form of an assassin's knife when she's asleep - then, no, I wouldn't give tuppence for her chances."

TWENTY-THREE

Aballava Tablet No. 8, Inventory No 13.27 (Morris Archive)

Caeluibianus, Cohort Tribune and Praepositus of the Company, to Julius Rufinus, Tribunus Laticlavius and commander-in-chief, I send my greetings. In the matter of determining the fate of Galla Placidia (undertaken in the utmost secrecy as directed) I have done so in full accordance with your wishes and have set out my findings below. Since my last report I have finally completed my passage to Volubilis, a journey undertaken at a fearsome pace, and under such trying conditions that I fear my health may have been injuriously affected. As you will surely attest, my Lord, I am the least likely man to succumb to melancholia or morbid feelings, or given to indulging in misplaced self-pity. However, since my arrival in Mauretania Tingitana, the hot and dry conditions have aggravated my choleric humor, thereby provoking the following symptoms (among a number of others that are too numerous to bore you with): a sluggish digestion; a sallow, jaundiced complexion; soft, sticky, yellow stools; burning urination; putrid flatulence. Far worse than these purely physical ailments, my Lord, are the debilitating effects on my temperament and mood. Anger, impatience, irritability, agitation, insomnia, restless sleep - all have become my constant bed-fellows. My physician, deceitful charlatan that he is, has diagnosed a phlegmatic corruption of yellow bile, blaming this for my current liver derangement and the imbalance in my humors. His advice for my cure is to prescribe the daily consumption of fennel and to recommend the avoidance of all greasy, unctuous food. May the Gods damn him and his false remedies! My nights have become a living torment of late and I am constantly fearful of falling under the sway of Somnus. As soon as I succumb to his influence, I risk being set upon by an unholy trinity of night terrors, violent fantasies and nightmarish visions. And the root of this torment is as unlikely to lie in an excess of yellow bile as the overthrow of Rome is to be provoked by the chirruping of a young chaffinch! The closer I get to Volubilis, the worse my affliction. The nearer I approach the source of my aggravations, Galla Placidia, the more extreme my agitation has become. My Lord, the diagnosis for my torment is clear. The cancer will have to be removed, once and for all. To that end, I have today paid my respects to a local magistrate, Gaius Modius Calvinus, and requested his assistance in locating and apprehending Galla Placidia. He is not personally aware of any reports concerning her whereabouts, but has insisted on introducing me tomorrow to a local grain merchant, Antalas Alfassi. This Berber Jew may have more information to impart about three Britons who have newly arrived in the city. If initial intelligence is correct, these individuals are all likely to be males, sadly. I fear tomorrow's visit may prove to be a wild goose chase, but I cannot risk offending our obliging local magistrate whose assistance I will certainly be availing myself of in future. May I not shrink from my purpose, my Lord. I will do whatever conscience and good sense dictates and at every moment of decision you can depend on me to be ready.

TWENTY-FOUR

Location: Volubilis, Mauretania Tingitana
Coordinates: 34° 03' 36" N and 5° 33' 00" W

Time and Date: 18.00: 28 August, 258 C.E.

To this day, the southern walls of Volubilis, or what remains of them, are bounded by the Oued Khomane. In the third century this small river was one of a series that helped irrigate the rich, fertile plain upon which the wealth of the city depended. From first light, Sands and Birch had been out inspecting the land that lay beyond the river, large tracts of which were owned and cultivated by Antalas Alfassi and his family. Accompanying the two Britons were Guenfan and Barthabbathas Males, the Syrian trader who had alerted Birch to the commercial possibilities of the hashish trade.

As well as familiarising themselves with the landscape and soil conditions, the Britons were planning to inspect a patch of uncultivated land that lay at the furthest edge of the arable plain. Like so much of the surrounding landscape, this plot belonged to Antalas Aflassi. After much prompting, the Berber had agreed to turn it over to the cultivation of a new cash crop – the cannabis plant.

Barthabbathas Males, meanwhile, had been pinpointed to play a critical role in the new venture. His contacts in the middle-east were going to be crucial. And his knowledge would be essential in sourcing the seeds and importing the know-how necessary to plant and harvest a commercially viable crop.

Barthabbathas and Sands spent the journey conversing in Greek. Sands apologised to Birch, who was straining hard to follow the conversation. "Greek's the language of the eastern Roman army. It's the easiest way for us to communicate."

"Ask him about the Syrians' cultivation methods. How do they prepare the hashish? Get as much useful practical information as you can."

Sands shot him an exasperated look. "What the hell do you think I'm trying to do?"

By mid-morning they'd arrived at their destination and were inspecting the fallow land that Guenfan had identified as being surplus to Antalas' immediate requirements.

"What do you reckon, Sands? It's about a hectare, I'd say. I wonder how much of the raw cannabis plant we could cultivate here?"

"Barthabbathas says the raw plant yields only a hundredth of its weight in pure hashish."

"Okay, so let's be pessimistic. Let's say we manage to grow only 2 tons of the raw plant per hectare. That would be equivalent to 2000 kilos and a hundredth of that would be..." Birch paused and looked at Sands for assistance.

"20 kilos of pure hash," she replied.

"Correct, 20 kilos of hash per hectare. That seem plausible?"

Sands racked her memory. "Remember when we were in Afghanistan in 2010? The U.N. published that Afghanistan cannabis survey and the press corps made a big thing out of it. We came in for a lot of stick at the time."

"Vaguely – run the details past me."

"You must remember. There'd been a massive sudden increase in cannabis cultivation in south Afghanistan, and we caught a ton of flack over it. The Yanks spun it as all being the Brits' fault.

"Oh yeah, I'm with you now. The Taliban growers were getting incredible yields per hectare: four times more than farmers in Morocco. It's all coming back to me. What was the yield of raw hashish per hectare?"

"150 kilos."

"That's very precise. You really sure?"

"Oh yeah. I shared a few beers with one of the UN researchers. Good looking guy. He was very helpful. He painted me a visual image of Norman Schwarzkopf with a massive hard-on and a sixty pound backpack. That was the yield in weight per hectare: one hundred and fifty kilos. I've always kind of cherished the image."

"I can see why the memory might be difficult to dislodge," Birch concurred with a shudder. "So, according to the U.N.'s comparison, Moroccan farmers were getting about 40 kilos per hectare."

"Yeah, in which case, your estimate of 20 kilos per hectare doesn't appear too off-beam."

"You'd be able to check that amount of luggage on a plane and not pay excess baggage charges."

"Handy to know, especially in the third century."

"At least it doesn't involve picturing one of Norman Schwarzkopf's humungous erections."

"True."

"So, has Barthabbathas explained how they extract hashish resin from the plant?"

"Yeah, but you won't like it. It's highly labour-intensive."

"Like how labour-intensive?"

"Let's just say it'll involve a sweatshop of workers dry sifting hashish plants 12 hours a day. I can't see *you* doing it."

"I've got no problem with supervising a sweatshop. What about the production process? How straightforward is it?"

"Tedious rather than complicated. First stage is reducing the flowers of the plants to a fine brown dust through sieving. Then the dust is baked and rolled a number of times in order to compress it into hard resin bricks. And there's your finished hash, easy to cut up and easy to transport. I've made it sound a whole lot simpler than it is in reality, though."

"It doesn't sound too hard. I reckon we could convert an olive press shed and oversee the work in town. What do you think? We'd have to transport the dried plants back and store them, though."

"God, is there no holding you back? I've got to admire your blind optimism, Birch."

"A man must have a dream, Sands. At least I'm not planning to cultivate tobacco."

Sands laughed. "Indeed, credit where credit's due. You've echoed my thoughts entirely. It's not as if you're promoting the delights of the grape either."

"God forbid."

"You know, if this takes off, the Romans are going to tax you to hell."

"I'll look forward to it. As far as I'm concerned, taxing drugs would be an enlightened policy. It'd put the Taliban out of business for starters."

"Pinch me, Birch – you're beginning to talk sense."

Birch smiled at his companion. "It's been known. You seem happy, Sands."

"I am happy."

"Good for you. You bloody well deserve it."

"Yeah, I do, don't I? I *do* bloody well deserve it."

"So, are you missing Azulay?"

Sands blushed at the unexpectedness of the question. "Why are you asking? He and Ojo will be back in a couple of weeks."

"You know what I mean. I can tell you do. There's something going on between you two."

"You think?" She was unable to keep a straight face. "Is it that obvious? Do you reckon anyone else has picked up on it?"

"No, only me and Ojo, as far as I'm aware. The rest of the family seem completely in the dark. You just come across like a nice, polite young man. Perfect son-in-law material, I'd say."

"Don't take the piss - it's too painful."

"Look, you're really going to have to deal with the fall-out."

"How do you mean?"

"Tufayyur has expectations. It's obvious." He stared at Sands in a schoolmasterly fashion

"Oh, God, poor old Tufayyur. What can I do?"

"What can you do? How about breaking it to her?" he replied. "It doesn't help that Ojo's now become besotted with her. At least you could clear the way for him."

Sands looked at him with amazement. "Clear the way for him? For Ojo? It wouldn't be as simple as that. He'd have to convert. Doesn't he realise?"

"He'd do it, he's told me."

Sands looked shocked. "What, convert to Judaism? Really? How come I don't know? Ojo and Tufayyur? Are you serious?"

"Your attention has been elsewhere. You may not have realised it."

"But converting would just be a flag of convenience for him."

"So what if it is? Hasn't that been the reality of religious conversion for most people?"

Sands shook her head as the impact of Birch's comments hit home. She could feel a stab of covetousness. "I didn't realise he felt like that about her. Ojo tells me everything."

"He's a big lad. He'll cope. Anyway, he'll have his mind on other things with this current delivery of produce to Tingi. If nothing else, it'll give him a chance to have a few man to man chats with Azulay."

Sands winced at the prospect. Her head was spinning. "That's what I'm afraid of. God knows what those two will dig up to talk about."

The next few hours passed in a daze. The mid-day heat intensified. On re-entering the city through the southern gate, Birch and Barthabbathas left their two companions and staggered off to the bath house. Guenfan and Sands dismounted and trudged back to Antalas' house. Sands walked in silence. She was deep in thought, wrestling long and hard with her conscience. How could she reveal the truth about herself to Tufayyur and her parents?

When she passed through the front entrance to the House of Oleanders, Sands was assailed by a delicious wave of refreshing air. The open inner courtyard had a miraculous capacity to circulate currents of cool ventilation like a giant convector fan. She groaned and swabbed the sweat from the back of her neck. Her head was beginning to clear. If only her conscience could be wiped clear with such ease. At that moment, she resolved to tell the truth. She would suffer whatever consequences fate flung at her.

"Kalius," a familiar voice called from the atrium. It was Tufayyur, wreathed in smiles, delighted to see that her friend had returned home. On seeing her approach, Sands' heart sank before she checked herself. Here was her chance to come clean and she had to seize it.

"Tufayyur, we need to talk privately. There's something I need to tell you. Can you come upstairs for a few moments?"

Tufayyur was alarmed by the earnest tone that Sands was adopting. "Of course, dear Kalius, but can't it wait? Father has instructed me to lead you to the *tablinum* as soon as you set foot in the house. He has important visitors and he wishes you to meet them straight away. Is everything alright? You look very serious."

Sands felt a wave of frustration tinged with relief. "Yes, everything's fine. Now, let's go and see your father and his visitors. Then we can talk after that."

Tufayyur slipped her arm through Sands' and hugged it. "I do love talking to you, Kalius, don't let those boring men detain you too long."

"I promise. There are important things I need to tell you."

"Oh, how exciting. Not bad news, I hope?"

Their conversation was interrupted by the sound of Antalas's voicing calling them from the *tablinum*. "Ah, you two, come through and join us please." The formality of his tone struck Sands. She could feel her body stiffening as she marched around the *peristyle*. Memories flooded back of her final year in the Army Air Corps and the constant reprimands she'd been forced to endure at the hands of her superiors.

Sands moved to the threshold of the *tablinum*. "You wished to see me, sir?"

Antalas wore a severe expression. He acknowledged her but bade her not to enter while he was conversing. Neither of the two male guests revealed any awareness of her presence.

Sands waited outside the room. As her eyes wandered around the space, her concentration focused on Antalas' expression. Her interest then shifted to the rear view of his two visitors. Unable to divine the topic of their conversation, Sands' attention moved next to the wall decorations of the *tablinum* before being drawn to the spectacular mosaics that adorned the centre of the floor. She examined the iconography with mounting fascination. She wondered how on earth she had failed to notice the subject matter before.

To Sands' dawning surprise, the central design – two concentric circles within a square - appeared to contain a classic zodiac motif that was divided into a dozen radial sections. Each of the twelve subdivisions contained a recognisable astrological symbol with a name assigned to it in Hebrew. The two symbols that faced closest to her at the bottom of the circle could be identified as Libra and Virgo, and she observed that the other ten followed sequentially in a counter-clockwise direction that echoed the order of the seasons. This impressive central mosaic was bordered at either end by two smaller rectangular ones. The top mosaic included a pair of monumental menorahs, a traditional symbol of Judaism. These seven-branched holy candelabra were just the kind of symbols that Sands would expect to find decorating the floor of an affluent Jewish household. However, she was particularly fascinated and puzzled by the large central image, a circular motif that lay within the zodiac itself. It appeared to Sands' untutored eye to represent a curious, Christ-like personage. The figure was adorned with a crown but was also ornamented with a halo that radiated shafts of bright light. To add to the enigma, he was represented sitting atop a golden chariot pulled by four horses. In his left hand he was holding a globe and a whip.

"Who is that figure?" Sands whispered to Tufayyur.

"That is Sol Invictus, the sun god. Berbers and Romans worship him alike."

"But how about Jews? Do you worship him, too?"

"To us Jews, Sol Invictus is a minor deity to whom we sometimes address prayers. Grandfather knows more about these things than I do."

Sands was fascinated by this open conflation of Jewish symbols, pagan astrological signs and Roman and Berber deities. She tried to imagine the likelihood of Ojokwu becoming assimilated into this religion. It was already clear that the cultural and religious melting pot of Volubilis had acted as a fertile breeding ground for tolerant interchange among its many pious worshippers. And these mosaics appeared to offer some form of documentary evidence that the city's local religions were not just capable of coexisting, but also of intermingling and, in certain respects, actually being receptive to the fusing of long-consecrated traditions.

Sands was roused from her reverie by the sound of Antalas's voice calling her from within. "Come, Kalius Placidius, please enter and meet my guests; they have a few questions they would like to ask you with your permission?"

At the mention of Sands' Romanised name, the neck of the younger of the visitors snapped to attention. He was standing with his back to Sands as she entered. The hairs on his arms suddenly stood erect. He appeared to be hovering, in a trance-like state, incapacitated on a gravity-free cushion of disbelief and yearning. He was disabled and tongue-tied. His inability to turn and face Sands full-on was obscured by the old magistrate, Gaius Modius Calvinus, who had leant across his companion in order to introduce himself to Sands. They greeted each other and exchanged the formal niceties associated with official introductions.

As he stepped back, the magistrate turned to introduce his companion, who was now standing behind him, and whose puce face was still obscured from view.

"Your attention, please, Caeluibianus Claudius Asinianus," the magistrate barked.

As Caeluibianus turned to face her full-on, Sands' face and deportment betrayed the shock of recognition that Caeluibianus had experienced moments earlier. He returned her stunned look. But now his face also wore an expression of confusion. Who was this young man standing in front of him? How could this be?

Sands was the first to recover her composure. "Greetings, Caeluibianus Claudius Asinianus."

Her apparent nonchalance disconcerted Caeluibianus. He nodded at her. He could not be mistaken, surely? Had he taken leave of his senses?

"I hope I can be of service to you," she said.

Antalas interjected. "Gaius Modius Calvinus is trying to track down the current whereabouts of a certain Galla Placidia, a fellow countrywoman of yours, who he suspects may by now be in Mauretania Tingitana, or may even be in Volubilis itself. Do you have any knowledge of this woman, Kalius Placidius? She may also be in the company of two male companions. That's right, isn't it, Caeluibianus Claudius Asinianus?"

"Indeed it is, Antalas Alfassi."

Caeluibianus stared at Sands as he spoke. "There were originally four other members of this gang of conspirators. Three we know are currently travelling overland to meet up with Galla Placidia in Volubilis." He studied Sands' expression for the merest hint of a reveal in her facial response.

She stared back at him.

"What news of the fourth member?" asked the magistrate.

"Oh him?" replied Caeluibianus. "We don't have to worry about him."

"And why is that, Caeluibianus Claudius Asinianus?"

Caeluibianus stared at Sands as he formulated his response.

"Because that skinny streak of traitorous shit has died the death he deserved, torn limb from limb by my own brave hunting dogs. He thought he was safe in the bosom of his family, tending his cattle and hens, but no traitor - no matter how far afield he, or she, may roam, - can escape the fearful justice of Rome."

Sands face showed barely a tremor of emotion. She stared back at him.

"Tragic, isn't it?" he mouthed.

Imperceptibly, her gaze was beginning to glisten. One single tear began to form in the edge of her right eye. She fought to hold back its inevitable descent across her cheek. She failed. Slowly, it traced a moist track to the corner of her mouth.

Caeluibianus smiled. "You bitch, it is you, isn't it?"

The blood pooled in Sands' stomach. She stood speechless, rooted to the spot, unable to respond or react. But instead of looking at her, the three other occupants of the room turned towards Caeluibianus. Antalas, Tufayyur and the magistrate appeared no less shocked by his outburst than Sands had been.

"How dare you, Sir?" reprimanded Antalas, outraged by the insult flung at his guest.

"I'll remind you to keep a civil tongue in your head, Caeluibianus," snapped Modius Calvinus. "What's the meaning of this outburst? In the name of Jupiter, compose yourself."

Caeluibianus glared at Sands. "That thing," he spat, "is Galla Placidia."

There was silence for a moment as the meaning of his words sunk in.

And then there was uproar.

Tuffayur was the first to cry out in protest. "Father, please! Stop him!"

Both older men started talking at once.

"Are you demented, Caeluibianus Claudius?" Antalas demanded, his crimson face betraying the depth of his anger.

"Shame on you. Retract your words at once and apologise to the young man," the magistrate instructed.

Caeluibianus turned to address Antalas. "Her disguise might persuade you otherwise, sir, but I can assure you she's no more a man than your daughter is."

"Liar," shouted Tufayyur. "And you are no more a gentleman than I am!" She struck Caeluibianus across his shoulder. "Have him flung out of the house, Father."

Antalas leaped forward to restrain Tufayyur. "Quiet, girl!" he urged, as she struggled to resume her assault.

"Throw the son of a dog out," she yelled. "How can you tolerate such an insult against poor Kalius?"

"I would caution you to restrain your daughter's language, sir," interjected the shocked magistrate. "This is men's business; there is no place here for a woman's hysteria. She risks making herself unwell."

Antalas nodded. "Leave the room at once, girl. Go to your mother."

"But, Father!"

"Do as I say, and be quick about it before I'm obliged to chastise you further."

Tufayyur shot her father a furious look and swept out of the *tablinum*, her insults and complaints echoing around the *peristyle* as she withdrew to the front of the house.

"Now what is this nonsense all about, Caeluibianus Claudius? You are mistaken in your assertion, surely? Apologise, and we'll say no more about it, eh? There's a good fellow."

"Ask her to deny it," Caeluibianus contested. "It's the easiest thing in the world to prove one's sex." He adjusted his clothing. "There," he said, pulling out his penis in full view of the assembled company, "I've just shown you how it's done. Now, it's your turn," he challenged Sands. "If you can match my cock with one of your own, then I'll be the first to apologise for unjustly accusing you."

"In the name of the Gods, Caeluibianus Claudius, put it away," the magistrate reprimanded his colleague. "This is most unseemly and obscene conduct on your part. Must I remind you that this is a reputable, private residence and not a bordello?"

"I apologise for the crude manner of my accusation, Gaius Modius, but in my defence, I'd quote of a line from the *Priapeia*."

"Which is what?"

Caeluibianus composed himself before delivering the quotation: *"I'd rather die than use obscene and improper words; but when you, Priapus, as a god, appear with your testicles hanging out, it is appropriate for me to speak of cunts and cocks."*

"Disgraceful!" Antalas protested. "I won't tolerate the use of such lewd and disreputable language in this house."

The magistrate also turned on the Roman tribune, but his tone was mellower than the Jew's. "Save your rhetoric for the law courts, Caeluibianus Claudius. Are you seriously attempting to hold Kalius Placidius responsible for the obscene manner of your accusation against him?"

"I am indeed. That woman is the author of her own downfall. If she seeks to gain advantage through assuming a man's appearance then she can expect no recourse to the indulgences normally accorded her sex."

"Villain, out of my house, now!" roared Antalas.

"Calm down, sir" Gaius Modius insisted to his host. "You risk overstepping the mark. Despite these open provocations, I would urge you to compose yourself. As a magistrate, I have a legal right - nay, a duty - to insist on questioning Kalius Placidius in order to ascertain the truth or otherwise of the wild accusations made against him. If he is the injured party here, as in all likelihood he is, then plainly he has nothing to fear from my scrutiny."

Sands meanwhile had been standing in silence. She had wiped the tear from her cheek. Now she turned to present a defiant face to the magistrate as he prepared to address her.

"Kalius Placidius, you have had a number of serious accusations laid against you, and I am obliged in my capacity as city magistrate to put them to you formally and in the presence of witnesses. Caeluibianus Claudius, here, maintains that you are, in fact, a woman and not a man, and that, in the guise of Galla Placidia, you were in contravention of the *leges maiestatis* and, therefore, guilty of the crime of treason against the Roman people, including, but not limited to, the murder of hostages, the occupation of public places, the meeting within the city of persons hostile to the state with weapons, incitement to sedition and the release of prisoners justly confined. In the name of the authority invested in me by the provincial *propraetor*, I call upon you now to answer these charges truthfully. Do you deny all or any of these assertions?"

Sands replied without hesitation. "I refute them all but one."

"Speak plainly, then. Truth is a balm to the conscience."

Sands looked down at the sign of Libra, the astrological symbol upon which she was standing. Her birth sign represented the scales of justice. "If destiny is pre-ordained then at least I've got righteousness in my corner. I admit it, I am a woman."

"Vindicated!" shouted Caeluibianus in triumph. "There she stands, the traitor, the mountebank, shorn of all disguise!"

"I am *no* traitor, Gaius Modius. All the other charges laid against me are false. Antalas, I appeal to you. I am innocent. You must believe me."

191

Antalas looked crushed. "But you lied to me," he cried in anguish. "You're a woman. You lied to me and my family."

"I wanted to tell you. Please believe me. The only crime I could be accused of is cultivating your friendship and hospitality under a concealed identity. But it was done for the very best of motives. I never intended to take advantage of you, trust me."

Caeluibianus laughed. "What a touching scene. There's no sight as pathetic as a credulous old fool brought to his knees by a conniving, duplicitous bitch. These two deserve each other, Gaius Modius. You should have them chained together and thrown to drown in the nearest cesspit."

"Hold your tongue, Caeluibianus," snapped the magistrate. "Your role here is concluded; it does not extend to passing judgement and dispensing justice. That's a matter for the courts."

"And what is to become of Galla Placidia in the meantime, if my role here is finished? I urge you to entrust her house arrest to me, and I will ensure that she is delivered safely into the hands of justice at any time determined by the courts."

Sands objected. "Caeluibianus bears me naught but ill-will, Gaius Modius. Left to his tender mercies, I will never see the light of a new day, never mind the inside of a court house."

"I am not inclined to disagree with you," the magistrate responded with practiced obliqueness. "Caeluibianus Claudius Asinianus seems to be under the impression that because he assumes something *is* so, then that is simply enough for it to *be* so. In that regard, he demonstrates a sophistry that flatters Protagoras' most notorious maxim: "Man is the measure of all things: of the things that are, that they are, of the things that are not, that they are not." I, on the other hand, stand firmly opposed to such casuistry. Gaius' treatise on the *Edicts of the Magistrates* is all the authority I require in order to implement the equitable jurisdiction of the *praetors.*"

"In which case," intervened Antalas, "may I humbly presume to offer to guarantee the secure house arrest of the accused until such time as she is called to trial?"

The magistrate stroked his chin while he pondered the suggestion. "I trust you understand that the court would impose a stringent bond upon you, Antalas Alfassi. The liberty of yourself, your wife and your children would be forfeit if Galla Placidia, as we are now obliged address her, was to fail to attend court to face any charges brought against her by the state. You do understand the condition of this surety, I hope?"

"I do, sir."

"I won't let you down again, I swear," Sands pledged.

"You won't be given a chance to let me down again," Antalas barked. "You will be secured under lock and key in the servants' quarters in the disused old store room, and that's where you will remain until the date of your trial. Your period of confinement should provide you with ample opportunity to reflect how shamefully you have wronged me and my family."

Caeluibianus snorted with derision. He turned to the magistrate. "And what of her accomplices, Gaius Modius? How do you propose to apprehend them? Or will Antalas, here, be permitted to provide them with free board and lodging too?"

"I will issue an order for their immediate detention," the magistrate retorted.

"The black-skinned African is the one you want. I witnessed him cold-bloodedly murder an unarmed jailer in Aballava. What name is he currently hiding under?" Caeluibianus demanded of Antalas.

"Titus Ojokwus."

"His current whereabouts is where?" enquired Gaius Modius.

"He is supervising the transport of a shipment of grain by the overland route to Tingi. He won't return to Volubilis for fourteen days."

"In that case he'll receive a warm welcome on re-entering the city," Gaius Modius confirmed.

"Only if he makes it back alive," glowered Caeluibianus.

The magistrate received Caeluibianus' words with an indulgent smirk. "On this occasion I have some sympathy with the sentiment of your remarks, Caeluibianus Claudius. I wouldn't be altogether surprised to hear that the Gods have intervened and exacted their own revenge in the interim."

Sands noted the sudden transformation in the magistrate's viewpoint. "I implore you, Gaius Modius," she said. "Roman law demands not only that justice must be done, but that it must be seen to be done. Titus Ojokwus has a right to the protection of the law, just like any free-born citizen."

The magistrate laughed. "A noble sentiment, young woman, and it's one that I will happily uphold in your case. However I can't possibly be held accountable for the excesses of local auxiliaries who may wish to avenge the murder of one of their own cohort. Surely, you can see that?"

"But what about justice?" she pleaded.

"He'll get what's coming to him. He'll get justice all right," laughed Caeluibianus. "There's no need to concern yourself on that score."

TWENTY-FIVE

Aballava Tablet No. 9, Inventory No 13.28 (Morris Archive)
Caeluibianus, Cohort Tribune and Praepositus of the
Company, to Julius Rufinus, Tribunus Laticlavius and
commander-in-chief, I send my greetings. In the matter of
determining the fate of Galla Placidia (undertaken in the utmost
secrecy as directed) I have done so in full accordance with your
wishes and have set out my findings below. Rejoice, my Lord!
We have her! Galla Placidia is detained under house arrest till
such time as she is called to stand trial for acts of treason against
the state. Less pleasingly, the local presiding magistrate appears
to be an over-promoted, provincial moralist of the worst kind,
and has already proved himself to be - it scarcely needs saying
– a veritable stickler for procedure. He insists on parading his
judicial superiority as if it were a legionary standard, flaunting it
for the world to see, whereas in reality the only thing masking
his lack of moral substance is a thin veneer of rhetoric and a
rudimentary familiarity with legal procedure. He has, however,
privately confided in me that a sentence of death is a formality
in cases such as these, and has reassured me that the crime of
treason removes immunity from the use of torture should it be
required in order to make the accused testify. I have therefore
proffered the services of Bostar in this regard. I would
volunteer to undertake the task myself, my Lord, as you can
well imagine, but I fear that my motives might be misconstrued
if I was to do so, especially given my intention to both act as
litigant and to bear witness against Galla Placidia. I have also
taken the liberty, my Lord, of providing your name as guarantor
against a loan agreed with the quartermaster of the local cohort
from the Third Augustan Legion. Our funds, as you may well
imagine, have begun to grow thin, and I anticipate having to
incur considerable additional expenses if we are to guarantee a

successful prosecution. As well as requiring money for *nomenclatares* (those usual claques hired both to applaud our advocate's oratory and to intimidate the opposition) I will also depend on substantial bribes in order to attract the good favour of the judges. Furthermore, I've had to pay a sizeable retainer to the province's most renowned advocate, Antoninus Opellius Macrinus. I'm told he is a master of moving the audience to laughter or tears depending on the needs of the case. Every gesture, from the rise of an eyebrow to the turn of a foot, is calibrated to excite the greatest support for his cause, and some venture to suggest that, as a member of the equestrian class, he uses the courtroom as the perfect stage for his political advancement. At any rate, his services don't come cheap, my Lord, and he flatly refuses to enter a public courtroom without the accompaniment of a sycophantic phalanx of *minores advocati, librarii* and *pragmatici,* all of whose costs must be met, surprise, surprise, by the hard-pressed litigant. In the name of Jupiter, I would flay the skins of every last member of the money-grubbing legal profession if it was within my power! Jurists, praetors, advocates, lictors, scribes, magistrates – all would rather suck the last drop of blood from an honest man than turn their hand to a decent day's toil. Alas, my Lord, I am driven to the conclusion that, in order for good to triumph, it is sometimes necessary for the virtuous among us to consort with the handmaidens of avarice. And to that end, I will grease the palm of any *praetor* in order to guarantee the implementation of justice and the rightful application of the death penalty for Galla Placidia's multiple acts of treason. In the event that my ministrations fail to affect the required outcome, it may be necessary to implement some darker arts and apply a cruder, more hands-on solution to the problem. I call upon the Gods to sustain me in the challenges that lie ahead. May my resolve be put to the test and may I not be found wanting; may justice and truth prevail! I will not shrink from my purpose, my Lord. I will do whatever conscience and good sense dictates and at every moment of decision you can depend on me to be ready.

TWENTY-SIX

Location: Volubilis, Mauretania Tingitana
Coordinates: 34° 03' 36" N and 5° 33' 00" W

Time and Date: 10.00: 30 August, 258 C.E.

There was a gentle knock on the door.

"Kalius, are you decently attired? It is I, Guenfan. I have brought you your breakfast. Are you prepared to receive me?"

He listened hard for a response. "I'm about to unlock, pray arrange your dress."

"Come in, Guenfan," Sands answered. She stood up to receive him as he entered with a tray of food and drink.

He averted his gaze as he laid out the breakfast on her table. "Here is your food. I will conduct you to your ablutions when you are ready." His awkward manner betrayed his discomfort.

"Thank you, Guenfan, you are a kind and decent man."

"Madam, by what name should I know you? I'm confused as to your real nature. How should I address you?"

Sands was surprised to witness his open anguish. "It is true, Guenfan, that I am not a man. I regret having deceived you. I was forced to disguise my gender by subterfuge."

"Your brother has told me the circumstances of your forced flight from Britannia."

"You've seen Sextus Placidius? What news of him? Has he been arrested too?"

"No, he is still at liberty. The master has banned him from the house, and he is now residing with the Syrian, Barthabbathas Males. He sends his greetings and has asked for me to act as your go-between if it should so please you?"

197

"Thank you. I will certainly accept your offer. As long as you're sure it will not place you in any danger?"

"Me? No, I am a free man. What's more, Sextus Placidius stands charged with no crime. And you, Kalius Placidius, if that is how I should still address you, are entitled to legal assistance and advice."

"My name is neither Kalius Placidius nor Galla Placidia, the alias foisted on me by the Romans. I would be pleased if you would address me as Kal, and continue to think of me as your friend."

"Kal it is, and Kal it ever shall be, and you will remain my friend to boot, on that you can depend, no matter what charges those bastards level against you." He looked away to avoid meeting Sands' gaze.

"All's not lost, Guenfan. I'll fight to prove my innocence."

"But the odds are stacked against you. The law favours the powerful, not the virtuous. And you have made some powerful enemies. The whole of Oualili is talking about your case."

"I'm used to dealing with powerful enemies. It's been the story of my life. But now I'm preparing to fight for my freedom with every tool at my disposal - as well as some that aren't."

There was a sound outside. "May I enter?" enquired a small voice from behind the half-opened door. A familiar face peeped around the door frame.

"Tufayyur!" exclaimed Sands. "I was hoping you'd come."

"I wanted to see you," she replied, averting her gaze, "but Father was against the idea. I had to prevail upon him the whole of yesterday to change his mind. He is very angry with you."

"I know."

"As am I."

"I know."

Tuffayur extended her hands in supplication. Now she was staring at Sands, directly and accusingly. "How could you do it?" she cried. "You were my friend. How could you deceive me so grievously? I feel such a fool."

Sands was desolate. She held out her arms to the young woman. "Please forgive me for my subterfuge. I never meant to hurt you like this, Tufayyur. I wanted to tell you. I tried to tell you but it was too late."

Guenfan coughed. "Maybe it would be best if I was to leave now, so that you can talk privately." He moved aside to allow Tuffayur to enter. "I will stand outside till needed."

Sands nodded her acceptance and half-smiled as he backed out of the room.

"I was in love with you, do you not realise that?" Tufayyur continued. "How do you think that makes me feel now?"

Sands hung her head in shame. "I know." That acknowledgement was all she could muster in response.

"Ever since I was fourteen I've had to fight off men by the dozen," Tufayyur continued. "They've continually swarmed around me like flies, irritating me, pestering me, never letting me breathe, and I feel like I've spent my entire life swatting them away. The remains of my rejected suitors lie scattered everywhere I go. I find myself walking knee-deep through the empty husks of their unwanted proposals and spurned advances. And then, finally, one day, something very remarkable happens. By complete chance, I meet a man who doesn't harass, hector and annoy me. He doesn't impose himself on me, or try to constantly impress me, or bore me with his boasts. In fact, quite the contrary is true. He is modest, gentle and considerate. Instead, it is I who becomes the adoring admirer, the love-struck suitor, the amorous predator. Me! And who is the subject of these advances? You! And do you know the biggest joke of all? You're not even a man! You're a woman. My obsessive love made me blind to your very gender. How can this be? How can this be?"

Tufayyur's anger quickly dissolved to tears, her body wracking with sobs. "I trusted you."

"Come here, Tufayyur, please. Let me hug you."

"No, don't touch me. You've lost the right to comfort me."

"Would you at least give me the chance to explain?"

"No, that is for another day, if ever," Tufayyur sobbed. "I don't need explanations. I have a broken heart; explanations won't fix that. Explanations are designed to make *you* feel better, not me."

"Is there anything I can do to make up for hurting you?"

"Yes, you can allow me to help you. I need for you to be in my debt. Do you understand?"

Sands looked at her in surprise. "Help me? But how?"

"That's for you to decide. Don't ask me. Just do it. Think of something, you heartless wretch."

Sands struggled for inspiration. Her mind was a complete blank for the first time in many months.

"You need to give me something useful to do," insisted Tufayyur. She was slowly beginning to regain her composure. "What do you need? There must be something?"

"Papyrus scrolls!" I need *volumina*."

"Good, what kind of scrolls?"

"Book-rolls on courtroom rhetoric and legal procedure. I had a visit from an advocate hired by your father yesterday. He gave me some suggestions."

"Wait," interrupted Tufayyur with astonishment, "Father has offered to pay for you to have an advocate?"

"Look, Tufayyur, I didn't ask him to pay. You must believe me. He just arranged it himself. He hasn't spoken a word to me."

Tufayyur shook her head. "I'll never understand him. First you dishonour him in his own house, and now he's paying for your defence in court?" She emitted a deep sighed, before returning to the issue at hand. "Now, which scrolls do you need?"

"There's quite a number. Will you be able to remember them all?"

Tuffayur shot Sands an offended look. "Just tell me their names!"

"*Controversiae* by Senecca the Elder: there's a set of ten books, but just get whatever you can."

"Next."

"Quintillian's *Institutio Orataria*: it's a manual for training the perfect orator, or so my advocate claims."

"I know of it. Any more?"

"Tacitus?"

"Which volumes?"

"*Dialogus* if you can find it. If not, *Historiae* or *Annales*. The latter may be useful for disproving trumped up charges. It might be particularly helpful in dealing with Caeluibianus."

"Who's Caeluibianus?"

"My accuser."

"Would it also help you if I was to have him taken care of?"

"What do you mean? Do not do anything rash, I implore you, Tufayyur. Promise me that you will do what I ask of you, and no more."

"Is it true, as Father maintains, that you are to be tried on the grounds of *laesa maiestas*?"

"It is."

"And you do realise that treason attracts the death penalty?"

"I do."

"And that Father says you are to be tried by special tribunal, by *duumviri perduellionis*?"

"Yes, I will be tried by just two officials."

"You have been told that this is a bad outcome for you? It means it is much easier for the accuser to bribe the judges."

"I know."

"And you would still rather I didn't arrange to take care of your accuser? I have many admirers who would jump to win my favour."

"Yes, it's not the way I want to do things. It's not your fight. Remember that, please."

Tufayyur shrugged. "The decision rests with you, of course, but why do you think Father has placed a permanent guard on your door? It's not to stop you escaping. He fears your life is in imminent danger. Your chances of surviving to see the inside of a courtroom are slim."

Sands shivered. "If I have to die like a rat in a trap then so be it. But I won't ever allow myself to sink to the level of hiring an assassin."

"Is that it then?"

"No there's one other favour you can do me."

"Name it."

"I'll need you to sit and translate for me. I will not be able to read and understand the texts by myself. I need help, Tufayyur."

"You can count on me. When I give someone my word, you'll discover I can be trusted."

"And where do you think you'll find the *volumina*? They are likely to be expensive. I can ask Guenfan to get some money from Sextus."

"You mean Birch?"

"Yes, I mean Birch."

"Both my father and grandfather have extensive libraries. But there is also a wide range of volumes on sale in the scroll shop in the *Via Decumana*. I will find something for you. And it won't cost you a single *as*, on that you can depend. Your friends, those you've wronged so grievously, will see to that."

Despite these words, Sands looked downcast. "If you are still my friend, Tufayyur, I beg you to address me like one. Your disapproval, your reprimands, even your tears, I can stand, but not your coldness."

"That's an easy demand for you to make. You extinguished my warmth." Tears formed in her eyes once more. "It can't be ignited as you decree it. Once you were the commander of my heart, my every emotion was subject to your authority, you held total sway over my passions – but not anymore. Now you are merely my debtor. And I, as your creditor, am entitled to expect compensation from you, requests even, but *not* demands. I will thank you to remember that in future."

Sands accepted the reprimand in silence. The two women looked at each other from a distance of four feet, but were separated by a chasm as wide as the Todra Gorge.

"Now you will have to excuse me. I have your shopping list to attend to."

As Tufayyur swept from the room and made her way back down through the arcaded external corridors of the *peristyle*, Sands could detect three distinctive sounds emanating from the courtyard: the rustle of her friend's heavy clothing, the tiptoeing echo of her light, hurried footsteps and the young woman's distraught cries as she made her way back to her private quarters.

The sounds made Sands gasp with distress. Her suppressed emotions could no longer be contained. She sat on the bed and allowed her body to shake with violent sobs. She felt utterly alone.

TWENTY-SEVEN

"First things first," Morris announces. "Do you reckon the Artificial Intelligence system is convincing or not? Remember, the criterion we've adopted is the one proposed in 'The Turing Test', but, in our case, as applied to a computer game."

Sterland Morris is about to be cross-examined live on air by a group of national competition winners, each one of whom has won the right to put a question directly to the creator of the *Pax Britannica* franchise.

"Ah, yes, 'The Turing Test'," repeats the studio moderator. "Maybe you can elaborate on that for the benefit of our subscribers, Dr Morris?"

"Certainly, if it would help."

Morris settles himself in his seat. "Eighty years ago, Alan Turing posited a simple question, and it was this: Can machines think? Three uncomplicated words and one apparently straightforward question, but it leaves us with a devilishly difficult conjecture to prove."

He scrutinises his audience, as if challenging them to respond, before continuing with his explanation. "Turing suggested that a straightforward social test might provide the answer. Put simply, it goes like this: machines can think when they are able to fool us into thinking that they're human. Now, in a computer games context, such as the one we're experiencing in the world of *Pax Britannica*, we are posing the same question, but in a slightly different way: Can games characters think? Using the proof that Turing suggested, we would have to be able to answer the question in the following way: "Even though they exist in a games environment, these artificial characters can think and are able to adapt intelligently to their surroundings in a way that convinces me that they are human." On a philosophical level that's the central proposition that the *Pax*

Britannica project has been attempting to address. Are we able to prove that assertion in exactly those terms? So it's over to you now."

"Right, who wants to kick things off?" the studio moderator asks. "Dr Morris has indicated he's open to all questions. Feel free to tackle him on anything."

"Right, so here's what I'd like to know," the first questioner begins. "How come the characters are able to act so autonomously? It's like they're assessing problems intelligently and responding with genuine human emotions."

"Okay, firstly, we've programmed the main characters, particularly Sands, so that they're loaded up with an unprecedented amount of pre-knowledge that puts them ahead of the game subscribers."

"Ok, that makes sense," the questioner interrupts. "So, simply put, they know more about what's going on than we do?"

"That's true, up to a certain extent, but they are also aided by what we call a 'sensing' capacity. This gives them the advantage of appearing to act autonomously, or to act intelligently without seeking permission or being under our direct control. This 'Free will' function, as we call it, is central to the gameplay of *Pax Britannica*."

"It seems to be working overtime. Are you pleased with the response so far?"

"We're astonished at the reactions we've been able to get out of the characters so far."

"So how does the 'sensing' capacity work exactly?"

"You won't be surprised to hear that the technology behind it is hideously complicated, but it's underpinned by a pretty straightforward concept. Let me put it in these terms. Supposing someone you knew was offering you bad advice, and you sensed it was bad advice, would you still act on it anyway just because it was well-meant? No, of course you wouldn't. And neither does Sands; it's as simple as that."

"But to continue your analogy, how can she sense it is bad advice? How can she judge situations better than us?"

"Because she's been imbued with a self-protection instinct

that allows her to overrule the controller's commands, if, and when, she thinks they run counter to her continued survival in the game."

"Ok, let me get this straight. You mean even if we wanted to kill off the characters they would fight for their own survival?"

"Yup, that sounds about right. I'd say you've summed it up rather well."

"So, is it possible that the characters could see the game controller as the enemy, instead of the combatants that they are facing on screen?"

"Yes, it's a very real possibility. And in my opinion we may be witnessing the first hints that it's not far off happening."

"Just suppose for a minute, then, that as far as the characters in the game are concerned, they do exist and we are merely illusory."

"In other words, it's their actions which give value and meaning to the world around them, not the other way around? That's a Marxist way of thinking. If the characters could reject false consciousness they would no longer see themselves as powerless."

"So it's the appearance of the world around them which is deceptive and like an illusion?"

"Precisely, they would no longer be inert and lifeless. They'd realise that they alone are responsible for the existence and nature of things."

"In other words it's their own actions which control their objective everyday reality?" the questioner asks once again, taking on board the implications of what's being said.

"Exactly."

"So do you think Sands has a sense of her own power and destiny? Is she in control?"

"I'm beginning to hope she is. Aren't you?"

Now it's another questioner's turn to step in. "I understand what you're saying, but I'm not too happy about it. The whole point, surely, is that I, as a subscriber, control the game? Isn't that the way it's supposed to be? I'm looking for more autonomy and control, not less of it. Plus, I'm not sure I want an over-assertive female countermanding me and deciding what she's gonna do in my game."

"Ok, let's examine what you've said in some detail. Look, on the face of it, yours seems like a perfectly reasonable objection, but all we're trying to give each of you - each subscriber – is a richer, more realistic experience. We all want the characters to act and behave intelligently, don't we, and sometimes we have to accept that that's what's going to bring them into conflict with subscribers who are sitting at home in the comfort of their own homes. Our central characters have been imbued with a series of behaviour-modification algorithms that give them real power for the first time. And that can be hard for subscribers to deal with. We know that."

Morris turns and appeals to the wider audience. "Come on, what do the rest of you think? You've all experienced this amazing transformation for yourselves. The characters in *Pax Britannica* are like real, living, breathing entities, aren't they? And how has this come about? It's happened because we decided to place a psychoanalyst, an evolutionary psychologist, a moral philosopher, an anthropologist and a behavioural theorist at the very heart of our research and development team. Professional practitioners and academics have taken the geeks and anoraks by the scruff of the neck and forced them to engage with real human behaviours and motivations. Haven't you got fed up with predictable, one-dimensional character behaviours which seem to be set in concrete and immutable?"

"Alright, alright, I agree with all that," replies a new questioner. "And I like what you've done to spice up the character responses. But let's not beat around the bush. What I really want, and what most gamers really want is a chance to play God."

"Ah, so now we're getting down to the nitty-gritty," challenges Morris, "now we're getting down to the 'God' question."

"That's right, I don't want to have my wings clipped. I want to be the ultimate boss."

"The ultimate boss, you say - but what kind of ultimate boss might that be? Ok, let's look at it this way. Imagine if you were playing God in your computer game, would you want to be a vengeful, angry deity determined to exercise control and impose restrictions and punishment over individuals who had broken the rules and challenged your authority? Or would you rather be a loving, understanding God who appreciates the inconsistencies of human nature and who grants opportunities for development, forgiveness and redemption to his characters?"

The questioner laughs. "Ok, I get your point, but whichever way it goes, at the end of the day, it's not really going to be my call, is it? In the context of *Pax Britannica*, who is getting to play God then? Because it doesn't feel like it's going to be me."

"Who's playing God? That's an interesting question. I'd say what we're trying to do here is to return the role of the divine to the game's characters, to Sands and the others, to make them responsible for their own actions and to be answerable to their own consciences, and, yes, to their own spiritual impulses."

At this point the studio moderator intervenes to ask her own question.

"But from a religious point of view I'd like to know what part you think God, however you define him, plays in any of this?" she enquires. "Isn't it down to the divine creator to combine a body with a soul, even if he's only working with a digital body?"

"Some might say so, but, theologically speaking, who's to guarantee that God would have any objection to giving a soul to a digital computer character? And even if you do think God would have a problem with it, Turing argued strongly against the assertion that "Thinking is a function of man's immortal soul", thereby rendering the whole question superfluous anyway."

The studio moderator leans forward. "And do you believe that God resides within these characters; that they're up to that challenge?"

Morris deflects the question. "That, I'm afraid, is ultimately a judgement for the subscribers to make, not me. Having said which, I think that the signs are encouraging thus far; but it rather depends on how one is inclined to define the divine. That said, I'd like to see how the chararcters' moral compass, their conscience, their soul, call it what you like, reacts under testing conditions, when the chips are really down. That's what counts ultimately."

"And could the upcoming trial of Sands be the moment of truth that produces those ultimate testing conditions?"

Morris looks uneasy. "I suppose it may well be. In which case, if he does exist, may God help her. Because if there's one thing that's certain, she's going to need all the assistance she can get."

TWENTY-EIGHT

Location: Volubilis, Mauretania Tingitana
Coordinates: 34° 03' 36" N and 5° 33' 00" W

Time and Date: 10.00, 6th September, 258 C.E.

It was mid-morning. Kal Sands and an escort of four Roman auxiliaries were making their way towards the Volubilis public courthouse. The streets were alive with spectators. Since first light, word had circulated among the locals that the infamous rebel, Galla Placidia, was facing eight counts of treason against the Roman people, a crime so severe that it was considered second only to sacrilege in gravity. As a consequence, it was widely assumed that she'd end up being burnt to death at the stake or eaten alive by wild beasts. The prospect of witnessing either of these two outcomes, plus the associated courtroom theatrics, guaranteed an excellent day's entertainment to any citizen with no better claim on their time. And a casual glance around the packed walkways was enough to indicate that such a pre-condition applied to a sizeable segment of the city's population.

On crossing the *Decumanus Maximus*, Sands was forced to duck as a ripe aubergine whistled past her head and struck the armoured shoulder of the Roman guard walking behind her. A huge cheer and a gale of laughter erupted from the throng lining the path to the courthouse. Violent insults were flung at her from the back of the crowd. These were followed by a litany of lewd remarks and a basketful of assorted rubbish.

The unremitting, burning sun and the glare of public attention were making Sands wilt. As she passed through the crowds the Roman soldiers jostled her. She appeared disorientated, friendless and vulnerable. Everywhere she looked, Sands was surrounded by a sea of prurient spectators, the innocent object of their casual interest and abuse. She reeled under the verbal assaults. She resembled a no-hope prize fighter forcing her way through a baying crowd to some distant boxing ring.

Suddenly, as if from nowhere, a lone, familiar voice shouted a message of support from the back of the throng. "May the Gods protect you, Miss!"

It was Guenfan. He jostled his way to the front, pushing aside the professional loudmouths. "Don't allow them to beat you down before you've started. Justice will prevail!"

Sands beamed and shouted her thanks.

"Ignore the Roman bootlickers," he yelled in defiance. Although he was addressing Sands, his remarks were intended for a wider audience. "Everyone knows these bastards are being paid to defame the young woman." A number of sympathetic heads began nodding in agreement.

A few more voices started to be raised in Sands' favour. Barthabbathas Males shouted his encouragement. And then, from nowhere, there was Birch, smiling and holding out his hand to her. The tide had started to turn. Soon expressions of support from ordinary Berbers were beginning to drown out the insults from the paid lickspittles, the army sympathisers and the rowdier elements in the crowd.

"I've been down to the courtroom, Sands," Birch shouted as he marched alongside her. "It's like a football crowd. They've packed it out with prosecution supporters. They're kicking up one hell of a stink."

"Is my advocate there, at least?"

"In body, but not in spirit. He looks terrified. He may turn out to be worse than useless."

"Birch, I want you next to me on the defendant's bench."

One of the guards struck Birch with his shield and sent him spinning into the crowd. "Beware, Sands, Bostar's in there!" They were the last words she heard from her comrade as his voice became engulfed in the general tumult.

Sands' heart sank. All external sounds were excised. "That bastard, Bostar, he's come all this way to torment me." Images of her former maltreatment at his hands flashed across her mind. His leering expression returned to haunt her. Suddenly, a violent dig in her ribs interrupted her reverie. "March on, girl," roared the soldier behind her.

"Treat her with respect, you swine!" yelled an anonymous voice from the surrounding throng. His reprimand was met with shouts of support from other members of the crowd. "It's one law for the Romans and another for the rest of us!" someone else shouted. A murmur of agreement bubbled up.

The guards accompanying Sands became less confident. "Move it, lads," ordered the corporal in charge. "We don't want to get stranded out here with this mob around us."

As the entourage picked up speed, the attention of the crowd became more focused on the guards. They spectators started to hiss, boo and openly insult the auxiliaries.

Audible cries of "May the Gods protect and preserve you, Galla Placidia," rent the air.

Sands acknowledged the crowd. "May the Gods protect and preserve Volubilis!" she replied to great cheers.

The closer the accused and her guards got to the courthouse, the denser the crowds grew. Sands' detail processed around the side of the basilica and through the forum. People strained on all sides to catch a glimpse of the young woman whose fate seemed sealed. But contrary to expectations, she no longer appeared cowed, and, instead, bore herself with dignity and impressive stature. The last hundred metres of her journey were completed in a hushed, almost respectful silence. She was about to enter the field of play, and it was as if the assembled onlookers acknowledged her right to the moments of calm needed to steel her resolve and gather her thoughts.

On reaching the far end of the forum, the procession funnelled through a passageway formed of armed soldiers. This led to a large open-air forecourt in front of the Temple of Jupiter where the trial was to be held. The location had been chosen in order to accommodate the greatest number of spectators and official witnesses. Sands was unprepared for the sight that greeted her as she entered the courtroom. On the steps of the temple, a rostrum had been erected to accommodate the presiding magistrate and two judges. Huge awnings had been suspended over the rostrum and the main body of the courtroom to provide protection from the intense Moroccan sun. In front of the judges' rostrum lay a sizeable debating space, the field of battle upon which the fate of Sands was to be settled. Sitting at right angles to the rostrum, and facing each other across the court, were the litigants' *subsellia*, the portable wooden benches upon which the opposing advocates and their clients would perch throughout the duration of the trial.

The public benches were arrayed in multiple rows facing the judges. It was clear from the moment that Sands appeared in the courtroom that the front seats were dominated by the accuser's supporters. They set up a hum of disapproval as she was accompanied to her bench at the front of the court.

Sands met her advocate. She then scanned the spectators for any sign of Birch. On the opposing benches she could see Caeluibianus, Bostar and an endless retinue of paid legal advisors, three rows deep. She was friendless, seriously outnumbered in the legal department and lacking any kind of support among the locals on the public benches. The front rows were stuffed with Caeluibianus' *nomenclatores*, the hired claques. These men were paid to applaud and swoon in delight at the oratory of the litigant's advocate. Many of these individuals were army veterans with too much time on their hands and no independence of thought. Their allegiance could be bought by an unscrupulous officer such as Caeluibianus, who only needed to combine a traditional appeal to their military loyalty with a generous financial inducement.

Bostar, however, was another kettle of fish altogether. He sat directly across the courtroom, and smirked at Sands in an unpleasant and intimidating manner. She had already suffered at his hands, and she knew him to be a cruel and vindictive opponent. And yet, and yet, by returning his stare, and by forcing him to look away first, she knew him to lack the moral fibre expected of a seasoned Roman corporal. As her memory replayed some of her dealings with him, she also recalled that he could become spineless and self-serving when the odds were swinging against his favour. Under certain circumstances he might even become traitorous, especially if the fates conspired to offer him a convenient way out of a tight spot.

Caeluibianus was a tougher act to read. His enmity towards her felt personal. There was an obsessive, psychological tinge to his pursuit of Sands that she found more disturbing. He was not a man to be bought off or intimidated. If she wanted to uncover the motive for his single-minded quest, she was going to have a tough fight on her hands. This odyssey of revenge, which he had embarked on with such fanaticism, made no sense to her. Unlike Bostar, he avoided looking at the accused in court, preferring, instead, to feign a lack of interest in Sands. He made a point of turning his back and chatting to the scribes sitting behind him.

Sands occupied herself by examining the layout of the open-air courtroom. The public benches were packed with upwards of two hundred spectators, most of whom were jammed together and likely to be caught in the crossfire of the sun's direct rays as it traversed across the sky. On either side of the external space, now serving as a temporary courthouse, were two long covered colonnades, each offering standing room only but guaranteeing shade from the sun. These were inundated with late-comers, among whom she could spot Birch, who was waving to her, and a poker-face Tufayyur, who merely nodded back politely in acknowledgement of her smile. Sands motioned to Birch to step forward, but her advocate stayed her hand. "We will seek permission from the judges first so that the court can recognise him properly, if that's your wish."

The presiding magistrate, Gaius Modius Calvinus, and the two judges walked through the body of the courtroom. They were preceded by two lictors carrying the *fasces*, the insignia of the magistrate's office and the symbol of his authority. Once they had perambulated, the three officials took up their seats behind the rostrum on the lower steps of the temple.

At the request of Sands' advocate, Birch was summoned forward by the magistrate, questioned and then permitted to sit alongside the accused. He exchanged a smile with Sands and gave her hand an encouraging squeeze as he sat down next to her.

"It's a show trial," she whispered.

"Justice as spectator sport."

Sands indicated the packed seats of partisans behind them. "Things couldn't look much worse."

"This is nothing," he countered. "Just wait till you see how many people turn out to witness your execution."

Sands smiled at Birch's nonchalance. This show of studied indifference was performed for her benefit. "Thanks, Birch, I appreciate the sentiment."

"You're welcome. Oh, look sharp, we're about to start."

One of the lictors walked forward into the well of the courtroom and called for silence. The presiding magistrate then addressed the assembled throng. He spoke in a practiced, deep, sonorous voice. Despite the outdoor acoustics, his words carried into every nook and cranny of the space and commanded instant attention and respect. Sands was immediately impressed by the declamatory, theatrical quality of his address. He projected himself with the technical virtuosity of a seasoned high jumper approaching the bar in order to clear an impossible height. His words sailed in a great arc over the heads of the audience, clearing every obstacle placed in their path.

"Bloody hell, I hope your advocate's as good as this bloke," whispered Birch. "I have to admit, though, he doesn't fill me with confidence."

Sands glanced to her left where she could already sense her legal representative's apprehension at the ordeal that lay ahead. Her advocate's anxiety levels began to rise a notch higher as the magistrate addressed the litigants and their lawyers directly.

"Cases in the public courts carry with them the harshest penalties and the most publicity," the magistrate boomed, "and thus demand the greatest efforts and talents from advocates. This court expects no less from the litigants' representatives today. Jurists from across the Empire will be dissecting the outcome of this trial and pouring over the oratory of its participants for years, if not decades, to come. Mark my words well. The eyes and ears of Jupiter himself will be the final arbiter."

The magistrate turned and bowed to the statue of Jupiter, which could be glimpsed behind him through the open doors of the god's temple. The assembled audience made the same obeisance. Once the courtroom had settled down again, the magistrate continued with his introductory remarks.

"The Digest and Codex *Ad legem Iuliam maiestatis* defines the crime of *maiestas* as one which is committed against the Roman people or against their safety. As one of the *publica judicia*, it is a crime that may be prosecuted by any Roman citizen. This special tribunal has been called to consider an accusation of treason, *Laesa Maiestas*, against Galla Placidia. The prosecution is brought by Caeluibianus Claudius Asinianus, Tribune to *cohors I Nervana Germanorum milliaria equitata with numerus Maurorum Aurelianorum Valeriani Gallienique*, and *Praepositus* of the aforementioned company, which is currently garrisoned at the fort of Aballava on the *Vallum Aelium* in northern Britannia."

At the mention of the *numerus Maurorum Aurelianorum*, a ripple of approval passed through the audience, many of who had served with distinction in the same unit. The cohort was often composed of local Mauretanian lads, regularly recruited as auxiliaries in Volubilis and Tingi. These boys were proud to serve their emperor in any way that was required, even if it meant a lengthy posting to a distant, inhospitable land. For this reason alone, the sympathy of the court lay firmly weighted in favour of the accuser.

Once complete silence had returned to the courtroom, and on a signal from the magistrate, Antoninus Opellius Macrinus

216

leapt to his feet with a flourish and bowed to the judges. His movement was deliberate and choreographed and conveyed a chivalrous respect for the tribunal's three officials. They all nodded back in acknowledgement of his flamboyant gestures. The studied elegance and grace of his movements caused a stir among the spectators. Appreciative sighs could be heard on all sides. The audience held its collective breath in anticipation of his opening address. He paused in a theatrical manner, gathered up the folds of his toga and started to perambulate. He appeared preoccupied, swamped with pained and troubled thoughts. It was almost as if the duties incumbent on him were too onerous and too perturbing for him to share with the court. Finally, and with a regretful sigh, he began to lay out the case against the accused.

"Your magnificent Eminence, your illustrious Excellencies, noble citizens of Volubilis, I am entrusted today with a responsibility so arduous and burdensome that I would not wish it on my vilest and basest enemy. But I should begin today with an apology. I should apologise in advance for what I am about to say in this courtroom."

He paused. He turned to stare at the audience seated in the body of the hall. They stared back at him in turn, transfixed and fascinated, unable to tear their eyes away from the famed advocate.

"Firstly, I must issue a warning to those of you of a nervous disposition. For your own peace of mind, flee the courtroom this instant, I say. There is the exit, there the way out, leave immediately, I implore you." He scoured the room for a hint of any takers, but, as expected, no one so much as stirred a muscle in order to depart. He smiled indulgently, before continuing. "Good, good, I knew the citizens of Volubilis were made of stern stuff - and you will need to be, my friends, in order to survive what's coming next. For I am going to detail a series of inter-connected crimes so hideous in their conception, so ruthless in their undertaking and so pitiless in their effect, that many of you who stand witness to the telling today will be unable to sleep securely for weeks to come."

His voice by now had dropped to less than a whisper, and yet the spectators, craning forward in their seats, were still able to hear every word. Suddenly they all jumped in surprise as he slammed his hand down hard on his lectern and shouted a last, impassioned warning. "Last chance, be gone those of you of a cowardly or anxious character! No one, least of all I, will think the worse of those who seize this last chance to flee back to the safety of the family hearth."

"What an old ham," Birch laughed.

Sands shook her head. "He's hysterical - what a drama queen"

"Think you can match that performance?"

"Match that? I haven't got a hope in hell. Something tells me he hasn't even got warmed up yet. You just wait."

Antoninus Opellius Macrinus approached the accuser's bench and invited him to stand. "Caeluibianus Claudius Asinianus, in the name of Jupiter, I hereby call upon you to lay your accusations against Galla Placidia before this special tribunal. Speak honestly and speak fearlessly, sir, and may the God's protect you in this onerous public responsibility."

Caeluibianus bowed to the judges, swore allegiance to Jupiter and began outlining the nature of his accusations to the tribunal.

"I, Caeluibianus Claudius Asinianus, invoke the right invested in me as a Roman citizen to prosecute Galla Placidia for the crime of treason of the gravest kind against the Roman people. I accuse her of the following treasonable acts: bearing arms against the state, incitement to sedition, the administration of unlawful oaths, hostage taking, conspiracy to murder hostages, the freeing of prisoners justly confined, the occupation of public spaces and the destruction and defilement of Imperial standards and insignia bearing the Emperor's name and image. Additionally, in the prosecution of these crimes of treason she also engaged in or encouraged six acts of murder against Roman auxiliaries, and committed numerous gross acts of sacrilege."

Sands listened with care to the charges being laid against her, and at the mention of the final two, her head snapped to attention. She prodded her advocate to intervene. "This tribunal only has the authority to pass judgement on acts of treason. It shouldn't be considering accusations of murder or sacrilege. Say something."

"I'd urge you to desist from raising complaints about court procedure. It is the height of incivility. It will only incur the ire of the *praetors* if I interrupt without due respect for their office. Remember, it falls to the magistrate to determine the conduct of this court, not you. And I'll inform you when you are required to speak. So, it would be best if you do strictly as I tell you, and do nothing more. Is that clear?"

"But Caeluibianus can't be permitted to bring wild accusations of murder to this court without a challenge."

"Mark my words well, young woman. Your job at this tribunal is very simple - and it does not involve questioning my judgement. So let me spell it out for you. You have one job to fulfil and one job only, and it is as follows. At a given signal from me, and from me alone, you will be called upon to kneel as a petitioner before the mercy of the judges, and to clasp their knees in supplication as the situation demands."

Sands laughed in astonishment. "That's it? And I can expect to have no further say in the case?"

"Absolutely not. My reputation as an advocate rests entirely on the outcome of this case, and I have no intention of letting you soil my prospects any more than is humanly possible. And if it's not asking too much, I'll thank you to remember that I'm being paid a pittance to represent you. And, anyway, I've only agreed to take the case as a favour to my old friend, Antalas Alfassi, not that it's likely to do my career the slightest bit of good in the long run. I hope that's clear enough for you. Now, unless you wish to challenge my authority further, keep quiet, do as you're told and attend on my further directives."

Sands was dumbfounded by the peremptory and disrespectful nature of the exchange. She looked shocked and offended, a fact that did not escape the scrutiny of some of the spectators who whistled and jeered her reaction.

"Fucking outrageous," Sands protested to Birch. "Did you hear that? He told me to shut up and smile at the judges. He's got another bloody thing coming."

"Keep cool, Sands. He's not your biggest problem, not by a long shot."

"But he's a wanker."

The lawyer ignored Sands.

She addressed him in English. "You, sir, are a fucking useless wanker."

He stared ahead in a state of serene indifference.

While this exchange was going on, Caeluibianus began detailing some of Galla Placidia's alleged crimes. Encouraged by the shameless theatrics of Antoninus Opellius Macrinus, Caeluibianus staged a *Grand Guignol* re-enactment of the night time ambush and murder of her first victim, the auxiliary who was pitilessly slaughtered on the beach in the fog. The paid *claques* among the spectators shook and wailed on cue while others appeared to listen in genuine horror to the unfolding tale.

Sands could detect the mood in the courtroom turning against her, and the mood was being orchestrated by Caeluibianus, the man who hated her more than anyone else alive. Finally, she could stand the submissiveness of her advocate no longer.

"If you won't get to your feet and defend me, then I'll have to do it myself."

"Hold your tongue, woman. You'll only make things worse for yourself."

"How much worse could they get?"

"Interrupt the judge's proceedings and you'll soon find out. Now, be quiet. I don't want to have to warn you again."

Sands suddenly leapt to her feet. "Your Excellencies!"

The magistrate and judges looked at her in astonishment. Caeluibianus stood frozen in mid-sentence. Her outburst was greeted by a bewildered silence across the courtroom.

Sands pointed at her squirming lawyer. "I wish to relieve this man of his duties as my advocate. Do I have the permission of the court to do so?"

"This is most irregular. On what grounds?"

"On the grounds that I could do a better job representing myself. He is worse than useless."

The advocate rose to his feet to defend himself. He made a mewling apology for his client's disrespectful outburst.

The magistrate's face turned a threatening shade of purple. "Sit down, sir, and be quiet," he bellowed. "I do not wish to hear from you again. You are hereby dismissed."

The advocate collapsed onto his bench, unprepared for the public humiliation he'd just received. As he scuttled from his seat, his departure was accompanied by a low hum of opprobrium and sarcasm from the public galleries. Then the magistrate duly conferred with the two judges. "If the accused so wishes, then she is entitled to make her appeal to the tribunal herself."

Sands bowed. "Thank you, your Excellency."

"You've got some kind of nerve, Sands, I'll give you that," Birch whispered.

"In for a penny, in for a pound – what've I got to lose? That guy was a complete liability."

Antoninus Opellius Macrinus stepped forward once more. He wore an amused look, as if to emphasise that he could hardly believe his good luck. "Verily, your Excellencies, the Goddess Fortuna smiles down on us today, but I scarcely dare ask Caeluibianus Claudius Asinianus to continue outlining the charges levelled against the accused in case Galla Placidia is minded to dispense with my services, too."

The court erupted in delight. Great waves of laughter rolled up and down the rows of spectators. The magistrate and the two judges chuckled with glee at the advocate's wit. The merriment went on and on and on, forcing Sands to wait for her riposte.

Finally, after a verbal instruction from the magistrate, the public galleries comported themselves in a fashion more befitting a Roman courthouse.

Sands stood still, took a deep breath and readied herself to address the tribunal. Thanks to Tufayyur's assistance, she had a speech prepared for just such an eventuality.

"Your Excellencies, if Justice depends solely on the application of casual witticisms then I fear my case is already lost. I cannot hope to compete with the verbal joustings of my opponent, Antoninus Opellius Macrinus. However, if the scales of justice are applied with a respect for the law of *laesa maiestas* as propounded by Rome's greatest jurists, rather than weighted in favour of empty, flamboyant rhetoric and crude theatrical flourishes, then I have every faith that this tribunal will reach a judgement in my favour."

The courtroom drew an intake of breath. "I see the cat has claws," Antoninus Opellius Macrinus interjected. "Miaou!" he purred, as he shot a poisonous glare at Sands.

"Speak plainly, Galla Placidia," the magistrate instructed. He swept his arm around the room to encompass all the spectators. "If you have an objection to the conduct of this tribunal, then state it clearly so we all may hear."

"Your Eminence, the law of *laesa maiestas* makes no allowance for the inclusion of other public offences, no matter how grave, to be heard by a special tribunal such as this."

"You are entirely correct, Galla Placidia, but no such charges will be laid against you in this tribunal. Only those encompassed under the *Ad legem Iuliam maiestatis* can be prosecuted here."

"But why is Caeluibianus Claudius Asinianus being allowed to allege crimes of murder that do not fall within the authority of this tribunal to consider? It will be prejudicial to my defence."

The magistrate looked at Sands in confusion. He conferred with the two judges sitting on either side of him before responding. "The tribunal recognises that no such conflict exists. The practice of informing a court of all details relevant to an accusation is well accepted across the Empire. On what grounds could you possibly object to all facts being known, other than to thwart the application of justice?"

"I object on the grounds that these details are not facts at all. They are being presented to the court as such, but are simply no more than half-truths or lies. The accuser is exploiting these alleged crimes as a pretext in order to defame me in the eyes of the tribunal."

"Aha, a clear acknowledgement of guilt, if ever I heard one!" cried Antoninus Opellius Macrinus. "In my experience, whenever a litigant assigns to themselves the right to pick and choose which facts should be presented to a public court then it can be taken as a clear sign that they are guilty as accused. Suppress the facts and the truth will out, she says, and I riposte that it is by such means that justice is turned on its head!"

The magistrate sat back in his seat with a satisfied smile. "Well refuted, Antoninus Opellius Macrinus. What say you to counteract that logic, young woman? Do you not agree that false accusations, if that's indeed what they are, are best addressed by direct rebuttal, not censorship?"

"False accusations have no place in any courtroom, especially when they are vindictively prosecuted for personal gain. Rome has long-since grown sickened by the bringing of false charges against the accused," she continued, glancing down at her own hand-inscribed papyrus notes. "Tacitus specifically warned about men like him," she said, theatrically pointing at Caeluibianus, "*delatores* who make a practice of bearing false witness against innocent parties. Tacitus described these men of bad faith as being driven by "stealthy informations, following which beggars become wealthy, the insignificant, formidable, bringing ruin first on others and finally on themselves." The warning explicit in Tacitus' words should be well marked in this courtroom."

The magistrate absorbed Sands' appeal with mounting irritation. "I am overly familiar with the works of the noble jurist, particularly the *Annales* to which you refer, and do not require instruction from an untutored woman as to the proper application of their strictures in my own courthouse."

"My apologies, Your Eminence, I merely sought to clarify my concerns not merely on a judicial point but also on ethical grounds of grave concern to Roman jurists everywhere. The eyes of the legal experts will soon be poring over every line in the transcription of this trial. I notice that the scribes already have their attentions fully focused on the proceedings."

The magistrate looked discomfited. The sight of the scribes scribbling away gave him pause for thought. He turned to the two judges for advice. After a few moments of conferring, he turned his attention back to Sands. "You seek to play a very clever game, my girl, but I would warn you - do not abuse the licence you are being granted in this courtroom."

Sands smiled. "Nothing could be further from my intention, your noble Eminence."

The magistrate peered at her closely. "Am I right in saying that you have no possessions to speak of, no land, no inheritance, no funds?"

"That is correct, sir. I am a woman of few means. I own the clothes I stand up in and precious little else, perhaps half a dozen book-rolls on legal procedure."

"In which case, perhaps you could kindly explain the motive for Caeluibianus making false accusations against you? In a successful prosecution he would expect to be awarded the largest share of your estate. Tacitus, whose opinion you seem to value so highly, makes special mention of the greed of the *delatores*. But in your case, your self-proclaimed poverty would appear to preclude such a motive from Caeluibianus Claudius Asinianus' actions."

A great sigh of satisfaction swept around the courtroom. The spectators leant forward as if united in a single body to hear what devilish strategy Sands would employ to wriggle out of the trap laid for her by the magistrate.

She examined her enemy across the courtroom. Caeluibianus was perspiring under the glare of her scrutiny. His skinny features looked callow and clammy, sweat dotted his brow and upper lip. He licked his lips. His earlier self-assurance had now evaporated, leaving in its wake a peevish and crotchety alter-ego.

"He is motivated by a need to do me harm. I can't explain it any better than that."

Antoninus Opellius Macrinus leapt to his feet. "Oh, is that really the best explanation you can offer the court, Galla Placidia? You intimated so much and yet – let me put this as delicately as I can to spare the blushes of the ladies present - like any prick-teaser you failed to deliver the anticipated climax that your promises augured."

Bouts of riotous laughter greeted these words, the tribunal panel members relishing the crudity of the remark more than anyone. Sands, for her part, was enjoying seeing Caeluibianus sweat. She didn't mind being the butt of a few jokes if it suited her purposes. And while the courtroom was rocking with merriment, Sands seized the opportunity to examine Caeluibianus closely once more. He glared at her. His apparent animosity towards her reminded Sands strangely of Tufayyur's openly resentful manner. The connection hit Sands with the force of an electric shock. "Of course!" she thought. "He doesn't hate me. He resents me!"

Antoninus Opellius Macrinus waited for silence to return before addressing the magistrate once more. "In the absence of any coherent explanation as to why Caeluibianus Claudius Asinianus would profit from making a malicious accusation against Galla Placidia, I suggest we proceed, your Eminence, by asking my client to continue laying out the facts as he knows them to be."

The magistrate looked at Sands in a quizzical, patronising manner. "Ah, yes indeed. The facts. What with all the digressions, I'm afraid we're rather in danger of overlooking them altogether. I trust you don't have any objections, young lady, if we return to the matter in hand?"

"There's just one question I'd like to put to Caeluibianus Claudius Asinianus, your Eminence. I think his response might help shed some clarity on this entire matter."

Antoninus Opellius Macrinus leapt to his feet once more. "Oh, this is really too much!" The paid *claques* groaned audibly in support of their man. "She is making a mockery of this trial."

Cries of "Shame!" and "Sit down, in the name of the Gods!" could be heard echoing around the courthouse.

"Silence!" the magistrate ordered the public galleries. "This is your last indulgence," he instructed Sands. "I will allow you one question. That's one question, and one question only, and then we must proceed, do you understand me?"

Sands nodded her agreement to the magistrate. She paused for a moment and took a deep breath. She looked Caeluibianus up and down and then waited for complete silence to descend before asking her question. "Caeluibianus Claudius Asinianus, do you owe me your life, and, if so, is your persecution of me motivated by a need to avenge this debt that you owe me?"

The courtroom erupted in uproar.

"That's two questions," shouted Antoninus Opellius Macrinus, "two questions! Your Eminence, I implore you to reject this provocative line of questioning."

"I did say you could put one question only," agreed the magistrate. "Caeluibianus Claudius Asinianus, feel free to ignore the second question, but I must insist you address the first one. Do you owe Galla Placidia your life? A simple yes or no will suffice."

"Really, Your Eminence, I must protest," the advocate interjected, but his appeal was waved aside by the magistrate. His supporters threw up their hands in dismay and set up a rumble of disapproval.

Caeluibianus, by now, was appearing to look unwell. He was derailed by the question put to him by Sands. His physical reaction to the unexpectedness of it was shocking to those sitting next to him. He looked at his advocate for support but none was forthcoming. "You must answer the question, as instructed by the magistrate," Antoninus Opellius Macrinus reminded him. "A simple no will suffice."

Caeluibianus looked dumbly at his advocate. "I don't understand the question."

226

Antoninus Opellius Macrinus repeated his advice to his client. "Just say no, Caeluibianus Claudius Asinianus, if that is the truth."

Caeluibianus stood up and started to wobble. "Forgive me, I'm not well. I need some water. She is poisoning my mind." He gestured towards Sands.

"Answer the question," she demanded.

"I am ill, Your Eminence."

"Pull yourself together, man, you're a cohort Tribune and a company *Praepositus*. When you're in my courthouse, you'll acquit yourself in a manner demanded of your rank and status. You have the reputation of your unit to protect."

"She's done this to me," he replied, pointing at Sands once again. "She's rendered me unable to speak."

Sands turned to the three tribunal members and appealed to them directly. "These accusations are an insult to your reason. If he has become ill, it's only because of his obsessive need to revenge himself on me. His illness is simply an expression of an inner conflict that he cannot come to terms with through rational means."

Caeluibianus staggered forward and collapsed. He appeared to be suffering violent convulsions.

The spectators rose from their seats in shock. This was a dramatic *coup de theatre*, even by Antoninus Opellius Macrinus' notorious standards.

"He's not faking it, Sands," whispered Birch. "He looks like he's really having a seizure."

"You're not wrong, there. Penny to a pound it's non-epileptic, though. I bet his seizure's provoked by an emotional crisis. It was triggered by my question just now."

"You can say that again."

"Yeah, it's got bugger all to do with abnormal electrical activity in the brain. That's what makes his animosity so scary. It's irrational."

Meanwhile, the general hubbub in the courtroom continued unabated. The noise, if anything, appeared to be intensifying. Finally, the magistrate succeeded in making himself heard over the tumult. "Lictors, clear the way to allow Caeluibianus Claudius Asinianus to receive medical treatment. We will suspend further consideration of the case until he is fit to continue outlining his charges against the accused. The business of this court is hereby duly suspended."

TWENTY-NINE

Location: Volubilis, Mauretania Tingitana
Coordinates: 34° 03' 36" N and 5° 33' 00" W

Time and Date: 12.00, 6th September, 258 C.E.

Sands cast an anxious glance at Birch. For an hour they'd been detained in a stuffy cell in the basilica, passing the time dissecting the morning's events. Now they were growing impatient.

"I'll tell you what, Birch, Bostar's clocked you. You need to watch your back."

"You need to stop thinking about other people, Sands, and start worrying about yourself."

She ignored his advice. "Is there any news from Tufayyur about Ojo and Azulay?"

"Not yet. Antalas has sent out a warning that there's a shit-storm headed their way. He's got contacts in every village between here and Alexandria."

"You think they'll get the message?"

"If anyone can find them, he can."

Sands looked unconvinced. She turned to the window.

"Birch, I need to thank you for something."

Birch was taken aback. "Thank me? What for?"

"Tufayyur told me you've been watching the rear of the house every night."

"Oh that? That's no big deal," he mumbled. "I ran a security check on the property. There was one vulnerable entrance. Anyone wanting to harm you would've had to get in through the back door."

"I just wanted to say thanks. I didn't expect you to do that every night."

Birch adjusted his position. "Like I said, it's no big deal. What else am I going to do with my time?"

"Really, you didn't have to do that." She placed her hand on his shoulder.

"Yes, I did," he shot back. "You don't seem to realise you're all I've got."

Now it was Sands' turn to be taken aback.

"Are you serious? I'm all you've got?"

"Apart from Ojo, I guess."

Sands shook her head. "I'm not sure how to react, Birch. I know we've never seen eye to eye, exactly."

"That's an understatement."

"I don't know what to say."

"Don't say anything. Just win that case in there."

"I just don't get you. For some reason you've always played the officer jackass. Your bullshit has worn me out."

He shrugged. "It's my inheritance, my legacy. I can't seem to help myself."

Sands shot him a dubious look. "Just can't help yourself, huh?"

"I suffer from the same condition as Stogdon."

"An interesting comparison."

"I've never been able to express myself as easily as you have."

"This is no time to act the victim," she replied. "Own your feelings. Start taking a few risks."

He shook his head. "Nice try, Sands, I wish I could. I've blown it."

"Blown what? Now you're being melodramatic."

"Don't you regret not having done certain things?"

"Where are you going with this? I'm facing a death penalty and you're tiptoeing around like a fucking teenager. Come on, get to the point. Take a risk."

"Like not having told certain people how much they mean to you."

"Here we go. Is that your roundabout way of referring to me, Birch?"

"You know it is. Don't milk it."

"Yay, you like me," Sands smiled.

"Stop taking the piss. I knew I should've kept my bloody mouth shut."

"I'm not entirely stupid, Birch. I knew you didn't really hate me, despite all your off-handedness."

"I bloody well did, though. You could be a self-righteous little prick when the mood took you."

"Okay, so maybe you did at first. Yeah, you really hated me back then. But at least you've said it now. Now you actually quite like me. Fancy that! Birch quite likes me!"

"Well done me, yeah? A bit late in the day, though."

"I told you, it's never too late. I'm the one facing an imminent death penalty, not you."

"I'm lost. I mean it. I don't think I'll be able to cope without you, Sands."

"Don't be morbid. Fingers crossed you won't have to."

"But you're all that's got me through this last year."

Sands could feel her body respond. She couldn't quite identify the strange cocktail of emotions that began to stir in her. A feeling of guilt, mixed with equal measures of irritation and regret, seemed to be the principal ingredients. But there was another less identifiable emotion mixed in there. And she didn't want to put a name to it. She responded in the only way she felt capable. She put her arms around his shoulders and gave him a reassuring hug. She could feel him exhaling long, cathartic breaths.

"It's okay, Birch, we'll get through this - you and me."

"You and me and Ojo. Don't forget Ojo."

"Yeah, let's not forget dear old Ojo."

Birch sighed, drew in a few deep breaths and sat down with a look of bemused satisfaction. He wore the wistful expression of a man who'd become reacquainted with an old friend after many years of separation.

Sands needed to refocus. "I've got a strange question for you, Birch."

"What other kind is there?"

"Do you believe you are real?"

"Last time I checked."

"I mean do you believe what is happening to us is real?"

Birch's demeanour changed suddenly. "Okay, that's an altogether different question. I'd answer yes to the first question, jury's out on the second one. Why do you ask?"

"That's interesting," Sands mused to herself. "You see, I'd say the exact reverse. I'd say no to the second question, jury's out on the first one. I do feel real, but it's a strange sort of reality"

"What are you getting at?"

"I feel like I'm living in a huge experiment. The more I think about it the more I'm sure of it. So are you."

"Thanks, that's reassuring."

"But I'm not so sure about everyone else, though. What about Caeluibianus, Tufayyur, Antoninus Opellius Macrinus and all the rest of them out there? Are they definitely real?"

"Who knows?" he replied. "I can only speak for myself. *They* may not be real, but how about *us*?"

He paused, as if intending to answer his own question. And then a different thought occurred to him. "Can you ever remember feeling so *alive*?"

"How do you mean?"

"It's been bugging me."

"What has?"

"It seems so clear. I've never felt so alive, ever - not even when I was a kid, or a soldier in Afghanistan. I've never felt as alive as I do now, right this minute."

"Bloody hell, Birch, you're right."

Sands squatted down next to him in order to engage him. "You're right, we've never been so alive. It's the environment that's lifeless! Everyone else simply *acts* as if they're real."

Birch wiped the sweat from his brow. "But if they're not real, they're pretty damn convincing."

"That's exactly the point. When in the real world did you ever describe a human being as being "pretty damn convincing"?"

"Never."

"Never would be my guess, too."

Birch nodded. "So on what side of the equation do the two of us belong then?"

"You mean are we real or are we fake?"

"That's the question. Are we shape-shifting clusters of binary information or human beings with souls?"

"I know what I'd say. Don't forget all the rest of the baggage we traditionally carry around with us. I may not have all the answers, but there's more to me than a bunch of zeros and ones. And I know there's something out there that wants me to behave like I'm a convincing human. I've just no idea what the hell it is. But it's out there and it's trying to control me."

"But what about those guys back there? Don't forget about them," Birch added, pointing back to the courtroom. "Don't you think they're a big enough threat to be going on with?"

"What, you mean Caeluibianus and the others? Yeah, I believe they can hurt me. But do they feel like the ultimate threat to me? No, not particularly."

Birch looked concerned. "That's dangerous talk, Sands. I'm worried you're taking your eye of the ball. Ultimate threat or not, you're still going to have to fight for your life in that courtroom. Your guerrilla tactics may have helped you edge things so far. But you need a proper strategy if you're going to survive that tribunal."

Sands leant forward in a conspiratorial manner. "Here's what I'm thinking. I'm facing an external existential threat, but it's not manifested in these Romans. It's coming from somewhere else."

She glanced around to indicate to Birch that she feared being overheard. "It's emanating from something else. It's a mysterious, all-encompassing force. Or it likes to think it is."

"You think people are eavesdropping on us?"

"Not those guys," she replied, gesturing towards the two guards standing outside their cell.

"You mean out there?" he asked, raising his eyes heavenwards.

"Uh-huh."

"Are you really serious?"

Sands nodded.

"In that case, you'll have to juggle with fighting on three fronts at once. Not only have you got to contend with the judges and placate the rowdy spectators, but you've also got to offset this other mysterious force. The spectators can be swayed, so they're the easiest to deal with."

"How do you come to that conclusion?"

"There's no doubt. Just keep banging on with the oratory and rhetorical flourishes. Treat them like they're a rowdy music hall crowd – they'll lap it up. Go all Shakespearean on them; they'll be none the wiser, but they'll love it."

"But I still don't see how I can get them on my side. They don't like me. I can feel it. As far as they're concerned, I'm a traitor who's been slaughtering their sons and brothers. And I don't entirely blame them."

"When you put it like that, neither do I."

"So what do I do?"

"Keep it local, Sands, make it relevant to things that will touch them."

"Like what?" The sweat was beginning to trickle down Sands' back.

"I don't know – anything – storks, camels, oleanders. You'll think of something. If you're going to go all metaphorical and allegorical, at least talk about something they can relate to."

Sands pulled a face. "Ok, I'll give it a shot. I have had a thought about the best way to deal with the judges, though."

"Excellent - let's hear it."

"I'm never going to win by arguing points of law. It'll be like trying to whip Deep Blue at chess – it's just not going to happen. Those guys are programmed to the nth degree."

"I agree. So what're you thinking?"

"I'm not going to get anywhere by disputing the small print of Pliny the Younger's correspondence with Trajan, because the details are a matter of public record. There's no point arguing with the tribunal panel about what's been said by whom. If I'm right, they've already been fully programmed with complete knowledge of all classical sources."

"That's a fairly big assumption."

Sands ignored his warning and ploughed ahead. "However, this strength could also be their Achilles' heel. They don't know what they don't know. I think it's something I could try to exploit."

Birch sat up. Now he was getting interested. "You mean their weakness is what they *don't* know?"

Sands nodded. "How can they check the accuracy of facts that don't exist? They'll be flummoxed."

Birch lit up. The tempting nature of the hypothesis was beginning to intrigue him. "You're saying they're capable of arguing with what *has* been said, but they can't dispute what's *not* been said?"

"Exactly, it's worth a try, isn't it? Let's see how adaptable they can be. Let's see if they can respond intuitively when tossed an unexpected problem. Can they respond like real humans?"

Their conversation was interrupted by the sound of shouts coming from the corridor leading to their cell. A guard was bellowing instructions from outside the doorway. "The magistrate wants you back in the courtroom now."

Sands rubbed her hands on her knees. "That's us, Birch." She shot him a determined smile. "Caeluibianus must be back on his feet and raring to go."

Birch leapt up. "Good luck, Sands. That bastard's got no choice but to hit you with everything he's got."

As they moved to the door he gave her an encouraging pat on the back. "Remember, he needs to get this over and done with as quickly as possible. Let him get started, and then take him down - once and for all."

And within ten minutes they were back in the courtroom. The magistrate instructed the prosecution to continue with vigour. "If the accusations are proved then we can proceed straight to the implementation of the sentence this afternoon. The bonfire for the execution is already being constructed."

The public gallery nodded in general approval of the magistrate's ruling. Birch glanced at Sands in alarm.

Antoninus Opellius Macrinus took heed of the tribunal's wishes and responded with suitable robustness. "That bitch, that traitorous harlot, incited an act of sedition that directly led to the death of six brave sons of Mauretania. The mother of one of these poor boys you can see sitting next to me – destitute, heartbroken and inconsolable." He gestured to an elderly woman on his right who burst into tears.

The spectators emitted a great sigh of pity, a rolling wave of contrived sympathy, while the distraught mother wailed and tore at her clothing.

"Oh, my god, this is so disgusting," whispered Sands.

The Roman advocate was basking in his element. "But, fellow citizens, it gets much worse than this. These abominable crimes - tragic though their effects were - merely serve as appetisers when compared with the seditious treachery that Galla Placidia has practiced against the safety of the Roman people." He paused, just long enough to milk the suffering of the bereaved mother and to leave the spectators hanging in suspense at the nature of the heinous crimes that were yet to be revealed.

Sands could tolerate no more. She rose from her bench with a cry of frustration. "Your Eminence, if proof does exist of my alleged treason then the court must demand that it is sourced from the mouth of a reliable witness, rather than being plucked like an oleander flower from the fanciful imagination of an over-paid lawyer."

A spontaneous round of merriment greeted her remark. The odd cheer inter-mingled with the laughter. The magistrate called for silence but found it difficult to make himself heard above the hubbub.

Birch lent across and whispered. "Nice one, Sands, the crowd liked your spirit. Look how it's put the judges on the back foot."

The magistrate called for silence once more. He addressed Antoninus Opellius Macrinus. "Has Caeluibianus Claudius Asinianus recovered sufficiently to give evidence in support of his accusations of treason against Galla Placidia?"

Caeluibianus nodded his assent.

"In that case, let the truth be told," the magistrate pronounced.

Caeluibianus continued giving evidence but seemed very out of sorts. He rocked on his heels and swore with a reckless abandon. The floor around his feet became pockmarked with droplets of sweat from his brow.

"These things I have witnessed with my own eyes. Firstly, the freeing of justly confined prisoners and the murder of their jailer, secondly the seizing of hostages, thirdly the violent occupation of a military *Principia*, fourthly the conspiracy to murder hostages, fifthly the destruction and defilement of imperial standards and insignia bearing the emperor's name and image."

"Let's deal immediately with the fifth accusation," Sands demanded. "You say you witnessed this act of desecration with your own eyes?"

"I did."

"In which case, perhaps you'd like to explain to the court exactly how I was able to perform this alleged crime?"

Caeluibianus' eyes darted around the courtroom. "Through the application of witchcraft and fire."

The crowd emitted a shocked cry.

"Through the application of witchcraft and fire," she repeated. She turned to the public gallery with an indulgent smile. "Really, you expect this courtroom to believe that that's what occurred? I am a woman. You are twice my size. Why did you not try and stop me from defiling the Emperor's image, if what you claim is true?"

Caeluibianus' eyes darted around the courtroom. "I was unable to stop her, Your Eminence. I was powerless to intervene in the face of such sorcery."

"Really?" Sands countered. "You were powerless to intervene? What were you doing – cowering in the corner next to your commander-in-chief? Shame on you!"

Sands paused to allow the power of her condemnation to sink in. "In your testimony, you ascribe great powers to me. If what you say is true, why would I not choose to immolate you now and walk freely from this courtroom?"

The implicit threat made Caeluibianus stagger backwards.

"You stumble, Caeluibianus Claudius Asinianus. When asked a direct question, I would expect a cohort tribune to be as sure-footed as a camel. Why does the nature of my interrogation disturb your equilibrium so?"

Sniggers could be heard from the gallery. Some spectators were exacting pleasure from Caeluibianus' discomfiture.

Caeluibianus turned to the tribunal panel in desperation. "Your Excellencies, that bitch is attempting to confound me with her trickery. You can see the evidence with your own eyes. She is a sorceress and a seditious conspirator."

Sands observed him with a cold detachment. Now she had him where she wanted him.

"I'm no physician, Caeluibianus Claudius Asinianus, but it would appear to me that the apparent imbalance in your humours can be ascribed to an internal conflict for which you are alone responsible. Your unjust persecution of me has created a surplus of choleric bile that conflicts with your naturally sanguine humour. Your natural element is air, not fire. Beware you don't tumble from the sky altogether."

"Any imbalance in my humours is directly attributable to the malevolent effects of your proximity to me in this courtroom, and nothing else."

Sands shook her head. She turned to show the extent of her concern to the public gallery. "If that's what you are determined to believe, then so be it. But please don't be convinced for a minute that the rest of this courtroom is deluded enough to share your misapprehension."

"Go fuck yourself, you shameless whore! Your Eminence, this is an abomination. I am a man of honour. I have come here to fulfil my civic duty as a Roman citizen. And yet the accused has been granted license to make *me* the subject of a ritual, public humiliation. Where is the justice in that?"

Antoninus Opellius Macrinus attempted to stem the tide that was running against his client. He urged his paid *claques* to respond with sympathetic applause.

Sands waited till there was complete silence in the courtroom. "You'd do well to mark the migration patterns of the stork,

Caeluibianus Claudius Asinianus. The physical laws of nature are immutable and you challenge them at your own personal risk. As everyone in Volubilis knows, the stork thrives when living in harmony with the constraints imposed by nature, not by attempting to overrule them. When flying overland our native storks are borne aloft on clouds of warm air, but when they encounter the vast waters of the *mare nostrum* the atmospheric conditions change dramatically. They must divert their migration course in order to pass over Tingi, where the straits are narrowest, or risk descending into the watery depths. And the moral of this story? Maintain a proper balance in all things, as nature and the gods intended, and happiness is the guarantee, a life lived in delicate harmony with ourselves and our fellow men the result. But attempt to disturb the equilibrium by a single particle of dust, alter the balance of the weighing scales by the tiniest measure, and behold what unhappy disharmony ensues."

Utter quiet descended upon the courtroom. The public gallery held its collective breath. Sands' oratory had cast a spell over the audience. And then a lone individual dared the other spectators to respond. He stood up and shouted, jolting everyone else out of their stunned silence. Soon he was joined in enthusiastic applause by the others in the seats next to him, and then by those in the rows in front and behind. Finally, it seemed that the whole crowd, excluding the inscrutable *claques*, was united in response. Sands' rhetoric had struck a chord that echoed across the courtroom.

"Excellent, Sands," echoed Birch, "Shakespeare couldn't have put it any better."

"I think you'll find he already has, but thanks anyway."

The magistrate called the courtroom to order. His broad grin suggested he was enjoying the unfolding drama as much as anyone.

Antoninus Opellius Macrinus rose to his feet once more. "Yes, yes, yes," he pronounced, as if dismissing the excesses of a hyperactive child, "I do hope the public gallery is marking well this final serenade." He pointed at Sands. "Just look at her in

239

all her glory. The accused resembles nothing so much as a plump young peafowl. She's so mesmerised with the glory of her own display and the iridescence of her plumage, that she's conveniently forgotten that at any minute she'll be whisked away to the kitchen where she'll be plucked, gutted, trussed up and roasted to a crisp in the oven. *Sic transit gloria mundi.*" The advocate paused to allow Caeluibianus and his *claques* to hoot with laughter. "However, no amount of distracting warbling can detract from the cold facts in this case. Galla Placidia is guilty, as charged, and will soon be paying with her life. The crime of treason demands and deserves and will receive the death penalty."

"Did he just say "*Sic transit gloria mundi*'?" whispered Sands.

"Yeah, I think so."

"It may be Latin, but it's not Roman. It's Roman Catholic. Someone's screwed up. I'd swear that expression dates from the middle ages."

"Are you sure?"

"Completely certain. It's part of the Christian ritual for the coronation of a new Pope."

"In that case, you're assessment is right, Sands. This is all an elaborately staged ritual."

The next witness was Bostar. He gave his evidence in staccato bursts. Evidently, he was having great difficulty in both remembering his lines with any accuracy and delivering them with any conviction, although neither consideration appeared to be of the slightest concern to the tribunal panel. He danced to the tune of the advocate, making up stories here, lying there, and generally having a field day with the truth. Sands attempted to cross-examine him. She was shouted down by the magistrate, who appeared eager to get things wrapped up by lunchtime and to have the execution bonfire roaring by mid-afternoon.

"He's moving towards passing judgement," warned Birch. "Just look at the three of them up there – they're eager to get this over with."

Sands looked at the magistrate. Birch was right; she could sense what was coming. It was now or never. She had to act.

"Your Excellencies," she shouted. "I wish to invoke my right as a Roman citizen to be tried in Rome."

The magistrate looked at her in stunned amazement.

"If accused of treason, a Roman citizen has the right to be tried in Rome," she repeated. "I wish to invoke that right."

A murmur of surprise went up from the public gallery.

Caeluibianus and his advocate both leapt straight to their feet. "This is an outrage, Your Eminence," protested Antoninus Opellius Macrinus. "The accused refers to a right that is intended expressly for a noble-born individual of status, not for some low-born trickster who presumes to push their luck at the expense of natural justice."

Sands responded with vigour. "In the second year of his reign, the emperor Marcus Aurelius Severus Antoninus Augustus, whose noble memory is consecrated in the nearby arch erected in his name, passed an edict declaring that all free men in the Empire be given Roman citizenship."

Antoninus Opellius Macrinus appealed in desperation to the magistrate. "But Galla Placidia is a woman, Your Eminence. This is a fact that she conveniently tends to disguise, I'll grant you, but she is a woman, none the less, and as such, she is not entitled to claim any right to Roman citizenship under the terms of the said edict."

Sands protested. "Under the terms of this very edict, free women were also granted the same rights as Roman women."

"Ah, but not the right to Roman citizenship - the two things are entirely different."

The magistrate nodded his head in agreement. "I'm inclined to agree with Antoninus Opellius Macrinus' interpretation on this point."

"Time to play your trump card, Sands," whispered Birch.

"But, Your Eminence," she countered, "that specific inconsistency has now been eradicated with the edict passed during the second year of the joint consuls Publius Licinius Valerianus Augustus and Publius Licinius Egnatius Gallienus Augustus. I'm sure you would agree with me on this point."

Sands shot Birch a knowing glance.

The magistrate and the two judges looked startled. They huddled in furious consultation, unsure as to how to respond to this perplexing question.

"Your Excellencies," Antoninus Opellius Macrinus appealed, "this is an entirely fallacious and duplicitous argument. I call upon you to reject it."

"On what grounds, Antoninus Opellius Macrinus?" asked the magistrate. He was relieved to be given the chance to shift the responsibility on to the advocates' shoulders rather than to make a ruling himself. "Can you rebut the legal arguments advanced by the accused?"

Antoninus Opellius Macrinus was engaged in frantic consultations with his legal team. He turned around and addressed the magistrate. "I wouldn't dare to impugn the legality of any imperial edict, Your Eminence. But, in this case, I suspect that the motive of the accused is not an honourable one; she is simply attempting to exercise her rights in order to evade the justice of this court."

"That's as may be. But are you able to prove that what she says is not true?"

The advocate was floundering. His sweating, purple face was cruel evidence of his discomfiture. "But she can't be allowed to get away with it," was all he could muster by way of a response. "Your Eminence, I implore you to cast aside any doubts and find against the bitch."

"I think you might have got him," laughed Birch. "Squirm, you bastard!"

The magistrate called for calm in the courtroom. "I have to satisfy myself on one more point before I make my final judgement. I will only agree for this trial to be heard in Rome if Galla Placidia can prove to the satisfaction of this court that she fulfils the one remaining requirement of Caracalla's edict that she has so far failed to address."

Sands looked stunned. "I don't understand, Your Eminence, what else is there to prove?"

Caeluibianus detected a sudden chink of light. He sat up with a start. Maybe all was not yet lost on the prosecution's side. That bitch could burn after all.

"We've already established that all free men in the Empire were granted the right to Roman citizenship under the edict passed in the second year of the reign of Marcus Aurelius Severus Antoninus Augustus. We've also agreed that women were subsequently granted the same right to citizenship under the terms of the same edict and these rights were then reinforced two years ago under the joint consulship of Publius Licinius Valerianus Augustus and Publius Licinius Egnatius Gallienus Augustus. What is not in doubt in this case is the fact that a Roman citizen, which is what Galla Placidia claims to be, has the right to be tried in Rome when accused of the crime of treason."

Sands looked at him in confusion. "Everything you say is correct, Your Eminence, so what other proof could you require of my eligibility to invoke such a right?"

"There's one final, crucial piece of the equation missing, Galla Placidia. Without this evidence, you will not be leaving the confines of this jurisdiction. In fact, I can guarantee that, without this proof, you will be summarily sentenced to death by means of public burning."

The shock of his statement caused Sands to emit an involuntary cry. The blood drained from her face. "What proof do you require of me?"

"Proof that you are, in fact, free-born. Without this proof you would have no right to citizenship."

The magistrate's words hit Sands like a rock. She felt a jolt of fear shoot through her system.

"I have no proof," she whispered to Birch. "I'm done for."

Birch looked scared. "I'll do it."

"Would you accept the word of my brother, here?" she asked in despair.

The magistrate laughed. "And who would you recommend to vouch for your brother's status as a free-born man? You perhaps?" Guffaws of amusement could be heard from the public gallery. "No, Galla Placidia, you'll have to do better than that. I'm not allowing you to submit your own testimonial. I will require a sworn authentication from a respected, upstanding Roman citizen, someone well known in the city and beyond, a man of substance, a man of moral rectitude, a man of honour who is true to his word."

Suddenly there was a commotion at the back of the court.

"Is my word sufficient?" cried a loud, anonymous voice.

The litigants leapt up. There was uproar among the spectators.

"Who said that?" demanded the magistrate. "Speak up!"

"I'll attest to her free-born status," the disembodied voice shouted in response.

Four hundred necks craned in unison to see who was speaking.

"Show yourself, whoever you are!" ordered the magistrate. "And the rest of you, sit down."

A middle-aged, balding man rose wearily to his feet. The crowd emitted a hum of recognition.

"Antalas Alfassi, is that you?" the magistrate bellowed, as he peered through a sea of turned heads.

"It is indeed, Your Eminence," replied the Berber.

Sands beamed in bewilderment to see her old friend struggling to his feet on her behalf.

"Come forward and testify at the front where you can be identified clearly," the magistrate ordered. "This is not some kind of market place. We don't conduct our dealings under the cloak of anonymity in this courtroom."

Antalas vacated his seat slowly and made his way to the front of the courtroom. His dignified bearing was greeted with approving nods from the majority of the spectators. A few opponents, rather predictably, took a different approach; they hissed and whistled rudely as he took his oath and prepared to give his testimony.

"You are a Jew, are you not?"

"I am, and a proud Berber."

"How long have your family lived in Mauretania Tingitana?"

"My family have lived here for over twenty generations, Your Eminence; they moved here from Judaea long before the destruction of the second temple in Jerusalem. My great grandfather was granted Roman citizenship under the edict of the Emperor Caracalla. I'd remind the court that, along with many other new citizens of Oualili, he was forced to pay for the city's ceremonial arch that was erected in the Emperor's honour."

A rivulet of heads bobbed up and down in silent acknowledgement.

"So what are the circumstances that enable you to confirm the free-born status of Galla Placidia?"

"I have known her father, Quintus Placidius Scapula, for many years. He is a respected and wealthy wool merchant from Eboracum in the province of Britannia. Our two families have had business dealings for several generations."

Antoninus Opellius Macrinus threw his hands up in mock outrage. "What proof is there of this claim?" he demanded.

"Do you doubt my word, you scoundrel?" Antalas barked. He turned on the advocate with a look of implacable fury. "If so, you should be prepared to defend a suit of defamation."

"Compose yourself, Antalas Alfassi," the magistrate warned, "the prosecution is entitled to subject your testimony to proper scrutiny." He then turned to Antoninus Opellius Macrinus, to whom he directed his next questions. "Do you have any reason to doubt the word of Antalas Alfassi? Do you have any proof that what he claims is not true?"

The advocate looked at a loss for words. "Do I have any proof that what he claims is not true?" he echoed.

"Yes, well done," the magistrate replied, "that is what I asked, but in case you're still in any doubt, let me repeat the question. Do you have any proof that what he claims is not true?"

Antoninus Opellius Macrinus spun around and sought frantic assistance from his legal team. Bostar leant forward and shook his head in response to a series of urgent enquiries from the advocate. Finally, Caeluibianus entered the fray and began disputing with his legal representative, much to the amusement of the spectators in the public gallery.

"Antoninus Opellius Macrinus, do not make me ask you again!" shouted the magistrate.

The advocate jumped in alarm. His appearance seemed fraught and dishevelled, a far cry from the dapper and urbane façade he'd earlier presented in court. He stared at the tribunal panel with a look of deep embarrassment, unsure of how best to frame his response. Finally, with an agonising display of reluctance, he opened his mouth and spoke three simple words, "No, I don't," and then sat down again.

The public gallery erupted with unconcealed delight. Even the *claque*s appeared to be enjoying the drama of the moment.

The magistrate nodded to the judges and delivered his judgement. "In that case, and in the absence of any compelling argument to the contrary, I have no option but to suspend this prosecution and to uphold the accused's right to stand trial for treason in Rome."

Sands whooped with delight and punched the air. The sound of her celebration carried across the court. The spectators thrilled to her exultation and paid tribute by saluting her victory in a similar manner. Soon the whole court was jumping with glee.

Caeluibianus, however, was implacable. He thrust his advocate's commiserations aside and eyed Sands with a vengeful glare. Bostar made threatening gestures towards her and shouted obscenities across the court. Birch put a protective arm around his colleague and ushered her towards Antalas.

The magistrate struggled to make himself heard and summoned additional guards to restore order. "This is disgraceful behaviour," he complained to little avail. "I command you to compose yourselves in a manner befitting a Roman courthouse."

Sands was exultant. She could acknowledge that she'd been moments away from being burned alive at the stake. Although she knew her moment of triumph might be short lived, she had scored a substantial victory. As the guards surrounded her once more she shouted some final instructions to Birch. "All I've won is some breathing space, Birch. You're going to have start organising things to secure my release."

"Stay brave, Sands, we won't give up on you, I promise."

She squeezed his outstretched hand.

"I must thank Antalas. Where is he?"

"There," pointed Birch.

"Antalas, my friend, thank you!" she shouted, "I owe you my life. I will never be able to repay you."

He acknowledged her thanks with a sad bow of his head. She could see that tears were staining his cheeks. "Thank Tufayyur, not me," was his only response.

By now order had been restored in the court and the magistrate rose once more to issue a proclamation.

"I order that Galla Placidia will be taken into custody and transferred immediately under armed guard to Rome. She is not to be released under bail and will not be permitted the further luxury of house arrest. Her security falls under my jurisdiction for as long as she remains in detention in Volubilis. I will hand over responsibility for her transfer to Rome to the provincial governor, a move which will be expedited in the next few days. Guards, remove the prisoner to a place of detention."

"This isn't over, Sands," shouted Birch, as she was led from the court under armed guard, "not by a long shot. Keep your head up, girl."

As she was pulled from view he could just make out her last yelled instructions to him, "Thank Tufayyur, Birch. Tell her I'll never forget what she's done for me."

THIRTY

Aballava Tablet No. 10, Inventory No 13.29 (Morris Archive)

Caeluibianus, Cohort Tribune and Praepositus of the Company, to Julius Rufinus, Tribunus Laticlavius and commander-in-chief, I send my greetings. In the matter of determining the fate of Galla Placidia (undertaken in the utmost secrecy as directed) I have done so in full accordance with your wishes and have set out my findings below. I can scarcely bring myself to impart the news, my Lord, but Galla Placidia has contrived to escape the executioner's torch, at least in the short term. Instead of facing death, she is to be transported to Rome for trial, a judgement that defies all logic and rational understanding. Throughout the hearing she regarded the courtroom as little more than her own private fiefdom, a playground in which she felt free to play the bully and exercise her own rules. I'll concede that she played a devilishly clever game, this treacherous little harlot, one minute assuming the part of the simpering ingénue, the next the role of the cold eyed assassin, all the while camouflaging her intentions behind a subtle curtain of concealment. She was more than a match for our over-paid advocate, who she tied up in knots and left whimpering for mercy on the floor of the courtroom. And as for our so-called magistrate, the less said about that incompetent buffoon the better. His failure to correct Galla Placidia with the firm hand that her outrageous behaviour clearly warranted, was one of the principal reasons for her evading justice. It is a source of grievous regret, my Lord, that the only individual who will survive this sorry mess with his reputation and honour intact is me. You, of all people, need no reminding of my natural disinclination to claim credit where credit is not amply due. Having said which, I regret that you could not have been in court to witness my performance at first hand. The magistrate, no less, complimented me on the bearing and oratory with which I presented the case for the prosecution. I blush with modesty at the prospect of repeating the exact terms of his praise, which was far more fulsome than I truly deserved. But please believe that if I do appear to extol my own virtues, I do so not to bask in my own superiority but merely to illustrate the shortcomings of others by way of comparison. At one point during the proceedings, Galla Placidia's damnable trickery forced me to feign a debilitating illness in order to evade her questioning on a particularly thorny issue. She had the temerity to open a wound that we presumed had been sutured and bound a year since. By the Gods, it was only through my alertness of mind that our shameful little secret was not exposed to public scrutiny. Rest assured, my Lord, that she will not be repeating the same claim, neither here nor in Rome. I have been granted special licence to accompany her transfer overland as far as Tingi. The magistrate has made it clear that his jurisdiction over her safety extends no further than the city walls of Volubilis. Beyond the walls' perimeter, he has no interest in Galla Placidia's fate, a fact that he has made abundantly clear to me, and one that I fully intend to exploit to her detriment. I will personally dispose of her at the earliest opportunity that the God's see fit to grant me. On that you have my word, my Lord, and I will not shrink from my purpose. I will do whatever conscience and good sense dictates and at every moment of decision you can depend on me to act fittingly.

THIRTY-ONE

Location: Gilda, Mauretania Tingitana
Coordinates: 34° 14' 43.56" N 5° 56' 43.81" W

Time and Date: 22.00, 10th September, 258 C.E.

The present-day town of Sidi Slimane lies forty kilometres north-west of Volubilis. It is a scruffy, dispiriting place with a population of 75,000 mainly rural migrants, and has long been plagued by the triple effects of illiteracy, wretched housing and high unemployment. Through the middle of the town runs a small *wadi*, or streambed, the waters of which are controlled by the El Kansera Dam, thirty kilometres to the south. Beyond the squalor of the town's outskirts, this *wadi* soon reveals itself to be a rather lovely watercourse, bounded by sandy beaches and rich agricultural land on one side, and borders of thick, impenetrable vegetation on the other. Two thousand years ago, the waters of the *wadi* flowed far less predictably, but even in the height of summer the muddy brown stream would have been deep enough to facilitate the drowning of a bound and tied young woman. And if an individual was to carry a shovel down to this same location, walk inland twenty meters and dig down a metre and a half, one would still have a good chance of discovering the two thousand year-old remains of the victim. The wrist bones would still be tied with leather thongs and the body contorted into hideous realignment, clear evidence of the violent and contemptuous manner in which it had been interred. Sad to say, the distorted skeletal remains would be those of Lieutenant Kalahari Sands, late of the Army Air Corps, and only daughter of Peter and Isobel Sands.

This was the pivotal fate that Sands was preparing herself for. She'd thought of little else during the twelve hours that the locked and heavily-guarded *rheda* had been making its way to Gilda, the Roman precursor of Sidi Slimane.

"I thought that we might have one final chat," Caeluibianus had whispered to her that morning. "I want you to have a chance to prepare yourself properly."

Sands had recoiled in alarm. "Prepare myself for what?"

"Your death tonight."

"My death? What are you talking about?" she'd gasped.

"Yes, face down in a muddy stream," he'd mocked, "just you and me. I can picture it now. Can't you? It won't be pretty, but it'll be lots of fun."

"You bastard. You have no right," she'd disputed desperately, the blood draining from her face. "I'm under the protection of the state. You wouldn't dare."

"Calm down," he'd taunted. "It's a long road ahead. I'm just trying to be helpful. I thought it might help you take your mind off the journey."

As the wagon bumped along for mile after mile in the immense heat, Sands suffered as she'd never suffered before. On the few occasions that she was able to erase visions of the horrible death that awaited her, she was brought back to her senses by the sound of Caeluibianus' voice barking orders at the accompanying guards. She dozed fitfully but each time awoke in a pool of sweat and gasping for breath. She begged to be given drink but had to endure the taunts of Bostar who took great delight in spilling cupfuls of water onto the excreta-stained floor of the wagon. "Lick it up like the dog you are," he mocked.

She cried bitter tears of rage. When she'd appeared as a defendant in court, at least she'd had some form of authority she could to appeal to. She'd possessed some sense of autonomy. Now, she felt bereft and powerless. She could feel the last dregs of her resolve ebbing away. What good had her resolve done her anyway? Now she was facing this final, desperate lowering of the curtain. A sordid, pitiless climax loomed, enacted with no spectators in the auditorium, with no friends in the wings and with no hope of redemption backstage.

If she could've broken through the fourth wall and appealed to the wider audience that existed out there, she would have done.

On arrival in Gilda, the sun was already starting to set. An orange light bathed the landscape. Caeluibianus ordered the guard detail to pitch camp on open ground near the settlement. Vegetation for the horses appeared to be plentiful, a free-flowing stream ran nearby and the site was off the beaten track. All the same, the auxiliaries were puzzled by his decision not to overnight at the township's military outpost. Apart from Bostar, none of the accompanying guards entertained any initial suspicion of Caeluibianus' murderous intentions towards the prisoner.

The only drawback of their selected campground was the sudden, unexpected appearance of a huge caravan of wagons transporting wild beasts to the market in Tingi. Sands found the chaotic arrival and proximity of the animals a reassuring distraction. The guards, in contrast, were unsettled by the beasts' overpowering odour and the noise of their ceaseless growling. Some feared that the animals' arrival represented a bad omen, and they glared at Sands, as if to imply that her baleful influence was the cause of their current discomfiture. She was quick to exploit their fearfulness. "A caged lion never sleeps," she warned.

"Don't talk to her," shouted Caeluibianus. "I told you to refuse all communication."

The soldiers leapt to attention at the sound of the officer's voice. "Now get over to the mess tent and have some food," he ordered. "I'm going to interrogate the prisoner and I have no desire to be disturbed. You men ignore any shouts or cries you may hear. I trust I'm making myself clear?" he enquired.

The soldiers averted their gaze and nodded. Now they all divined his meaning.

"Soldiers, don't go," Sands implored. "You all know what crime he's planning to undertake. He won't have the courage to do it in front of witnesses."

"Oh, she's a crafty one, make no mistake," Caeluibianus countered, "but she's not going to pull a fast one with me. Now, men, be off with you."

"Come on, lads, let's go and eat," muttered the oldest auxiliary. "She deserves whatever's coming to her." The men picked up their packs and stumbled off into the dark.

"Come back, you cowards. You'll all pay for this," she yelled in despair. "You'll all be just as guilty as he is."

Caeluibianus laughed. "Now, Galla Placidia, finally, it's just you and me. All alone, just like I promised."

Sands felt consumed with panic. Her head pulsated with intolerable pressure. There was no way out. Finally, this was to be the moment of truth, here in this roadside clearing, out of sight and out of mind. The trial had merely been an entertaining distraction, a sideshow. Now it was time to make her final plea. Time to face her nemesis.

"You owe me your life," she protested in desperation. "Your conscience won't permit you to kill me in cold blood. You'll be unable to live with what you're about to do."

"You do me a disservice, Galla Placidia. My capacity for depravity is infinite. There are no depths to which it can't sink."

"That I do not doubt. But even the most depraved must answer to their conscience."

"Oh, no," he giggled, "are you really hoping you can appeal to my conscience? Oh how touching." He pulled a face in mock disappointment. "And I thought you knew me so well."

"I know you well enough to assure you of one thing. Any pain you inflict on me will be negligible compared with the suffering you'll be forced to endure in retribution."

Caeluibianus sneered with derision. "I hate to gloat, young lady, but you've made a fundamental miscalculation. You seem to be suffering under the misapprehension that I am incapable of dealing with the nebulous debt of life that you think I owe you. How wrong can you be?" He wagged his finger at her admonishingly. "No, let me tell you what I cannot tolerate, and will not accept. I can't abide the thought that I owe my life to anyone who is at liberty to remind me of such a humiliation.

253

That is what has provoked my pursuit of you. The path to my redemption is clear. It can only be attained through your death."

Sands stared at him in appalled recognition. "You are ill, Caeluibianus, don't you understand? Killing me doesn't resolve anything. It's only going to make matters worse for you."

"Quite the opposite is true. A *haruspex* confirmed me in my course of action through the careful inspection of sacrificed sheep entrails. It was the diviner's opinion that the imbalance in my humours cannot be corrected for as long as you remain alive. The remedy is a simple one."

"Listen to me, Caeluibianus, your collapse in court was an augury. It was a clear omen of what lies ahead in a much worse form if you persist in your plans. Let me go, and I swear you can resolve the inner conflict that presently afflicts you."

"You were the cause of my collapse in court. No one else was to blame, there was no other cause but you! Enough of this casuistry."

"But you don't have to kill me," she pleaded in despair.

"Me, kill you? Why, I have no intention of killing you."

"You don't?"

"No, the *haruspex* was quite clear on this point," Caeluibianus replied, before pausing for theatrical effect. "Bostar will have to do it for me."

"Bostar?"

"Yes, he should be with us in a moment or two. He's presently down by the *wadi*, digging a nice deep grave for you."

Sands face was transfixed in horror. "Help!" she screamed at the top of her voice. She banged the door of the wagon with her fists. "Someone, help me please!"

"You didn't realise? Oh, how remiss of me. I gave him strict instructions. "Dig down the height of a man," I said. "We don't want her bones to be flung all over the countryside by a pack of jackals."

Caeluibianus took great delight in watching the horrified realisation on Sands' face. "Oh, I can assure you that Bostar's very attentive to his duties, so you shouldn't worry yourself on that score. Anyway, you'll soon be able to judge his workmanship for yourself."

"You're fucking insane," Sands screamed at him in English. Her fists were bound in front of her and she used them to pound on the door of the wagon. She could feel her blood pressure raging in protest. There must be someone, somewhere who'd be prepared to help her.

Caeluibianus ignored her frantic pleas and prepared to open the wagon. "No one hears you. And no one cares. Now, let's not keep Bostar waiting."

Sands emitted a long scream for help. No human voice was raised in response, but somewhere out in the darkness her anguished cries seemed to stir a response in the caged beasts. A series of roars and muffled bangs could be clearly heard. Now human voices could also be identified; Sands could definitely hear shouts of alarm amid the ferocious snarls and growls of the lions and leopards.

Caeluibianus suddenly stopped dead in his tracks. He'd already unlocked the door of the wagon but was now frozen in his movements. He appeared to be sniffing the air. He could sense that something was wrong.

Sands shrank back into the corner of the wagon. She was preparing to fight for her life.

Suddenly, screams could be heard coming from the direction of the guards' camp.

Sounds of pandemonium erupted all around them in the dark. The reverberation of shouted warnings and shrieks rent the evening air. On and on it went. Out there in the dark, a terrifying wrath, some unnamed fury, was being unleashed.

Caeluibianus recoiled from the sound of the uproar. His men were being attacked but he shrank from offering any assistance. Figures could be seen running through the distant trees, flying from some unseen foe. Flames leapt high into the air as tents caught fire. Screams of agony and fear echoed across the camp.

A blood-soaked auxiliary ran past the wagon in a state of abject terror. "The lions are loose!" he screamed. "We're ambushed. All is lost. Run for your life!" He stumbled off through the dense bushes that lead down to the *wadi*.

"The lions?" Caeluibianus bellowed at the fleeing auxiliary. "Come back, you swine, you're deserting your post!" But his rank carried no more authority in the dark than his dismembered voice. "Where are the other men?" he shouted in desperation.

The screams of injured and dying soldiers provided a vivid answer to his question. He looked around him in anguish. "Bostar, where's Bostar?"

"You're on your own now, Caeluibianus. Get out of here while you still can," Sands urged. The balance of power was shifting in dramatic fashion; now she'd regained her place at the negotiating table.

"I may be many be things in your eyes," he retorted, "but I trust you'll concede that I'm no coward, unlike these scum who flee into the woods at the first sign of trouble."

Sands was no longer watching her antagonist. Now she was staring through the bars of the wagon at a dark form crouching on the sand no more than twenty metres away. "Caeluibianus, don't look around," she whispered. "Don't make any sudden movements. There's a lion behind you."

The deep growl of the gigantic beast resonated through the camp. Every bone and sinew in Caeluibianus' body was immobilised. He froze in trepidation. He stared at Sands through the bars of the wagon.

"Help me," he whimpered. "I implore you."

Sands made an instant calculation. "I'm going to ease the door open," she whispered. "Here we go. Nice and slowly. Then you're going to get in. Don't rush it – remain calm." Sands opened the door towards her adversary. "The inside of the wagon's your only sanctuary. But don't move till I say."

The great beast rose up on its haunches, spitting and snarling, and began to sway, its tail lashing from side to side.

Sands tensed her muscles.

"Ok, jump now!"

As the Roman leapt head first onto the floor of the wagon, she slammed the door hard behind him and scrambled to secure it from the inside. Caeluibianus scuttled into the far corner, panting hard and swearing aloud.

Sands leapt forward. "Quick, Caeluibianus, undo my bindings. We can use them to fasten the door."

The Roman scrambled to his feet in desperation. "Hold out your wrists," he shouted.

Sands glanced behind her. "Quick, man, quick!" But in a split second he'd grabbed the leather thong with both hands.

"What are you doing, you bastard?" Sands shouted. She grappled with him in a vain attempt to free herself. "Let me loose!"

"Out you go, you bitch," he yelled in triumph. He kicked open the door and hurled her onto the ground. "That's where you deserve to be, down with the beasts."

He raised his arms in exultation. "And I have a front-row view of the combat!"

Sands lay face down in the soil, dazed and winded. She fought hard for breath and struggled to sit up.

Caeluibianus yelled and banged on the walls of the wagon in an attempt to provoke an attack by the lion. "Now, let battle commence," he laughed.

Sands struggled onto her knees, wheezing hard and gasping for air. Her head was spinning. She was conscious of her desperate need to breathe, but little else. She could hear shouting and banging. Somewhere above her head she had a vague awareness of a halo of sparks and flames engulfing her in its protective embrace. She bent double, gasping hard for breath. Slowly the picture started to become clearer, the fog began to lift. A ferocious snarling noise brought her to her senses. She struggled to focus on the source of the mayhem. It looked as if the lion was engaged in extreme combat with a blazing ball of flame. The conflagration swept in a great circular arc above her head. A man stood at the epicentre of the bedlam, his legs a few feet away from where she crouched. His powerful arms swung the ball of flame in ever-increasing circles, forcing the lion to retreat with each revolution.

"Get up, Sands. We gotta get outta here," he shouted above the roar of the conflagration.

Sands was stunned. She looked in confusion at her saviour.

"Stogdon, is that you?"

"It's me," he shouted, as he released the fireball with a great flourish in the direction of the fleeing lion. "Who the hell else d'you think's gonna save your arse?"

"I can't believe it," she sobbed. "I thought I was a gonner. I've never been so pleased to see anyone in my whole life."

"I told you I bare had your back," he laughed.

"You wonderful man."

"Here, hold your wrists out so I can cut your ties."

Sands felt overwhelmed as she embraced Stogdon. Tears of fear-induced gratitude sprung from her eyes. "What are you doing here? You've saved my life."

"Come on," he whispered, "we ain't got time for that now."

She wiped her cheeks and fought to regain her composure. "What are we going to do?"

"We're getting' you outta here, that's what. Come on, follow me, we gotta find the others."

Stogdon cast a final glance around him. And then he froze in his tracks.

"Hang on," he whispered.

He wiped the sweat from his eyes and peered through the shadows. He'd seen something.

"Hello, who's that in the wagon?" he asked, a malevolent tinge to his voice.

He stared harder though the gloom.

"Well, well. Is that little shit-bag in there who I think it is?"

"Come on, forget him, Stog, he's not worth it."

"Ah-ha, would you just look at who it ain't," Stogdon exclaimed in delight.

Caeluibianus' features were frozen with fear.

Stogdon chuckled with glee as he met the Roman's rigid stare. "I reckon you and me have some unfinished business, me old son."

Stogdon drew his sword and advanced on the wagon.

"No, Stog!"

"I'll just be a tick, Sands. You really gotta grab these opportunities when they crop up in life."

"Watch yourself Stog, it's not worth it."

"Oh, it'll *definitely* be worth it. This is for all them lads in Charlie fireteam."

Sands cast about her in desperation. "This is not a good idea, Stog. Let's get out of here, please."

But Stogdon was on a mission and there was no turning back. One way or another, retribution would be served.

Caeluibianus' pathetic pleas for mercy were the last thing that Stogdon heard. As he reached for the door of the wagon, Bostar appeared from out of the shadows and delivered a shattering blow to the back of his skull with the sharpened edge of his short spade. Stogdon was dead before he hit the ground. His massive body collapsed in on itself, his palpable bravery and steadfastness undermined and corroded by the countless regrets, endless conflicts and incalculable grief of centuries.

Sands had screamed a warning. But it had been too late to save her comrade. As Stogdon collapsed, she could hear herself emitting a cathartic howl of despair. Somehow, she'd foreseen this tragic outcome. The sordid predictability of it simply added to her agony. In the split second that it took Bostar to wield the death blow, her survival and Stogdon's demise had become inter-dependent. Paradoxically, both conditions were able to co-exist, in the form of an interpenetrative object/subject relationship, but only in transition, with one state flowing inexorably into the other. Stogdon's death appeared inevitable, unchallengeable, and had been pre-ordained as a condition of her own survival.

"By the gods, Bostar, we'll make a soldier of you yet," shouted Caeluibianus as he burst out of the wagon in exultation.

Bostar appeared stupefied, shocked by the savagery and perfect triumph of his assault. He swayed, the blood and bone from Stogdon's devastated skull dripping from his spade.

"Quick, man, head for the river," Caeluibianus shouted. "More assassins are upon us."

The two men ran helter-skelter for their lives, brushing past the prostrate Sands as she lay slumped on the ground, distraught and disoriented. They were blind to her presence and immune to the devastation they had wrought. They scrambled, jumped and stumbled their way to safety through the thicket of bushes that lined the banks of the *wadi*. They, at least, would live to fight another day, of that they'd make damn sure.

Crawley, Rattigan and Ojokwu, meanwhile, had wreaked a terrible vengeance on the other auxiliaries. Marauding lions, too, had played their part in scattering the troops and grievously injuring a number more. By the time the three comrades stumbled upon Sands and Stogdon, the bodies of their dead and dying foes lay scattered far and wide around the perimeter of the campground.

"Stog's dead," Sands wept.

The three men slumped onto the ground next to his body. Crawley crossed himself. The others stared in dumb disbelief at the corpse of their indomitable comrade. Rattigan inspected the wound to the back of his skull. "Jesus, Stog," he muttered, "you poor, careless bastard."

Ojokwu turned a sorrowful gaze on Sands. "What happened?" he asked. "Was it that bastard, Caeluibianus? His fingerprints are all over this."

"No, it was Bostar. He hit him from behind. Stog never saw it coming."

"Where is he?"

"He and Caeluibianus have fled."

"What the hell are we going to do with the poor fella?" Crawley asked. "We can't just leave his body here. Not for the likes of Caeluibianus to dispose of."

Sands pulled herself up and stumbled over to inspect the corpse. She looked at her fallen comrade. Tears were falling freely. "There's an unused grave, freshly dug, down by the river. It was intended for me, but Stog's welcome to it." Her voice was choking with emotion. "It should have been me lying in that grave, not him. He died saving me."

Rattigan shook his head. "It don't stack up, Kal," he contradicted. "Saving you? Look at his wound, look at how he's fallen. Stog had other priorities when he met his maker."

"Sarge is right, Kal," concurred Ojokwu. "Don't blame yerself. One thing motivated Stog more than loyalty. And that was extracting vengeance."

"Especially vengeance for fallen comrades," added Rattigan.

Sands couldn't face an inquisition. She averted her eyes.

"I bet he was going for Caeluibianus," Crawley postulated. "I bet he was. Birch said that bastard even boasted about killing young George McKay."

Sands nodded her head. "I couldn't stop Stog," she said. "I owe him my life."

"Ain't that just Stog the trog all over?" replied Rattigan with a sad smile. "None of us could ever stop him. Made him the man he was. He was an insubordinate fucking nightmare, but he was a great soldier."

"Right, Ojo, let's take a leg each," instructed Crawley suddenly. He leapt to his feet. "Sarge, why don't you nip over and tell Birch so he can pay his last respects? Azulay can look after the horses by himself."

Sands looked around her with sudden urgency. "Azulay?" she queried. "Is he here, too?"

"Relax, we've kept the lad well out of it," Crawley replied in a business-like manner. By now, he and Ojokwu were starting to drag Stogdon's body towards the *wadi*. "And Kal, chop-chop, you're gonna have to get a grip. You've gotta help us find that empty grave before Roman reinforcements arrive."

THIRTY-TWO

Aballava Tablet No. 11, Inventory No 13.30 (Morris Archive)

Caeluibianus, Cohort Tribune and Praepositus of the Company, to Julius Rufinus, Tribunus Laticlavius and commander-in-chief, I send my greetings. In the matter of determining the fate of Galla Placidia (undertaken in the utmost secrecy as directed) I have done so in full accordance with your wishes and have set out my findings below. My Lord, I am ashamed to have to report that disaster has befallen us all. Although it pains my heart to do so, it is my sad duty to relate the tragic events of last night. The twin hand-maidens of *hubris*, in the form of retribution and excessive violence, visited our camp after dark and exacted full retribution for the impiety shown by one of our own. Bostar - for it was he! – must bear sole culpability for our downfall; he was not merely the author, but also chief perpetrator of the crime that provoked the vengeance of our assailants. Without my knowledge, and in clear contravention of my explicit directives, Bostar felt impelled to dismiss the guard. He then indulged in wanton acts of sexual violence against our defenceless prisoner, Galla Placidia, for no other reason than to satisfy his own personal gratification. While he enacted his hideous crime in full view of the Gods, their retribution was to unleash, without warning, an unholy alliance of wild beasts and spectral assassins, all unified in outrageous accord against our terrified troops. The result, as you can well imagine, was mayhem. The wild beasts scattered our men to all parts; we later found the remains of dismembered and disembowelled auxiliaries spread far and wide across the countryside. By the time we recovered the bodies, packs of jackals and other scavengers had already had their fill of our dead. The soil was baked in dry blood and strewn with unidentifiable body parts. By mid-morning, the sun's intense early rays had already caused the victims' skin to discolour and the internal organs to display unmistakeable signs of putrefaction. Eight men have been slain, possibly more. Three others are currently missing, presumed to have fled the scene or to have cleared off into the bushes to die. On a brighter note, I can confirm that the dreaded Galla Placidia is no more, slain by my own hand while attempting to flee. I also put paid to that giant champion of hers, Tiberius Stogdanus, whose tracks I have been doggedly following since he departed Londinium. His physique, although truly of heroic proportions, was never alone going to match my Roman zeal and valour. And, as forsworn, I dedicate his death to you as a measure of my highest esteem and comradeship. But his body, alas, is no more, removed most likely by his comrades before they flew the scene. The search for the attackers, I have been informed, will be undertaken by the commander at the local fort in Gilda. I can hold out no realistic prospect of their apprehension, my Lord, neither now, nor in the near future, especially given the nature of the wild, uncivilized and lawless land into which they have fled, and the profound indolence of the fort commander. Despite the bloodletting, or, perhaps, as a result of it, my choleric humor is suddenly much relieved. At first light, I was attentive to the fact that my early morning stools were of a less sticky, yellow complexion and were pleasingly free of the putrid aroma so regularly attendant on their production, for which gracious intervention I am deeply indebted to the Gods. Our journey is almost at an end, my Lord. Our principal foe is vanquished and justice has been served. I will submit my penultimate report to you on arrival back at Volubilis, where I intend to make life intolerable for that rebellious Jew, Antalas Alfassi. In my humble opinion, both he and his benighted family have ridden far too high in the saddle, for far too long. It would furnish me the greatest pleasure to unseat them all, and to send them tumbling back into the city's cesspool where they so evidently belong. I thank the Gods for sustaining me in the challenges that have confronted me. When my resolve has been tested I trust that it has not been found wanting; under the divinities' jurisdiction, justice and truth have prevailed. I will continue to persevere in the fulfilment of my purpose, my Lord. At all times I have aspired to do whatever conscience and good sense dictated and at every moment of decision I hope that history will validate my actions and show me to have been worthy of your trust and admiration.

THIRTY-THREE

Location: Imazzouzane, Rif Mountains, Mauretania Tingitana
Coordinates: 34° 51' 37" N, 4° 32' 34" W

Time and Date: 11.00, 15th September, 258 C.E.

A string of eight horses breeched the surface of the mountain's skyline, their silhouettes etched hard against the blinding luminance of the morning sky. As they filed in fluid sequence along the undulating ridge, the string's path gave the illusion of ascending and descending in the manner of a digital waveform, their altitude recorded on the vertical axis, and the distance they'd travelled on the horizontal plane.

Seven riders could be seen mounted atop the eight horses. An unidentified Berber appeared to be leading the way, followed in succession by Azulay, Sands, Birch, Ojokwu and Crawley, with Rattigan last. The riderless horse at the rear had belonged to Stogdon. It was a sturdy beast, but with no soldier to carry, it had been reduced to the irksome and undignified role of packhorse.

The riders had been on the move for five days now. They'd journeyed a hundred miles over hostile and unforgiving terrain. It had been as arduous and dangerous an undertaking as it had been possible to make, one that had been completed by saddle mainly, but also on foot when circumstances had dictated. Now they were deep within the mountainous region of Arrif, a wild and forbidding landscape so named by the Berbers who had been settled here since time immemorial, and who still held unchallenged jurisdiction over the terrain. The Rif, to give it its widely-used contemporary name, covers a huge area stretching from Tangier in the west to the Algerian border in the east, and from the Mediterranean in the north to the Wergha River in the south. The landscape that confronted Sands and her companions was densely forested in parts, with vast groves of Atlas cedar, cork oak and Moroccan fir. Navigable tracks were as few and far between as properly paved roads are today. Most of the time, they were travelling above an altitude of 5000 feet. As they approached their final destination, Mount Tidghine, the highest mountain in The Rif, loomed over them at 8000 feet.

"Aksil says we'll be there by midday," Azulay shouted over his shoulder. The Berber guide had been leading them towards their journey's end for three exhausting days. He had traded with Antalas for many years and knew both the land and Azulay well.

"Just look at this landscape, Sands," Birch repeated for the umpteenth time. "Some of these lower slopes look ideal for cultivating hashish."

"I hope you've got the seeds safe?" Sands enquired with a tired smile. Ever since Birch had received the shipment from Ojokwu, he'd talked of little else.

Birch patted his saddlebag with satisfaction. "Don't you worry yourself on that score, the little darlings are safe and sound. They haven't made it all the way from Syria for nothing. Commercial cultivation in The Rif is a mere six months away, gentlemen, you mark my words. And it's all been down to Barthabbathas Males' good offices."

"Oi, don't forget the part played by your overland courier," interjected Ojokwu.

"Ojo, my friend, with your contacts and my business acumen, the world is our oyster."

"You think you can run an operation like this without a bit of muscle?" Rattigan intervened from the rear. "I'm telling you, Birch, security has to be your first consideration. Everything else flows from that. No bullshit. Ain't I right Mal?"

"It's just like the geezer said," responded Crawley with a laugh. "Without security, you ain't got fuck-all."

"So you boys are in then?" asked Birch for the tenth time, although he already knew the answer.

"What else we gonna do to earn an honest crust? Kal's always said we need to diversify."

"But we get the locals to do the backbreaking work, right?" said Crawley.

"Just remember that it's the locals who are going to be offering you protection," Sands replied. "Think about that before you get any big ideas about exploiting them. This is their land."

"For the time being, perhaps," Rattigan muttered to Crawley. "Let's not rush to judgement."

Azulay pulled his steed up so he could ride alongside Sands. "You know I have to head home soon with Aksil, don't you? I fear for my family's safety, and any reprisals that the Romans might exact."

"I know, Azulay. I've caused your family so much pain and suffering. You should be with them now, not me."

"But you don't understand, it was my father's wish that I help you escape. He ordered me to ensure your safety."

Sands looked at him in astonishment. "He did? But how? You were on the way back from Tingi with Ojo. How could he have ordered you?"

"Tufayyur acted on his behalf. She tracked us down on our way back, just before we met up with the others."

"Tufayyur did this, and with Antalas' permission?"

"No, she did it with his agreement but not his permission. My father would never have permitted such a thing. She risked her own life to save yours. Without her help we would never have managed to find you."

"She really did that for me? I thought she'd grown to despise me."

"You lied to her. You disappointed her. But she doesn't despise you. She's devoted to you. You should have seen the look in her eyes when she implored us to save you."

"Will you thank her for me, Azulay? I may never see her again, but I want her to know that I will always remember her." Sands weather-beaten face began to crumple in an effort to stem the tears.

"You may have turned my family upside down, Kal, but none of us regret having known you, least of all Tufayyur."

Azulay leant over and passed a small tightly-bound purse to Sands. "My father asked me to make sure you received this with his blessing."

"What is it?" she asked, half-anticipating the answer.

"It's the proceeds from the grain sale we transacted in Tingi. The gold's yours. He knows you'll need it and use it wisely."

"How can I repay your generosity to me and my friends?"

Azulay smiled at the young woman. "In another time and place this would all have turned out so differently, don't you think?"

Sands nodded her head. Her body shook with repressed sadness and regret.

"Hey, Sands, here's a question for you," shouted Birch without warning. He had a habit of throwing disconnected challenges into the mix.

"If you could take one object back with you from the 21st century, what would it be?"

Sands sniffed loudly to clear her airways. "Sanitary towels. Next question."

"That's disgusting," shouted Rattigan. "If that's how you want this to go, then I'm going to say bog paper. My arse can't take no more of sponges, leaves and lichen."

They all cheered in sympathy.

"What about you, Birch?" asked Sands, suddenly grateful for the chance to engage in a bit of light-hearted male banter. "What are you missing most?"

"Dark glasses. It's a fucking nightmare without them. Don't know how the hell the ancients coped. What about you, Ojo?"

"Me? That's simple: it's gotta be a box of matches. If I never have to use a flint and a knife again, I'll be a fucking happy man."

They all nodded in sympathetic agreement.

"You next Mal," Sands shouted to Crawley.

"You guys are serious? Not one of you has mentioned tobacco?"

"Yeah, good shout," conceded Rattigan with an appreciative nod. "Fuck the toilet paper, I'm changing my vote."

"A pair of squaddies, through and through - you guys'll never change," Sands laughed. "I bet Stog would have made it a hat-trick if he was here right now."

"No doubt. God bless him wherever he is," said Crawley.

"Don't you two wish you'd stayed in Londinium?" Sands asked. "Stog might still be alive if you had. Don't you miss the old place?"

"Nah, it was a right shit-hole. We'd all three be well dead by now if we'd stayed. Ain't that the truth, Sarge?"

"Yeah, 'The Smoke' may have done for my old man, but it weren't gonna finish me off too. There's plenty of fight left in the two of us yet."

Azulay listened to these strange exchanges in wonderment. He may not have understood a word of the idle repartee as it bounced back and forwards between his companions, but he wore a wide smile nonetheless. There was an easy-going bonhomie, a palpable sense of community among this oddball collection of itinerants that he responded to with appreciation.

Sands was aware of it too. She was beginning to feel a kinship with this weird clan of time travellers. It wasn't the kind of family she would have wished for. If such a prospect had ever existed anywhere, it now lay in pieces, out of reach and irreparable, back in Volubilis. Immutable decisions had been made that had led, inevitably, to the destruction of that dream. She wasn't entirely to blame for the chaotic outcome, she knew that, but she found herself enduring a heavy burden of responsibility for the disorder that had been visited upon the House of Oleanders and its many occupants.

Still, life had its compensations. Stogdon's death had taught her a powerful lesson about the primary importance of loyalty and comradeship. Ojo and Birch had proved themselves capable of sustaining Sands through her many bouts of self-doubt, and both had come up trumps, in their very different ways, through their sense of optimism and their indomitable faith in the future. Even Rattigan and Crawley had moved up

269

in her estimation. She knew them both to be ruthless and callous killers, but this awareness had also blinded her to their many qualities, chief among which was their remarkable capacity for adaptability and their resilience in the face of unimaginable challenges.

As she gazed across the endless Moroccan landscape, Sands began to reflect on the nature of the anxieties that had afflicted her over the preceding three months. Since setting off in a canoe from that bleak Scottish beach, she'd had no opportunity or space to view things in any meaningful context. And the more she now began to reflect on recent events, the calmer she felt. In truth, she was a born survivor, not matter what fate threw at her. Even when she contemplated the extraordinary, relentless stress that she'd had to bear, the persistent threats to her life that she'd endured, and the debilitating existential crisis that she'd overcome, she felt empowered, not cowed. Guiltily, she'd never felt so alive, despite the ever-present shadow that death cast over her shoulder. Certainly, she mourned the passing of Stogdon, whose violent murder she still felt somehow implicated in. However, on a more positive note, she also felt able to luxuriate in the intensity of her feelings for Azulay and Tufayyur, and to acknowledge the strength of her growing bond with Ojo and Birch. The resonance of her relationship with Antalas, whose paternal protection she so valued, and her deep-felt affection and admiration for the Berber people and culture, also afforded her great consolation.

As she looked to the horizon, she felt suffused with a warm glow of well-being. A combination of the thin atmosphere, the sun's glare and the warmth of the day left her feeling a touch giddy. She embraced the glorious morning; it appeared to promise so much. Light-headed and light-hearted, she gazed at her travelling companions with joyful acceptance. She smiled to herself. And as she did so, she stroked her stomach in broad, protective sweeps. Rather than the end of a journey, this felt very much like the beginning of something - something wondrous, and something life-enhancing.

THIRTY-FOUR

Aballava Tablet No. 12, Inventory No 13.31 (Morris Archive)

Caeluibianus, Cohort Tribune and Praepositus of the Company, to Julius Rufinus, Tribunus Laticlavius and commander-in-chief, I send my greetings. In the matter of determining the fate of Galla Placidia (undertaken in the utmost secrecy as directed) I have done so in full accordance with your wishes and have set out my findings as to her fate in the previous tablet, despatched to you in utmost haste from the field of battle in Gilda. Since that momentous encounter, I really have very little of consequence to report. On returning to Volubilis, I was summoned to spend a tedious afternoon in the company of the resident magistrate who seemed wholly unconcerned by the death of the prisoner for whom I held personal responsibility or, indeed, the slaughter of the poor auxiliaries, but appeared most put out by the loss of the wild beasts in which he had a substantial financial interest, a fact that he did not cease to remind me of on at least half a dozen occasions. Really, my Lord, the venality and corruption of these provincial officials lies beyond all acceptable bounds. If it were not for my own tolerant nature – my worst vice, I am assured by those whose judgement I respect most – I would have cautioned him to show greater respect for the poor lads who were dismembered by the object of his investment. Alas, as is often the case with your humble subordinate, my soft heart was moved to spare the magistrate my harshest reprimands. Truly, my Lord, I am often my own worst enemy – a rebuke, I hope you won't mind me mentioning, that you have also regularly levelled against me. I'm bound to say in my defence that I've grown heartily sick of this endless escapade, and now that the subject of our hunt has been well and truly plucked, drawn and roasted I am determined to return to Britannia and be of service there once more. As my mission draws to a close, I wish to record the depth of my heartfelt gratitude to you, my Lord. My task was rendered possible, in the first place, by the great tolerance that you have displayed in my judgement, and, secondly, by the constant flow of rebukes you delivered in an effort to temper my wilder excesses. Truly, my Lord, even your harshest reprimands were welcomed and acted upon. They proved to be quite as instructive to me as the outstanding quality of the intelligence forthcoming from our spy ESEM. In my humble opinion, this anonymous source has no equal in the empire. At every twist in the road his advice and foresight has proved to be uncannily prescient. If weather conditions prove favourable, you can expect to see my return within forty days. Unless circumstances change dramatically, or unless important new information is forthcoming, do not be alarmed if you receive no further reports from me in the interim. Till we meet again, if the Gods be so willing, I salute you and will continue to persevere in the fulfilment of our joint enterprise, my Lord.

THIRTY-FIVE

"Do you have any idea what bloody time it is?" Sterland Morris barks.

He's just been woken up from a deep sleep. His colleague, *A*, is voicing him.

"I'm sorry, this can't wait."

Morris fumbles for a light switch. "Just hang on, will you?"

"I've just had a tip-off," *A* continues. "The folks at *Digital Screamer* seem to think they've got their teeth into something."

"Not that bloody outfit again," Morris replies with a stifled yawn. "Our PR people can deal with it in the morning."

"Not this time. This time, you deal with it."

There's a hint of weary irritation in *A*'s voice that Morris doesn't much care for. "For heaven's sake," he insists, "*I'm* not the one going around waking people up at four o'clock in the morning. If you've got something to say, just say it, will you?"

"Have you ever come across a Jed Baker?"

There's a long pause before Morris clears his throat. "Have I ever come across who?"

"Baker - Jed Baker. Says he's a farmer from Cumbria or somewhere. Name ring a bell?"

"Baker - no, never heard of him. Should I have?"

"Well, he seems to know you, or says he does."

"Bully for him."

"He's levelled a couple of worrying allegations against you."

"Has he now? He's just the latest in a long line of professional complainants to shoot off unfounded accusations against me, as you well know. And he won't be the last, I can promise you that."

"He says you found the Aballava tablets on his land."

There is another long pause.

"Sterland, are you still there?"

"You know I can't comment on that."

"It's true then?"

"As a matter of principle, I've always refused to comment on where the location is. There's an overriding imperative to protect the site for posterity. I've told you that repeatedly."

"But this fella, Baker?"

"These chancers are always trying their luck. They think they'll flush you out if they keep hammering away at it."

"You do know him, don't you?"

"I've already explained my position on this matter."

"Look, Sterland, I can understand if you're trying to cover your tracks. I'm only trying to help here. If there's a problem then we need to deal with it. You can't just bury your head in the sand and say 'no comment'."

"No comment."

"Look, this bloke's saying you didn't find the tablets five years ago like you've claimed. He said they were dug up at the same time as the Aballava hoard over twenty years ago."

"No comment."

"And he never received a penny in reward for them, despite the fact they were found on his land."

Morris tuts loudly. "*A*, it's the middle of the night, and this is really getting exceedingly tedious."

"I'm sorry to be boring you, but if half of what he says is true, the consequences are going to be mad serious – and not just for you."

Morris strikes a more defensive tone. "It's his word against mine. If this man Baker is indeed the owner of the land where the original hoard was found, then of course I may have had some fleeting contact with him twenty years ago, but only in my capacity as a representative of the British museum. I mean, how old is he now, anyway? He must be well into his eighties. I seem to recall he wasn't the brightest spark back then. God knows what his mental state is now."

"Look, Sterland, whatever happened back then, is done and dusted and beyond recall. But I need to know that I can trust what you're telling me now."

"Look, the bottom line is that everything is real; the hoard is real, the finds are real, the tablets are real. Interpretation, however, is open to conjecture."

"But something's missing. There's something you're not telling me."

"Grow up, A. The evidence is all there. It's not my job to draw your conclusions for you. Now, if you don't mind, I'd like to get back to sleep."

"One final thing. Let me read you this section from Baker's interview."

"Make it quick. You've got one minute."

"Okay, this is from the transcript that *Digital Screamer* has sent me. It reads as follows:

"One thing that don't make no sense," said Baker, "is where's the missing tablet?"

"What missing tablet?"

"When I handed them over to him there was thirteen of the buggers, not twelve."

"Thirteen? How can you be certain it was thirteen after all this time?"

"Cos of my name, see - Baker. He [Morris] joked that there was a baker's dozen, thirteen, like my name. You never forget a thing like that"."

"What's your response to that?" A asks.

There's a long silence. "He's right, there are certain things that you don't forget." Morris can be heard chuckling to himself. "Sometimes it's the most innocent remarks that come back to haunt you."

"So there was a thirteenth tablet?"

"Evidently."

"So why didn't you publish it along with all the others."

"It's a very embarrassing explanation for a historian. It got destroyed in the conservation process. It was in much worse condition than all the others and we overdid the processing to compensate for its illegibility. The result was one almighty cock-up. It's inexcusable, I know, but that's the size of it, I'm afraid. Not my proudest moment."

"Have you any idea who ESEM is?"

"Who?"

"Come on, you know what I'm talking about. ESEM – the intelligence source who Caeluibianus refers to in the twelfth tablet."

"No idea. He's only mentioned once."

"It's been puzzling me," prompts *A*. "I've been wondering whether more information about his identity wouldn't have been revealed in the thirteenth tablet?"

"We'll never know, sadly."

"We've only got your word for it that the final tablet was destroyed under the circumstances you described."

"And why on earth would I not be telling the truth?"

"To protect the anonymity of ESEM? Who or what is ESEM? Maybe the final tablet would have provided the answer."

"I think you'll find ESEM is a minor Assyrian divinity - hardly a meaningful or particularly relevant discovery."

"That's exactly what I thought," replied *A*. "But the more I've dug up about the cult of ESEM, the more I've begun to think it's simply an elaborate red-herring masking a blatantly obvious identity. You know what I reckon? The answer's staring me in the face."

"I'm sure you going to share it with me."

"Take the phonetic name, ESEM, boil it down to its figurative identifiers, and you're left with a pair of initials. It's like stripping away an external mould to reveal a bronze statue."

There is silence in response.

"Sterland, did you hear what I just said?"

More silence.

"Sterland, just what the hell have you been up to?"